The Case

of the

Clever Secret Code

All the Best!

Cindy Vincent

Also by Cindy Vincent

The Case of the Cat Show Princess:
A Buckley and Bogey Cat Detective Caper

The Case of the Crafty Christmas Crooks:
A Buckley and Bogey Cat Detective Caper

The Case of the Jewel Covered Cat Statues:
A Buckley and Bogey Cat Detective Caper

The Mystery of the Missing Ming:
A Daisy Diamond Detective Novel

The Case of the Rising Star Ruby:
A Daisy Diamond Detective Novel

Makeover For Murder:
A Kate Bundeen Mystery

Cats Are Part of His Kingdom, Too:
33 Daily Devotions to Show God's Love

The Case
of the
Clever Secret Code

A Buckley and Bogey
Cat Detective Caper

Cindy Vincent

Whodunit Press
Houston   Bozeman

The Case of the Clever Secret Code

A Buckley and Bogey Cat Detective Caper

Published by Whodunit Press

A Division of Mysteries by Vincent, LLC

For information, please contact:

Whodunit Press

c/o Mysteries by Vincent

Mysteriesbyvincent.com

This is a work of fiction. All events, locations, institutions, themes, persons, characters and plot are completely fictional. Any resemblance to places or persons, living or deceased, are of the invention of the author.

ISBN: 978-1-932169-31-7

Printed in the United States of America

Dedication

To Mocha Marie and Elisabeth.

*Sometimes "greatness" comes in small packages.
You will always be in my heart.*

CHAPTER 1

Holy Mackerel!

For as long as I live, I'll never forget the day when that really, really long, black car drove right into St. Gertrude. It was on a Monday morning, and the sun was already blazing way up high in the sky. June had been extra hot, and I didn't think things were going to change for a while. It wasn't exactly a good time to have extra layers of fur like I did. And it wasn't exactly a good time to be afraid of the water, like I was. And like most other cats are. Because jumping into a swimming pool probably would have cooled me off pretty nicely.

But let me tell you, if I thought things were hot then, well, that was nothing. Because things were about to get a whole lot hotter! And I don't mean because of the temperature. No, it was because of that long, black car that rolled onto Main Street and went straight through our downtown! In my short time as a cat detective, I had never seen anything like it. That car must have been the size of three or four cars put together. In fact, I wasn't even sure it was a car at all.

I turned to ask my brother and best friend, Bogart — or "Bogey" as we call him — if he knew what it was. He was sitting beside me on top of an old oak dresser in our Mom's antique store.

But Bogey knew what I was going to ask even before I got

the words out. I guess that's the way it is when you're one of the best cat detectives in the business.

"It's a limo, kid," he told me. "That's short for limousine."

"Oh . . . well, there's nothing short about it." I crinkled my brow. "I wonder why they don't just call it an extra, extra long car?"

Bogey shook his head. "Beats me, kid. Some things just don't make sense."

He reached a lean arm into a vase next to him and pulled out a bag of cat treats. They were fish flavored. Some of my favorites. He passed one to me and then took one for himself. We munched on our treats while we watched that long car drive slowly toward our Mom's store. We had a perfect view of it all since we were sitting in the gigantic front window. Right under the big sign that read, "Abigail's Antiques." It was one of the places we liked to sit when we worked the security detail at our Mom's store. As cat detectives, that was part of our job.

Of course, the humans aren't exactly aware of our detective duties. Probably because us cats always switch to cat language whenever humans are around. Plus, some people have no clue what cats are capable of. But Bogey always says we can use that to our advantage.

Though to be honest, I'm not completely sure what he means by that.

I squinted as that big, black car continued to creep closer. The bright sun bounced off the shiny hood and it was blinding. Especially when that limo stopped for a moment, smack dab in front of our store.

"Put the treats away, would ya, kid?" Bogey said under his breath.

"Um . . . sure," I told him. Then I grabbed the treat bag and stuffed it back into the vase where Bogey always stashed it.

When I turned back to my brother, I saw he was now sitting up very straight and tall. His ears were tilted forward and his tail flicked from side to side. And he didn't take his eyes off that limo even for a second.

I could tell his senses were on full alert, so I figured maybe mine should be too. So I sat up nice and tall and stared at that car. Just like he did.

That's when I realized that if we could see the limo, well,

whoever was in that limo could see us. The only thing was, we couldn't actually *see* them. That's because the windows were tinted so dark that no one could see inside.

And even though I'm supposed to be a big, brave cat detective like my brother, I, Buckley Bergdorf, suddenly started to shake in my paws. To tell you the truth, I didn't like the looks of that black limo, with its dark, eyeball-like windows. It looked sort of like a big, scary monster crawling up the street.

So I decided it might be a good idea for me to scrunch down and try to be invisible. The only problem was, being invisible wasn't exactly something I'm good at, considering I'm a Maine Coon cat. If you've never heard of Maine Coon cats, well, let me tell you, we're really, really big. And I do mean big! I'm only two years old and I'm already twice as big as Bogey. And Bogey is a full-grown guy!

Then again, sometimes I'm amazed at how different Bogey and I really are. Sure, we're both black cats with gold eyes. But I'm huge and fuzzy with gigantic paws that always seem to get in my way. It seems like I barely get used to them when they grow some more. Then I have to get used to them all over again.

But Bogey doesn't have that problem. Bogey is sleek and lean, and he can run so fast that some even say he can fly. Bogey never has any trouble getting his paws to go where he wants them to go.

When he wants them to go there.

Yet even though we're different, we're both cat detectives. Together we run the Buckley and Bogey Cat Detective Agency. I'm the rookie and he's the pro. He's been teaching me everything he knows since the day I was adopted into our forever home. That's when he took me under his paw, taught me the business, and helped me to become a real cat detective.

Now I only hoped I could be as good a cat detective as Bogey was some day.

But today probably wasn't going to be that day.

Especially when I heard a loud squeal behind us and I nearly jumped to the ceiling. It was our twelve-year-old human sister, Gracie. She is the only daughter of our human Mom and Dad, and we love her like she was our real sister.

She is always so sweet to us cats.

"Mom, Mom!" Gracie yelled as she swished around in her favorite sundress that had big pink, yellow, and red flowers on it. "There's a limo outside on the street."

A few seconds later, our Mom strolled up to join us. Her long, dark hair floated around her shoulders. She had on a white cotton sundress, and I could see some of my black fur on the bottom of the skirt.

"Sure enough, honey," she said. "It's a limo. We don't see a lot of those in St. Gertrude. At least not in the middle of the day."

"I wonder who's in it," Gracie whispered.

She had her own long, dark hair pulled into a ponytail today. Her dark eyes sparkled and she began to dance around. Then she stopped and grabbed me up into a nice, tight hug.

She pointed out the window. "Do you see that, Buckley? There must be someone very important inside that car."

Well, I had to say, "important" sure was a lot better than scary.

Seconds later, our Mom's two employees, Millicent and Merryweather, ran up and joined us, too. Millicent had short, curly gray hair and dark-framed glasses that she wore on the end of her nose. Merryweather was dressed in a pink dress with a big skirt from the 1950s. Her dress went really well with her red hair and her pink, pointy cat-eye glasses.

"I'll bet it's a rock star," Merryweather said. "Maybe they're on their way to a big concert somewhere."

"Or it might be a TV star," Millicent added.

Now the limo started to move forward again and inched up our street.

"Maybe it's the Governor," Gracie suggested. "Because of our Fourth of July celebration this weekend. Maybe if I win the essay contest, he'll be there to hear me read it. At our town picnic on Saturday night."

Our Mom put her arm around Gracie's shoulders. "It's probably not the Governor," she said gently. "I don't think he rides around in a limo quite as large as that one."

"Well, whoever it is, they must be really rich and famous," Merryweather said. "To be sitting pretty in those fancy wheels."

"Whoever they are, I wonder what they're doing in downtown St. Gertrude," our Mom said.

Bogey meowed over to me. Like I said, us cats always switch to cat language when humans are around.

"I was wondering the same thing," he told me. "Why is a limo driving up our street? And why are they looking at our Mom's store like that?"

I shrugged. "I don't know. Maybe they want to buy some antiques."

Then I glanced back at the huge main room of our Mom's store. Our Mom sure had plenty of antiques for them to buy. Her store had rows and rows of old tables and chairs and sofas. Antique glassware and dishes were displayed on old bookshelves. Plus there were paintings and toys and all kinds of things on display for sale, too. I always loved the days when our Mom brought us to work with her. The whole store was full of wonderful smells and lots of great nooks and crannies for us cats to explore.

Millicent picked up my brother and cuddled him. "Bogey, you're the only 'big star' that I need. You do your namesake justice. Maybe one day you'll be riding in a limo."

I wasn't sure if Bogey would like to ride in a limo or not. And I sure didn't know what Millicent meant by a "namesake." But Bogey didn't seem to care one way or another. He just grinned and purred up at her.

"Be careful," Merryweather warned. "Don't get taken in by his charm. Buckley and Bogey may be as dashing and handsome as any big stars, but they're also very sneaky. They've tried to fool me and sneak out the front door many times. And they know they're not supposed to go out."

Bogey reached up and put his paw on Millicent's cheek. All the women laughed before Millicent kissed Bogey on the head. Then she set him back on the dresser. Gracie kissed me on the head and set me down beside him.

Just in time for us to see a whole bunch of people walk by. First there was a woman who worked at the store a few doors down. Then another couple of ladies walked by in a hurry. After that, a man and two girls a little older than Gracie hurried past. Before long, there were more and more people passing by our store. They were all rushing in the same direction.

But nobody stopped in.

I noticed Bogey sat at attention again.

"Now what's happening?" I asked my brother.

"Don't know, kid. But I don't like the looks of this," he meowed back.

"Mom, can I go see what's going on out there?" Gracie asked.

"No, honey," our Mom laughed. "You're supposed to be practicing. You know the Fourth of July essay contest is tonight and you have to read your essay out loud. At the library."

Gracie started to bounce up and down. "I know, Mom. But I think something exciting is going on out there. And I want to see what it is. I won't be gone long. I promise."

Now more and more people raced past our window. That's when I realized they were all going in the same direction as that limo had gone.

"All right," our Mom sighed. "But don't forget you've got to practice if you want to win that contest."

"I'll take her," Merryweather said. "It's time for my lunch break, anyway. Gracie and I can check things out and we'll grab a bite to eat, too."

Millicent glanced at her watch. "And I've got to get back to work."

I turned to my brother. "Do you think we should go check this out?"

Bogey shook his head. "Nope, kid. We'd better stay put and keep an eye on things here. We've gotta make sure our Mom's store is secure."

Seconds later, Merryweather and Gracie went through the front door. Then they walked right in front of our store along with a whole bunch of other people. Gracie blew us a kiss as she went by.

They had barely gone out of sight when the phone rang. Our Mom ran to answer it.

Then we heard her say, "Who? Oh right, him. What's he doing in St. Gertrude?"

Well, that sure made me wonder who "he" was. Especially since our Mom must have known him. And apparently that "him" she was talking about didn't live here.

More people went by, and they headed in the same direction that all the other people had gone. Pretty soon I figured the whole town of St. Gertrude must have passed by our window.

A few minutes later, a man holding a big news camera on his shoulder went by. A lady dressed up in a suit tripped along in her high heels in front of him. I was pretty sure she was holding a microphone.

Bogey nodded at them. "Must be something pretty big brewing out there, kid. For the local TV news to be here."

Holy Mackerel! Now TV reporters were running by our window, too?

I gulped. "Do you think it has anything to do with that limo?"

"That would be my guess, kid." Bogey squinted his eyes and moved even closer to the glass.

Not long after that, Gracie came rushing back. She had to dodge people on the sidewalk just to get into our store. She flung the front door wide open and ran inside.

"Mom, Mom!" she yelled. "You'll never believe it! You'll never guess who's here in town! It's Steele Bronson!"

Gracie had the funniest look on her face. She smiled kind of goofy-like and she sort of wobbled around the room. It reminded me of the way Bogey looked whenever he saw our friend, Amelia. She was a beautiful, longhaired calico cat, and for some reason, Bogey always went into a daze when he saw her.

Our Mom smiled at Gracie. "I know. I just heard from Velma down the street. She heard it from the store next to hers."

Millicent gasped. "Steele Bronson? Did you say Steele Bronson? Oh my goodness! I can hardly believe it! He's here? Right here in St. Gertrude?"

"Oh Mom!" Gracie gushed. "Steele Bronson is so hot."

"You've got that right," Millicent agreed. "He's the most handsome man alive. I can't believe he's really here."

"I saw him, Mom! I actually saw him!" Gracie squealed.

"That's nice, honey," our Mom told her. "What happened to Merryweather?"

"She saw him, too. And then the crowd got so big that she told me I should come back. She took some pictures on her phone and she almost fainted. So then she went to lunch. She said she wasn't sure if she was hungry or in shock."

I turned to look at my brother. "Do you know who Steele Bronson is?"

Bogey shook his head. "Haven't a clue, kid. But apparently he's very handsome."

"And hot," I added. "Maybe if he's so hot, he should come into our store. After all, our Mom has air conditioning. That might cool him down."

Bogey kept on watching out the window. "Could be, kid. Could be. Though I'm not sure we want all the hubbub that seems to go with this guy."

Millicent and Gracie joined hands and started to spin around and around. I had never seen them so excited before in my life.

Now I had to wonder, who in the world was Steele Bronson?

Holy Catnip!

CHAPTER 2

Holy Catnip! Before long, Merryweather returned to our store, carrying a plastic bag with some sandwiches. She passed one to Gracie and then started eating one herself. But Gracie completely ignored her lunch. Instead she stood there with Millicent, and together they talked so fast I could hardly understand a word they said. As near as I could tell, they were pretty wound up about this Steele Bronson guy. Funny, but the only one who didn't seem excited about him was our Mom.

"His last movie was the best!" Merryweather said when she was halfway through her sandwich.

"Personally, I liked his earlier movies," Millicent chimed in. "Before he became such a big star. And before he started dating that waitress."

Merryweather took the last bite of her sandwich. "*And* broke up with that waitress. Then started dating that model. And broke up with her, too. It made all the news."

I glanced over at my brother. "It made all the news? I never saw anything about this guy in the news before. Did you?"

Bogey shook his head. "Different kind of news, kid. We mostly stick with the crime beat. Not movie stars and what dames they're dating now."

"Hmmmm . . . It sure seems like an awful lot of people are

interested in what this guy does," I murmured just as Gracie came dancing over to us.

She put her arms around me and picked me up. "Did you hear, Buckley? Steele Bronson is right here in St. Gertrude! He's a really famous movie star and I got to see him. It's a dream come true!"

Holy Mackerel! Gracie acted as thrilled as everybody else did about this movie star guy. Just like Millicent and Merryweather. Maybe there really was something special about him. And well, I did have to say, I sure liked it when dreams came true.

I reached up and gave Gracie a kiss on the nose. My biggest dream came true when my family adopted me from the cat shelter. Especially since my first humans weren't very nice and they abandoned me in a park. After that, I was out on the mean streets before someone *even* took me to the cat shelter. Back then, I didn't know where my next meal was coming from. But now that I have my forever home, I have food, and toys, and a bed, and a nice house to live in. Plus I have my brother, and a family of both cats and humans. They all give me lots and lots and lots of love. And a guy like me is thankful for it every single day.

Gracie hugged me tight and I hugged her back. Then she started spinning around with me in her arms. For some reason, she'd been going through this spinning phase for a while now. I was really looking forward to the day when she grew out of it. And I do mean *really* looking forward to it! In the meantime, I just wrapped my arms around her neck and hung on for dear life. Around and around we went. The whole room went by in a blur!

"Gracie, you've got to quit spinning Buckley." Our Mom's voice floated over to us from somewhere. "It's time to practice reading your essay for the contest."

Gracie stopped spinning. "Okay, Mom! I'll practice it in front of Buckley and Bogey."

She kissed me on the head and put me back on the dresser. Right next to my brother. But even though I was no longer being spun around, the room still seemed to be going in circles. I could barely make out Bogey standing over me with a cat treat.

"Here you go, kid," he said. "This'll get you going."

And sure enough, it did. I munched on the turkey-flavored treat while he helped himself to one, too.

I glanced over to see Gracie skip to the back of the store, where our Mom had her office. She'd barely left us when the front door opened. Then it opened again and again. One by one, customers walked into the store and started to shop. As they did, they all talked about that Steele Bronson guy. It seemed the more they talked about him, they more antiques they bought.

Millicent and Merryweather and our Mom had their hands full at the cash register. They had to work really fast to take care of all the sales. We watched the whole thing until Gracie came skipping back to us. She had her essay in her hands.

"Okay, boys," she said. "Do you know about the contest? Every year the city of St. Gertrude holds a Fourth of July essay contest. They ask school kids from grades six to nine to write essays about how our country was founded, and about celebrating our country's birthday. Because that's what the Fourth of July really is — it's a big, giant birthday party for the United States. It's America's Independence Day that everyone celebrates all across the country."

Holy Mackerel! That really *did* sound like a big birthday party! And I sure liked birthday parties. A lot. At our house, we celebrated the birthdays of all the humans and all the cats in our family every single year. It was a lot of fun. Our Mom always made us cats a tuna fish cake to share. So let me tell you, I looked forward to every single birthday party.

Now Gracie smiled her brightest smile. "The theme for this year's essay contest is 'What the Red, White, and Blue Means to Me.' The people holding the contest got the idea because the colors of the American flag are red, white, and blue."

She pointed to the flag that our Mom had hanging in the front of her store. And sure enough, Gracie was right. There were red and white stripes, and white stars on a blue background. I had to say, it was a really pretty flag. I liked the stars the best.

Gracie twirled around. "After all the kids entered the contest, the judges picked the top ten best essays. And guess what? My essay made it into the top ten! Can you believe it?"

Well, I *could* believe it! Gracie worked so hard in school to get good grades. And us cats would know. That's because one of the cats in our house, Lil Bits, spent lots of hours with Gracie when she did her homework.

Now Gracie stood still but her dark eyes kept dancing. "Tonight, the kids with the best essays will read them aloud at the library. That's when the judges will pick the final winner. And the winner gets to read their essay at the big celebration on Saturday night. Right after the town picnic and before the fireworks start."

That made me shiver. Sure, I wanted Gracie to win the contest. But to tell you the truth, us cats don't really like fireworks. I'd seen a bunch last New Year's Eve. And as far as I was concerned, they were bright and loud, and way too scary for a guy like me. They weren't exactly the kind of thing I wanted to be around ever again.

Gracie started to bounce up and down. "Plus, the winner gets a big trophy. And their picture in the paper. But best of all, they get to ride on a float in the parade on Saturday morning! I want to win so much I can hardly stand it!"

Holy Catnip! Wouldn't it be fun to ride on a float in the parade? I glanced at my brother and he winked back at me. Then we both sat up as tall as we could and purred just as loud as we could purr. We wanted Gracie to know that we were so proud of her. And we wanted her to win, too!

She leaned over and gave us both a kiss on the forehead. "I sure wish you boys could be at the library tonight. Even though I want to win, it's kind of scary to read my essay in front of all those people."

I turned and meowed to my brother. "Don't they let cats into the library?"

He grinned back at me. "Don't sweat it, kid. We'll figure out a way to get there."

That was music to my ears. I reached up and gave Gracie a kiss on the elbow.

She giggled. "Thanks, Buckley. But now I've got to practice."

Then she stood up straight and started to read. "What the Red, White, and Blue Means to Me."

She paused and smiled at us. I always loved to hear Gracie

read out loud. She had such a nice voice, and she sure was a good reader.

"My name is Gracie Abernathy and I am proud to be an American," she started. "It makes me smile every time I see the red, white, and blue — the flag that is the symbol of our great country. When I see our flag, I am so happy that our forefathers and mothers started this great country, a place where people would have freedom. Of course, they risked everything they had — their homes, their belongings and even their own lives — to create this great nation of ours. Sometimes it's hard for me to imagine, but once upon a time, there was no country named America. In fact, the United States is less than two hundred and fifty years old! And while that seems pretty old to me, believe it or not, as a country, that's actually pretty young! Then again, it took a lot of years to grow and become this nation of fifty states. Especially since we started out very small, with only thirteen colonies — Massachusetts, New Hampshire, Connecticut, Rhode Island, New York, New Jersey, Delaware, Pennsylvania, Virginia, Maryland, North Carolina, South Carolina, and Georgia."

Gracie paused for a breath. "Sometimes I try to imagine what life was like back in those original thirteen colonies. At first, the colonies were under the rule of England and King George II. But then, when King George III became king, little by little, our history changed forever. You see, it all started when the king needed money to pay for the French and Indian War. And King George figured the best way to get some money was to take it from the people in America's thirteen colonies. So he did. He created something called the Tax Stamp, where he taxed every piece of printed paper that people used. Even playing cards. Well, needless to say, that made the people in the colonies very angry. Because they thought this tax was completely unfair, especially since they didn't even have a say in the matter. 'Taxation without representation,' was their cry."

Gracie squared her shoulders and kept on going. "The people of the colonies were also supposed to buy all their goods from England. Can you imagine someone telling you where you could shop? I can't. My Mom owns an antique store, and her customers all shop there because they want to.

Not because they're forced to. Anyway, the people in the colonies didn't want to buy all their goods from England, so they bought goods that came in from other places on other ships."

Gracie shook her head. "Well, King George didn't think much of that, so he made it legal for his soldiers to just search people's houses and look for goods that weren't bought from England. People were punished, some very severely, and of course, that made the colonists even more angry."

Gracie looked from me to Bogey and then back at her paper. "But King George didn't care what the people of the colonies thought. In fact, he just decided to punish them by adding more taxes and taking away more freedoms. Until finally, the people had had enough. Each colony sent delegates to Philadelphia to a meeting of the Continental Congress, so they could discuss what to do. Then on July 4th, 1776, the delegates adopted the Declaration of Independence. The document declared the United States to be a country unto itself, and no longer under the rule of England. It was a historic day and the Declaration of Independence is still one of the most important documents of our country."

Gracie took a deep breath. "Of course, King George wasn't about to give up control of his thirteen colonies. Oh no! Not without a fight. And that fight became known as the Revolutionary War. It was a long, hard war, but thanks to the leadership of General George Washington, the newly formed United States won the Revolution. And we became a country free from British rule. Because of those brave people who fought for our independence so many years ago, we now get to enjoy freedoms in this country. Freedoms like the freedom of speech and the freedom of religion. All things written down in the Constitution of the United States."

Holy Catnip! I had to say, Gracie's story sure was good. She had me on the edge of my seat. I could hardly wait to hear what was going to happen next. And I sure wanted to know more about this Declaration of Independence.

Gracie smiled and read on. "So when I see the red, white, and blue of the American flag, I think of those signers of the Declaration of Independence. And I proudly celebrate the Fourth of July, America's birthday and Independence Day."

She dropped her arms down and glanced at us for a moment. "Did you know, boys? The Declaration of Independence is on display in Washington, D.C. Someday I hope to go there with Mom and Dad and see it."

I'm sure my eyes must have gone pretty wide right about then. Because that document would be really, really old by now! I hoped Gracie got to go to Washington to see it someday, too. And I hoped she took lots of pictures so us cats could see what it looked like when she got back.

She lifted her essay up again and took a breath, all ready to finish. I scooted closer so I didn't miss a thing.

But I didn't get to hear another word. That's because a really big commotion suddenly sounded outside. It was coming from just down the street. It got louder and louder, and sounded like it was getting closer and closer. A few seconds later, I saw a big bunch of people walking our way. We saw the same lady TV reporter in her high heels. She was walking backwards and holding her microphone in front of her. Beside her, a man with a camera on his shoulder was walking backwards, too. Then there was somebody else holding up a big, long pole with a light on the top. Plus there was a blonde lady with a can of hairspray and a brush. And there were a whole bunch of people just talking and making noise. They were sort of gathered in a group and moving along.

But there also appeared to be someone in the middle of the entire group. Someone I couldn't quite see because of all the other people surrounding that person.

The group kept on moving up the sidewalk and they got noisier as they went. Bogey turned and stared out the window.

Gracie put her paper down and leaned forward to look outside. "What in the world?"

Then I watched as her jaw fell open wide. "Oh my goodness . . . He's coming here? To our store?"

"What's going on?" I asked my brother.

He tilted his head in my direction. "Looks like we've got company, kid."

I crinkled my brow. "The good kind of company? Or the bad kind of company?"

"We'll know in a minute," he murmured.

Gracie gasped and ran off. "Mom! Mom! I can't believe it! *He's* coming here!"

"Who, honey?" came our Mom's reply.

Before Gracie could say another word, the crowd passed by our window. They reminded me of a big bunch of bees swarming around a hive. That's when I remembered how I'd been stung by a bee once and how much it hurt.

I sure hoped this "swarm" wasn't going to sting me, too.

But I figured I was about to find out. Because the door suddenly flew open wide. And the next thing I knew, the man with the light on the end of the long pole walked in. He stepped off to one side while a tall, skinny lady with short brown hair came in, too. She put a big roll of something red on the floor. Then she held onto one end of that roll and gave the rest a shove. That roll tumbled forward and kept on going. Until it had rolled all the way out into a long strip of red carpet. It went right up the main aisle into our store.

Now the man with the camera moved into our store and stood to the other side. The reporter walked in backwards and kept her microphone in front of her face. Her shiny, black hair stayed perfectly in place the whole time.

Then, from out of nowhere, a few notes of music blared out. And let me tell you, that music was really, really loud! I nearly jumped to the ceiling when I heard it. It sort of sounded like trumpets playing, "*Dat-ta-dah-dah*!"

After that, a tall man strolled in with his arms open wide. He held some kind of golden trophy in one hand. He was wearing blue jeans and a faded, brown leather jacket. His golden hair glistened in the light coming from the top of the pole. In fact, his hair was almost as golden as the statue he was carrying. I don't think I'd ever seen hair that color of gold before.

Suddenly, he raised his arms up and hollered, "It's me! Steele Bronson! And this is my Academy Award! I'm here to do some shopping."

All at once, women screamed from all over our store. And they kept on screaming . . . and screaming and screaming and screaming. Gracie squealed and Millicent gasped. Then Merryweather fainted right into our Mom's arms.

I turned to my brother. "I guess that's Steele Bronson."

"Yup, kid," he answered. "It would appear so."

"Gee," I meowed over all the noise. "If he's so hot, then why is he wearing that jacket?"

Bogey stood up. "Beats me, kid. But I think we'd better check this out. I have a feeling the games are about to begin."

Games? Did he say games? I liked games. At home I really liked playing with our favorite feather toy on a string. But something in Bogey's tone told me I might not like the kind of games he was talking about.

I gulped. "What do you mean?"

He nodded in the direction of the commotion. "Time to go to work, kid. Something's suspicious here."

"Suspicious?" I repeated.

I stared at the crowd around Steele Bronson. I wasn't sure if it was suspicious or not. But I did know things were a whole lot different from how they normally were.

Bogey raised his brows. "Yup, kid. Of all the antique stores in all the towns in all the world, I'd like to know why he walked into ours."

Holy Catnip!

CHAPTER 3

Holy Mackerel!

I just kept on thinking about what Bogey had said. Especially the part about something being suspicious.

So when he leaped off the desk and down to the scuffed hardwood floor, I figured I'd better follow him.

"I don't like the looks of this, kid," he hollered over his shoulder. "I have a hunch there's more to this picture than meets the eye."

"Um, okay . . ." I said as I ran after him.

Though I still wasn't sure what he meant. But since he was one of the best cat detectives in the business, I trusted his hunches. And I sure hoped I would start having hunches someday like he did.

I raced to keep up with Bogey as we ran around bookshelves and china hutches and camelback sofas. I didn't exactly know where we were going, but I knew it was my job to stick close to my brother. Plus I was supposed to stay alert and keep my eyes open for anything out of place. As cat detectives, Bogey and I ran surveillance on our house every night. That meant we checked things out, like doors and windows, to make sure our house was locked up tight. And to make sure our family was safe. Then, on days like today, when our Mom took us to her store, we liked to keep up our security work here, too.

Bogey made a beeline for the group gathered around Steele Bronson. I followed along behind him. But it sort of seemed to me that we should be staying *away* from the crowd. Not running toward it. Especially since that crowd just kept on getting bigger and bigger. More women were coming in the door and joining the rest of the ladies who were already there. And I didn't exactly want to be underfoot when all those women had their eyes glued to Steele Bronson. That meant they wouldn't be watching where they were going. And they wouldn't be watching for any cats running along the floor. An extra big guy like me with an extra long tail was just asking for it in a mob like that.

To top it off, most of the women in the store had practically flocked straight to Steele Bronson. Including Millicent and Merryweather and Gracie. But before they could get close enough to actually reach him, two big security guards held out their arms so no one could touch him. Funny, but I hadn't even noticed those security guards before.

Bogey and I jumped up on another dresser and then to a taller cabinet to get a better view. The security guards started telling the women to move back and gather together. Then they commanded everyone to stand behind a line of dining room chairs. But they weren't exactly speaking in nice, normal voices. Oh no, instead they were sort of yelling at everyone like drill sergeants yelling to soldiers. In a very mean way.

I glanced back at the cash register counter and noticed our Mom was still standing there. She had her arms folded across her chest and a big frown on her face. She shook her head and then picked up the phone.

Eventually, the screaming crowd quieted down and got pushed back even farther into our Mom's store. That's when Bogey and I got a better view of Steele Bronson. The blonde lady with the hairspray and the brush hovered around him. She'd brush his hair a little and then spray it. I could see a little "puff" of hairspray up every time she did. All the while, the tall lady leaned in and talked into his ear.

Bogey nodded toward the movie star and his bunch. "Time for us to give Mr. Bronson a proper welcome, kid."

I blinked a couple of times. "A proper welcome? What do you mean?"

Bogey grinned. "Looks like the guy just waltzed in and took over. Let's go remind him that he doesn't own the place."

"Um . . . okay," I told him. "But how do we do that?"

Bogey pointed at the floor. "Follow me, kid. I see an opening between him and those gorillas he's got for security. Let's go show him who's really in charge of security around here."

Right about then, I'm sure my eyes went even wider than my food dish. "He brought gorillas with him? Where?"

Bogey shook his head. "Don't sweat it, kid. It's just an expression. It's a name they use for really big guys."

"Oh . . . okay," I told him. But I looked around anyway, just in case there might be some other gorillas running around. Ones that I didn't know about.

Then I glanced down to the spot on the floor that Bogey had pointed to. Sure enough, there was an opening. Right between the camera guy and the security guys who were holding back ladies who were all trying to get to Steele Bronson.

"I don't like these people pushing our Mom's customers around like this," Bogey went on. "This Bronson guy is bad for business."

Those were his last words before he leaped onto the floor and took off running in a black streak. Did I mention that Bogey can run so fast that some even say he can fly? Well, I think this must have been one of those times. Because I jumped down right after him and I raced for all I was worth. But no matter how fast I ran, I couldn't keep up with him. In fact, I lost sight of him for a moment or two. But I just kept on running until I spotted him again.

And when I did see him, I could hardly believe it. That's because he was sitting right smack dab in the middle of that red carpet! To tell you the truth, he acted like that carpet had been rolled out just for him. He sat about ten feet from Steele Bronson and he stared him right in the eyes.

A hush fell over the room. Especially when *I* came skidding in. Sometimes it's not easy for a big guy like me to stop really fast. Sometimes my big body just keeps on going long after I've put on the brakes. But thankfully, I was able to stop a few inches before I bowled my brother over.

Steele Bronson had been talking to the lady reporter. He was smiling into the camera while the lady held the microphone close to his mouth.

Or, at least, he *had* been talking and smiling. Right until Bogey and I showed up. That's when he made a slashing motion with his hand across his throat and yelled, "Cut!"

Then he turned his attention to us. In fact everyone looked at us. But that didn't bother Bogey one bit. While he stared at Steele Bronson, I could feel everyone staring at us. To be honest, it sort of made me squirm a little.

Steele Bronson laughed. "Well, well, well. What have we here? My, what a magnificent steely-eyed stare you have, Mr. Cat. I have practiced that very look a million times in front of the mirror. But I've never perfected it quite like you have. Wherever did you come from?"

Gracie ducked under the arm of one of the security guards. "Those are my cats," she yelled with panic in her voice.

She ran right over and picked me up. All the while, Bogey just kept on staring at Steele Bronson without even blinking.

Steele Bronson raised a dark eyebrow and looked at Gracie. "And who would you be?"

"I'm Gracie. My Mom owns this store. My big cat here is Buckley. The one sitting on the floor is Bogey."

Steele smiled and his teeth were so bright I even had to squint a little bit.

"Bogey," he repeated. "That wouldn't be short for Bogart, would it? As in Humphrey Bogart?"

Gracie nodded. "Uh-huh. That's what my Mom says."

"Well," Steele Bronson said. "Humphrey Bogart was one of the greatest actors of all time. And I can see that your cat here has a knack for the trade himself. He could be a great actor, too."

Gracie crinkled her eyebrows together. "Bogey?"

Bogey? I repeated inside my mind. Sure I knew he'd done some cat food commercials in the past. But I never really thought of him as a great actor.

A great cat detective, definitely. One of the best, in fact. But a great actor?

I glanced down at my brother to see what he thought. But he just kept on staring at Steele Bronson.

Now the two security guards noticed us.

"Would you like me to remove that cat?" asked the bigger of the two men.

"Yeah," said the other guard. "Maybe you'd like us to toss the chump out of here."

Suddenly my heart began to pound really loud. Were these two guys really going to throw Bogey out of our Mom's very own store? We belonged here, unlike all these other people.

But Bogey didn't even flinch. And he didn't quit staring. Finally, he held up one front paw and slowly flexed his claws. His very, very sharp claws. He examined them closely, raised his brows, and went back to staring at Steele Bronson.

Steele Bronson passed his big trophy to the tall lady. Then he put his arms out before him, and made kind of a "U" shape with his hands. His thumbs were touching together and his fingers went straight up. He closed one eye and sort of looked through that U-shape, right at Bogey.

"Ah, excellent!" he proclaimed. "The bone structure, the play of light and shadow, the set of the jaw! There is no question about it."

Gracie put me back down beside Bogey. "No question about what?"

"Why, little girl," Steele Bronson announced. "Your cats must be in my new movie!"

For a moment, I thought Gracie was going to faint.

"Wh-a-a-a-t . . .?" she sort of stammered.

He clapped his hands together a couple of times. "That's right, people! That is why I have come to this lovely little town of . . ."

He turned to the tall lady and spoke barely above a whisper. "What's the name of this place again?"

"St. Gertrude," she whispered back.

"Oh right," he said.

Then he stood up tall and looked at the reporter. "You might want to get this on film," he informed her.

Once the camera was on, he held his arms open wide and addressed the crowd. "Yes, ladies and gentlemen! I, Steele Bronson, have come here, into the very heart of America. Now I intend to make a movie about the very foundation of this great nation of ours. Yes, I plan to thrill audiences with a story about the very beginnings of these United States. It will be about the Revolutionary War and those brave persons who fought to make us independent. And I intend to film what will obviously become a blockbuster, right here in St. Gertrude."

Cheers and applause arose from all the people who were gathered around.

Steele Bronson pointed to the tall lady beside him. "And Nadia, my assistant here, will be making the arrangements. She might even interview people for small parts in this movie. But we'll know more as things progress."

More squeals and cheers rose up from the group.

Then he pointed to Bogey and me. "And my fine feline friends here will be given starring roles in my movie. Clearly they have the qualities that all leading men should have."

We did? Holy Catnip! I wondered what qualities those were. And how did we get them?

The cameraman turned off his camera, and he and the reporter started talking really fast. As near as I could tell, they wanted to audition for Steele Bronson's movie.

Gracie kneeled down and petted us both. "Did you hear that, boys? You're going to be in a movie! Isn't that exciting? You're going to be famous!"

We were? I wasn't exactly sure what that meant, but Gracie seemed pretty happy about it all. So I figured it must be a good thing.

Suddenly the door opened and everyone sort of sucked in their breath all at the same time. It made kind of a *waauuuuh* sound. Now what was going to happen? Were we going to have more movie stars come into our store?

Instead we saw Officer Phoebe Smiley of the St. Gertrude Police Department step inside. She had another officer with her. I saw her raise her arm and wave to someone in the vicinity of the cash register counter. I guessed she was probably waving at our Mom.

Nadia, Steele Bronson's assistant, stepped forward and made a beeline for Officer Phoebe.

"I'm so sorry, Officer," she said with a British accent. "I fear we have created quite a lot of commotion in your town today."

Officer Phoebe nodded. "Yes, we just received a

'Disturbing the Peace' complaint."

Nadia smiled. "It happens everywhere we go."

Officer Phoebe put her hands on her gun-holster belt. "I'm sure it does. But this is a place of business, and I'm afraid you're holding things up. We'd like you to set up this little dog and pony show somewhere else."

"Dog and pony show?" I meowed to my brother.

First I'd heard mention of gorillas. Now I was hearing talk about dogs and ponies. Pretty soon we'd have an entire zoo inside our Mom's store.

"Just an expression, kid," Bogey murmured out of the side of his mouth. "I'll explain it later."

Much to my amazement, Bogey was still staring at Steele Bronson and his crew.

Steele Bronson turned and practically waltzed over to Officer Phoebe. "My goodness, what a stunning young police woman! Such cheekbones, such glamour! And such a shiny badge. You must be part of my new movie, too. How do you feel about wearing clothing from 1776?"

Officer Phoebe's mouth fell open. "I-I-I . . ."

He stepped closer and stared directly into her eyes. "I apologize for setting your town into such an uproar. Things will quiet down in a few days. Once we've started filming."

Now Officer Phoebe's eyes kind of glazed over. "Um . . . Uh . . . Uh . . ."

I'd never seen her act like that before. I really wondered what was wrong with her. Was she sick or something?

Steele Bronson took her hand in both of his. "In the meantime, I would propose a compromise. I would like to shop in this lovely store in peace. Perhaps for an hour? Afterward, I will sign autographs for all who would like one. Right here, so all these lovely customers will return. I have an entire stack of glossy photos of myself out in my limo. After I sign autographs, I promise I won't interfere with the course of business anymore."

I leaned toward Bogey. "He carries around pictures of himself? Why does he do that?"

Bogey rolled his eyes. "Beats me, kid. I guess he likes them."

Our Mom didn't carry around pictures of herself. Neither

did our Dad. Or Gracie. In fact, I don't think I'd ever met anyone who carried their own pictures around with them.

Our Mom worked her way through the crowd and came to stand next to Officer Phoebe.

"That will be fine," our Mom agreed. "Let's let Mr. Bronson shop for an hour. When he's finished, everyone can come back and get autographed pictures."

Cheers and murmurs rose up from the crowd again.

Then Steele Bronson fixed his gaze right on our Mom. "And you must be the famous Abigail Abernathy."

She held her hand out to shake his. "I'm Abby."

But instead of shaking her hand, he grabbed it and lifted it to his lips. "Ah, such a beautiful woman. Truly, truly beautiful. A face that an artist would want to capture."

Gracie and Millicent and Merryweather all sighed. Really loud.

But let me tell you, our Mom did not look happy at all. Neither did Bogey.

Our Mom pulled her hand away and took a step back from Steele Bronson.

He took a step closer. "I understand you're an expert on antique furniture. Especially furniture from when St. Gertrude was founded. My sources say that was one hundred and fifty years ago."

Our Mom eyed him carefully. "Yes, that's correct, St. Gertrude *was* founded one hundred and fifty years ago."

He flashed her one of his blinding smiles. "I'm also told that you're such an expert on St. Gertrude history, that you're writing a book about it."

Our Mom's mouth fell open wide. "How did you know that? I've only told a few people."

He turned his smile up a notch. "I have my sources. I've also been told that you have some furniture from some of the first families of St. Gertrude. Right here in your store."

Our Mom inched closer to Officer Phoebe. "Yes, I do. I have several pieces."

He tilted his head. "I'll buy them. All of them. I don't care what they are or what they look like. Or how much they cost."

Now our Mom's eyes went even wider.

"I'll need it for . . . my movie sets," Steele Bronson said.

"Yes, that's right, for my sets. To make the background of the movie look more real."

I turned to Bogey. "If this is the way this guy shops, it sure isn't going to take him an hour."

Bogey shook his head. "You got that right, kid. But it doesn't add up. Gracie just read in her essay that the American Revolution was almost two hundred and fifty years ago. So if Steele Bronson is making a movie about the American Revolution, why is he buying furniture that's only one hundred and fifty years old?"

I did the math in my head. "I don't know. That would mean he's off about a hundred years."

Bogey gave me a paw bump. "You got it, kid. Something's not right here. And I have a very bad feeling about all this."

I gulped. "You do?"

Bogey nodded. "Oh yeah, kid. I have a hunch we're about to get a whole new case for the Buckley and Bogey Cat Detective Agency."

Another hunch from Bogey? And a new case on top of that?

I'm sure my eyes went really wide right about then. "We are?"

Bogey nodded. "Yup, kid. I'd bet my last cat treat on it."

Holy Catnip!

CHAPTER 4

Holy Mackerel!

A whole new case for the Buckley and Bogey Cat Detective Agency! Just the thought of it made my heart pound really fast and my fur stand on end. I had to wonder why Bogey was so sure we'd have a new case before long.

I wanted to ask more, but I figured *now* was probably not the time. Instead, I followed my brother as we ran from the red carpet and jumped up on old, oak desk. Bogey grabbed a bag of cat treats that he had stashed in a drawer. He gave us each a couple of treats while we watched Officer Phoebe organize the entire crowd. She even managed to get all the ladies to walk out of our store single file.

But they sure weren't very quiet about it. No, they talked and squealed and giggled the whole way out. Some of them even got on their cell phones. They called their friends and took pictures as they left. The cameraman, the reporter, and the man with the light at the end of the pole all walked out, too. Then they sort of situated themselves in front of our building and started filming.

"Abby's store will be open again in an hour," Officer Phoebe told the crowd. "We'll let you back in then. Please line up along the sidewalk."

I heard more squealing and giggling coming from the

women. Honestly, I thought they'd all just walk off and come back later. So I was pretty amazed when I saw most of them start to line up already. That meant they would be waiting outside for an entire hour.

Just to get an autograph from Steele Bronson!

Holy Mackerel! I could hardly believe it!

I turned to my brother. "Would you ever stand in line that long just to get some guy to sign his name for you?"

Bogey grinned and passed us each another treat. "Nope, kid. Not unless he was signing it at the bottom of a big, fat check."

Somehow I figured he probably wasn't going to do that.

Officer Phoebe locked the front door as soon as everyone was outside. Then she stood next to the door to guard it.

Gracie skipped over to Bogey and me. I think she'd pretty much forgotten about practicing her essay for the contest. She put her arms around us and kept her eyes glued to Steele Bronson as he walked around the store.

"I can't believe he's here," she whispered again and again. "Him. The guy every girl dreams about. And you boys are going to be in his movie! I can hardly stand it! This is the most exciting day of my life."

It was? Funny, but the most exciting day of my life was the day when I got adopted into my family.

I glanced over to see Millicent and Merryweather sticking close to our Mom. Steele Bronson stood even closer to her. It was strange, but she didn't seem very happy at all about his being here.

In the meantime, his assistant, Nadia, went out to the limo to pick up a stack of his pictures. Officer Phoebe unlocked the front door to let her out and then locked it again behind her. As soon as Nadia had gone, the blonde woman who always fixed Steele Bronson's hair let out a huge sigh. Then she sort of melted into a wing chair and closed her eyes. I guess she must have been really, really tired. Maybe it was a lot of work to keep Steele Bronson's hair perfect all the time.

One of the security guys walked over to us. He leaned against a desk that was right next to the one we were sitting on.

He nodded to Gracie. "I'm Tango. And that's my buddy, Bravo, over there with Steele Bronson. Nice store your Mom's got here."

Gracie smiled. "Thanks. She works really hard to have a good store. And she really loves antiques. I come down to help her in the summer and on weekends. We bring Buckley and Bogey with us some days, too."

Tango grinned at Bogey. "I like the way you handled yourself out there, cat. You showed some real courage."

Bogey grinned back and lifted a paw. Then he bumped his paw against the security guard's huge hand.

Tango's eyes went wide. "Did you just give me a fist bump, cat? If I didn't know better, I'd swear you just gave me a fist bump."

But Bogey just sat there and kept on grinning.

"You did give him a paw bump, didn't you?" I meowed to my brother.

"Sure did," he meowed back. "He's a good enough guy. He's just doing his job. Like we are."

I tilted my head and looked up at Tango. I tried to salute him but I only ended up poking myself in the ear with my big paw.

Then Tango's eyes went even wider. "Did you try to salute me, big cat? If I didn't know better, I'd say you tried to salute me."

I crinkled my nose and meowed up to the man.

"And now he's trying to talk to me," Tango said. "Gracie, did you see all that?"

Gracie giggled. "Aren't they the best cats ever? We've got three more at home."

"Whoa . . ." Tango said. "Your cats are kind of scary . . . it's almost like they know what I'm saying . . ."

At that point, Tango scooted away and headed for the front door. But not without looking back at us a few times.

Bogey passed us a few more treats. I munched on one of my treats and then turned to look at our Mom. She was busy pointing out different pieces of antique furniture to Steele Bronson.

She ran her hands over the top of a desk. "This is an especially beautiful piece. Note the wood. It's walnut."

Let me tell you, Steele Bronson sure looked excited about that desk!

He nodded his head very, very fast. "And you say it was owned by someone who helped settle St. Gertrude?"

"Yes, it was," our Mom told him. "They moved here from Philadelphia and brought all their furniture . . ."

But Steele Bronson didn't even let her finish. "I'll take it."

Our Mom wrote it down in her receipt book before she pointed to a china hutch. "And this piece was owned by the first mayor of St. Gertrude. In fact, he and his family moved here from Boston. His wife loved to host big dinner parties with . . ."

Again, Steele Bronson didn't even let our Mom finish. "I'll take that, too," he said.

She wrote it down in her receipt book before she pointed to a table. "Here we have a full mahogany dining table along with eight chairs that . . ."

He was right behind her. "I'll take them also."

Holy Catnip! He sure was buying a lot of stuff in our store. I figured this would make our Mom happy, but she still wasn't smiling.

As Steele Bronson picked out all the stuff he wanted to buy, Merryweather and Millicent worked as fast as they could to group all that furniture together. Bravo jumped in and helped, too.

Nadia knocked on the front door and Officer Phoebe let her back in. Then Nadia walked up the red carpet and came over to the desk next to the one we were sitting on. She slapped a big stack of photos on the desk with a loud *thwack*! It made quite a breeze and I almost jumped to the ceiling. But she barely even glanced our way before she strolled off to join Steele Bronson.

"I've sent the reporter and cameraman packing! Exactly like you wanted," she told him.

He smiled at her. "Good."

Then he just kept on following our Mom around the store and buying more and more furniture. Before long, he had a huge bunch of furniture picked out. I wondered how he was going to move all that stuff out of our Mom's store. Sure, his limo was big, but it wasn't big enough to carry all that stuff.

Finally, our Mom said, "And that's everything in my store that was owned by the early settlers of St. Gertrude."

"Excellent!" Steele Bronson proclaimed. "Now, are there any paintings or photo albums or anything else? From the people who founded this town?"

"Why, yes . . ." our Mom sort of stammered.

Then she took him around and showed him all those things, too. Just like before, he bought every single one of them.

"Is that it?" he asked when they were done. "There's nothing left in the store from the early families?"

Our Mom smiled for the first time. "That's everything I can think of."

She wrote down a few more things in her receipt book. By now the list of things that Steele Bronson had bought was pretty long. Two pages full of stuff.

Steele Bronson pulled a credit card from his pocket. "Charge it all to my card."

Our Mom took his card. "Thank you for your business," she said very politely before she headed for the cash register.

Seconds later, we heard a loud knock on the glass front door. We turned to see a man in blue jeans and a faded, gray t-shirt standing there. His hair was the opposite of Steele Bronson's hair. While every hair on Steele Bronson's head was perfectly in place, this man's light, brown hair was sticking out all over. Kind of like he had just gotten out of bed.

Officer Phoebe hollered to the man through the thick glass. "Sorry, the store is closed right now. It'll be open again pretty soon."

The man pointed toward Steele Bronson. "I'm with him."

Steele Bronson glanced at the door. "Oh right. It's Franklin Jefferson. You can call him Frank. He's my writer. He's writing the script for my movie. Let him in."

Officer Phoebe crinkled her brow. "All right."

Then she unlocked the door and let the man stroll inside.

He yawned and headed straight toward the blonde women who had fixed Steele Bronson's hair. I couldn't tell for sure, but I thought she might be asleep. Frank looked at her and then slid into a chair next to hers.

"You're late, Frank!" Steele Bronson yelled at the man before he pointed to us. "And by the way, I want you to write those two black cats into my movie. They'll give it a certain 'noir' quality." He pronounced the word "no-whar."

I leaned toward my brother. "Noir? What does that mean?"

Bogey shook his head. "It means bleak, kid. Sort of dark and unhappy-like."

That's when I sat up straight and swished my huge tail. Back and forth. I wasn't sure if I wanted to be in a movie that was bleak. Or unhappy. To tell you the truth, I really only liked happy things.

Bogey pulled a few more cat treats from the bag. "Anything here strike you as being fishy, kid?"

I glanced around the room. "You mean, like the cat treats?"

Bogey shook his head. "Nope, kid. I mean, does anything seem odd to you? Out of place?"

Well, I had to say, the whole situation seemed "odd" to me. Ever since Steele Bronson had shown up, things had gone from odd to odder.

"Uh-huh. It sure does," I told Bogey.

He squinted his eyes and scanned the room. "So what is Bronson going to do with all this stuff he's buying? And why only stuff from the first families of St. Gertrude?"

I crinkled my eyebrows. "He said it's for his movie."

Bogey tilted his head and stared at the movie star. "That's what he says, kid. But I have a hunch the guy's telling a big, fat fib.

Bogey had another hunch? Well, if there was one thing I'd learned, it was that Bogey was probably right.

I munched on my last treat. "I guess he is an actor. So he could probably lie really well. And people would believe what he's saying."

Bogey stashed the bag of treats back into the drawer. "You got it, kid. You're thinking like a cat detective."

Frank pointed to us and chuckled. "Do you want me to write lines for those cats? Or just action scenes?"

Steele Bronson shot the man a dirty look. "Very funny, Frank. Cats aren't that smart. So no lines for them."

Well, let me tell you, *that* made the hairs on my back stand up. "What does he mean by that?" I meowed to my brother. "The part about us not being smart?"

I wasn't sure if I was the smartest guy around, but I sure knew my brother was smart. And to top it off, we had a really, really old cat in our family who was probably smarter than anyone. That's why we called her the "Wise One."

Bogey put a paw on my shoulder. "Take it easy, kid. Let him think we're not too bright. It might just come in handy."

All the while, I noticed Nadia was talking on her cell phone. She put it to her shoulder for a second and turned to Merryweather. "Is there a back door to this shop? Where we can load all this stuff into a big truck?"

Merryweather pointed to the back of the store. "There sure is. Right back there. We'll even help you get it loaded up."

"Good," Nadia said. "We've rented an old warehouse on the edge of town. We're going to store this stuff there for a while. Until we're ready to put it on the set."

"My goodness," Millicent jumped in. "You've already got a warehouse and storage set up? That was quick."

"You'd better believe it," Nadia nodded. "Things will roll pretty fast around here. We plan to start filming right away."

And speaking of fast, it wasn't long before everyone had all that stuff moved to the back room. From the sounds I heard next, I could tell a truck had backed up into the alley. And all the stuff that Steele Bronson had bought was being loaded up.

"Gracie," our Mom called out from the cash register. "Have you been practicing your essay?"

"No, Mom!" Gracie hollered back. "But I'll get right on it."

With those words, she pulled her essay out from her pocket.

Let me tell you, that sure got the attention of Frank Jefferson. He pushed himself up from his chair and headed our way.

"What'cha got there, little girl?" he asked Gracie.

"It's my essay," she told him. "It's for our Fourth of July essay contest."

"I'm a writer," he told her. "Let me look at it. I know a lot about this Fourth of July stuff. I'm related to both Benjamin Franklin and Thomas Jefferson. Indirectly, anyway. That's why my name is Franklin Jefferson. But everyone just calls me Frank."

She handed her essay to him. "Oh that's so cool. You must

be proud to be related to the people who founded our country."

He shrugged. "It's okay."

Gracie smiled. "Well, you're going to love it here in St. Gertrude. It's a great town."

Frank laughed. "I'm sure I will. I accidentally learned about it while I was doing research for my book. You have no idea how happy I am to have found this place."

Then, without saying another word, he started to read her essay so fast that I could see his eyes moving. Back and forth. Back and forth.

"Needs work," he told her as he pulled out a red pen.

Before Gracie could say a word, he started making marks on her essay. He drew lines and arrows and wrote things all over her papers. Her mouth dropped open wide and, for a moment or two, she just stared at him.

But he didn't seem to notice. "You need to punch it up here. Add some 'zip' and 'pizzazz' here. And cut this and add this."

Well, I wasn't sure what the words "zip" and "pizzaz" meant. And from the frown on Gracie's face, I wasn't sure if she did either.

He handed her essay back to her just as our Mom walked over to Steele Bronson. She held his credit card in front of her.

"I'm sorry, Mr. Bronson," she said. "But I'm afraid your credit card won't work. It was declined when I tried to use it for payment."

"What!" he practically shouted at our Mom. "Then try it again. I'm sure that card is good."

Our Mom shook her head. "No, I'm afraid not. I tried it twice."

"Oh this is ridiculous," he kept on shouting. "I'm Steele Bronson. Obviously, I can pay for all this furniture."

Our Mom smiled. "Not with that credit card, I'm afraid. You'll either need to use a different credit card or I'm afraid we'll have to unload that truck."

Steele Bronson stomped his foot and yelled at the top of his lungs. "Nadia! Come here at once!"

Nadia came running from the back room. She stopped in front of Steele Bronson and wiped the dust from her pants.

Steele Bronson crossed his arms. "Nadia, I need to use

your credit card to pay for this furniture. Mine doesn't work."

Her eyes went wide and her jaw practically hit the floor. "Steele . . . I can't pay for all this . . ."

"It's just for now," he told her. "I'll pay you back."

"But . . ." she started to say again.

He shook his head and held out his hand.

Nadia frowned and reached into her pocket to get her own credit card. She handed it to him and then he handed it to our Mom.

"Go!" Steele Bronson yelled at our Mom. "Ring up my furniture."

Our Mom frowned, too, but then she turned and went back to the cash register.

"All right, Steele," Nadia said. "I will not forget that you owe me."

"Not to worry, little one," he said with a sparkly smile. "By the time we're done in this town, we'll be back on easy street."

I turned to Bogey. "Easy street? That's a funny name for a street."

But Bogey squinted his eyes and stared at Steele Bronson. "Just an expression, kid. It means they plan to make a lot of money here."

I crinkled my brow. "From their movie?"

Bogey shook his head very slowly. "Maybe, kid. Maybe. But I'm not so sure. There's something's wrong with this picture."

And by "picture," I don't think he meant Steele Bronson's new movie.

Holy Catnip!

CHAPTER 5

Holy Mackerel!

Right after Steele Bronson had finished his shopping, Officer Phoebe let people back into the store just like she had promised. Then Nadia kept all those women herded into one huge, long line. And I do mean huge! The front of the line led straight to the desk where Steele Bronson sat with his pile of pictures and a big, black pen. The rest of the line snaked out the door and all the way down the block. As near as I could tell, it even turned the corner. I wondered if it might have gone down another block and even turned another corner or two.

Bogey and I watched it all from the desk next to the one where Steele Bronson was seated.

Bogey glanced at the long line of women and shook his head. "Dames. I can never make heads nor tails of 'em, kid."

"Dames," I repeated and shook my head, too.

Though I had to say, I wasn't exactly sure what Bogey was getting at. But I did still wonder why all those ladies would wait in line like that. Just to get Steele Bronson to sign his name on his picture.

Especially since he said almost the same thing to each one of the women. He always told them they were pretty or beautiful or had nice, shiny jewelry. And they always said something about being his number one fan. Funny, but I always thought there could only be *one* number one fan. Yet we had seen a whole bunch of number one fans today. Somehow it just didn't quite add up to me!

After a while, Bogey nudged me and nodded to the front of the store. "Let's move to the big window, kid. We'd better keep an eye out."

And so we did.

We sat and watched as lady after lady came through the line. After those women got their autographed picture, they didn't leave the store. Instead, they stayed and shopped. Pretty soon I wondered if we'd have any room left in the store for more people.

Our Mom and Merryweather and Millicent sure had their hands full. They rang up purchase after purchase on the cash register, and put things into bags and boxes. Gracie jumped in to help, too, even though she was supposed to be practicing her essay. I wasn't sure she'd actually read her essay since Frank had written all over it.

It was several hours later before we finally saw the end of the line. It was just outside the front door.

Right about then, I could barely hear our Mom say to Merryweather, "I've got to get Gracie to that essay contest. She hasn't even had any dinner yet. And I don't think she ate her lunch."

Merryweather waved her hand. "Don't you worry about a thing, Abby. I can stay late and take care of this."

"Me, too," Millicent added with a smile. "Especially if Bravo and Tango will help us out a little."

Both the security guards grinned.

"We'd be happy to," Tango said.

"That's right," Bravo added. "All this has upset your day. So we'd be happy to pitch in and set things right."

Our Mom smiled for the first time. "Thank you so much. All of you. I certainly appreciate it. Gracie would be pretty disappointed if she missed her essay contest tonight."

That's when I realized the security guards weren't even sticking with Steele Bronson anymore. To tell you the truth, that kind of surprised me. But it sure was nice of them to help out.

Our Mom turned to Gracie. "We'd better get going, honey."

Gracie pointed to us. "What about Buckley and Bogey?"

Our Mom sort of sighed. "I guess they're coming to the library with us. We won't have time to stop at home. And we can't leave them here."

"And we can't leave them in the car," Gracie added.

Our Mom smiled at her. "That's right. People are never supposed to leave pets in the car. Especially when it's as hot out as it is today. It's very dangerous."

"But it will be so much fun to take them to the library, Mom!" Gracie giggled. "I won't be so nervous when I read my essay if the boys are there."

Our Mom let out a little laugh. "Let's hope the people at the library think it's fun, too."

Gracie picked me up and put her arm around my brother. "Did you hear that, Buckley and Bogey? You're going to the library! You're gonna love it! There are books everywhere. It's one of the best places ever. And now you're going to see it, too!"

Well, that sounded pretty good to me. I reached up and gave her a kiss on the nose. Bogey leaned in to her and purred.

Then before I knew it, we were in our pet carriers and being carted out to the car. The sun was still bright in the sky and the day was hot. Really hot. It made me wonder about all those ladies who had waited in line to get Steele Bronson's autograph. They must have wanted it really, really bad to wait outside for so long in that heat.

Our Mom started the car and turned the air conditioning on nice and high for us. Then she drove toward the library. Along the way, she turned into a fast food drive-through. She ordered hamburgers and french fries for Gracie and herself. And she got hamburgers for Bogey and me.

"It's not the best dinner," she said to Gracie. "But it'll have to do for tonight. Since we didn't have time for anything else."

"Don't worry," Gracie smiled. "I'm just so happy I got to meet Steele Bronson. And he was in our store! I still can't believe it! I never thought something like this would happen to me. Every time I close my eyes, I can see him!"

I had a feeling that, if we weren't inside our car, Gracie

would be spinning around by now. And she would probably have me in her arms while she twirled. She had a huge smile on her face as she put our hamburger patties in our pet carriers. Then she turned and started to eat her own food.

Bogey and I gobbled up our burgers right away. As hamburgers go, they weren't bad.

But they certainly weren't tuna fish.

I peeked out at my brother from my pet carrier. "Do you think Gracie is ready for this contest tonight?"

He shook his head. "I dunno, kid. There was a lot of commotion this afternoon. So she didn't get to practice much. Especially after that guy made mincemeat out of her essay."

"Mincemeat?" I asked my brother. "He turned her essay into meat?"

Bogey shook his head. "Just another expression, kid. It means he destroyed it. Or made a huge mess of it."

I nodded at my brother. "Well, he sure did that. And I didn't like that Frank writing on her essay. I thought her essay was really good the way it was."

Bogey sighed. "Don't I know it, kid. Don't I know it. Some things just don't need changing."

All of a sudden, my heart started to pound really hard. What if Gracie couldn't read his writing? Or didn't know how to pronounce some of the words? That guy really did make a lot of changes. Was Gracie ready to read them all?

I glanced at Gracie in the front seat. The funny thing was, she didn't seem nervous at all. In fact, she sort of looked like she was in a daze. She just kept on smiling and staring off into the distance.

Our Mom took a left turn and then a right turn, and pulled into the library parking lot. The library wasn't far from our house.

And it was also very close the old church where we have the Buckley and Bogey Cat Shelter. The cat in charge is our friend, Luke, the church cat. He is a black cat who wears a white collar. Of course, there are some humans who help out, too.

The first time I'd seen that church, I thought it was one of the prettiest buildings in St. Gertrude. But now that I could peek out and see the library, well, I thought it was even prettier.

Both of the buildings had been made from old stones that had been carved so they fit together. And both of the buildings had big, oak double doors at the entryway. They also had some nice windows with stained glass pictures. And they were both built when the town of St. Gertrude was founded, about one hundred and fifty years ago.

And even though the church was a big building, the St. Gertrude Library was even bigger! It was four stories tall! It had lots of windows and pointy peaks along the roof. Plus it had some little round tower sections that stood out on either side of the building. I thought it looked more like a castle than what I guessed a library would look like!

Our Mom pulled Bogey's pet carrier out of the car and Gracie took me in mine.

Gracie leaned down to me. "Isn't this exciting, Buckley. You're going to see the library! It's so wonderful inside!"

I couldn't even imagine how it could look *more* wonderful on the inside. Because the outside looked wonderful enough. Especially when I saw two stone lions sitting on either side of the wide, front steps.

Plus there was a big stone sign standing in the grass by the walkway. The words on the sign read, "Hide not your talents. They for use were made. What's a sundial in the shade?" This was followed by the name, "Benjamin Franklin." So I guess he was the guy who wrote that saying.

Well, to be honest, I wasn't exactly sure what he meant by that. But I did remember seeing a sundial in a picture once. It had to be out in the sun or it didn't work. Otherwise, you couldn't tell time from it. And with all the bright sunshine outside, I figured a sundial would probably work really well today.

After that, I saw an even bigger stone sign. This one read, "The Arthur J. and Emily R. Fartheringston Library."

Gracie leaned down to my pet carrier. "See, Buckley? That's the name of our library. It was named after the people who used to live here. This mansion was their home. But when Mr. Fartheringston passed away, his wife turned the building into a library. So all the people of St. Gertrude could read lots of books and learn new things. Wasn't that nice of her?"

It sure was. Because I figured there must be lots of things that people and cats could learn at the library. I hadn't even set paw inside the building yet and I'd *already* learned some things.

Gracie and our Mom carried us through the front doors, and that's when I first saw the inside of the library. I had to say, Gracie had been right! It *really* was pretty on the inside. There were wooden beams across the ceiling, and old, wood paneling everywhere. The floor was covered in red carpet, and lots of old paintings and pictures hung on the walls. I could see a gigantic fireplace with a carved mantle off on one wall. Right above that fireplace was a really old and really huge painting of a man. He had white hair and a long, white beard. And a big smile on his face. He sure looked like a nice man to me.

On another wall was a really old painting of a lady. She had reddish-brown hair piled on top of her head. She was wearing a pretty, blue dress and had blue ribbons in her hair. She looked like she was probably pretty nice, too.

Gracie pointed first to one painting and then to the next. "See, Buckley? There's Mr. Fartheringston and Mrs. Fartheringston. When Mrs. Fartheringston turned this mansion into a library, she stayed in an apartment on the fourth floor until she passed away. She was actually our first librarian in St. Gertrude. And kind of a teacher, too. She used to have Science Club for kids in one room and Math Club in another. She wanted to teach kids all she could about Math and Science."

Holy Catnip. This lady *really* did sound nice to me.

"And guess what, Buckley?" Gracie went on. "She had three cats and they lived here, too. They ran around the library any time they wanted. But after they passed away, there haven't been any more library cats."

Okay, now I liked the lady even more. Though I thought it was kind of sad that there weren't any cats who lived here now. This building looked like a perfect home for a family of cats.

I leaned to the side of my pet carrier and meowed to my brother. "Did you hear that, Bogey?"

"Every word, kid," he meowed back. "Every word. Gracie knows her history. The girl has a real brain in her."

Bogey sure had that right! I was so proud of Gracie. And I really hoped she was going to win the essay contest. Especially since she talked about history in her essay, too.

Now we moved toward a really big, antique desk that sat off to one side. Way behind that, I could see a huge, wide staircase. It had a cherry wood banister with fancy carvings on the posts. Plus I could see wood paneling that had wood rectangles set into the paneling for decoration. The staircase circled around and went above us.

Let me tell you, Bogey and I loved to run the stairs at home. It was a lot of fun. But I was pretty sure it would be even more fun to run those big stairs right in front of us!

A lady stood up from the old desk just as soon as we walked in. She had gray hair that was piled on top of her head and kind of curled over her ears. She was wearing a blue dress that was way too big for her and little half glasses that sat on the end of her nose. Her nametag read, "Mrs. Penelope Peebles."

"Good evening, Abigail! And Good evening, Gracie!" said Mrs. Peebles. Her voice sounded kind of like a bird chirping.

"Hello, Penelope," our Mom said with a smile. "So nice to see you. I'm afraid we're running a little behind this evening. We had some unexpected excitement at the store today."

Mrs. Peebles sort of shivered. "I heard! I heard! Apparently that dreamboat, Steele Bronson, was in town! If only I could have gotten away from my desk to come down and see him."

"Do you know what a dreamboat is?" I meowed to my brother.

He shook his head. "Dames, kid. I've heard them say it before. But I have no idea what it means."

I crinkled my brow. "Dames?"

Bogey nodded. "Yup, kid. Dames. They have a language all their own."

Mrs. Peebles put her hand on Gracie's head. "Gracie, you and your Mom can go into the auditorium. The other finalists are all there. The director of the program will be taking you around and showing you how the ceremony will go. Then you kids will each draw numbers to see what order you'll be reading your essays."

Gracie and our Mom started to carry us toward the door on the left behind the desk. There was a sign above the door that read, "Auditorium." And another sign on a stand that said, "Independence Day Essay Contest tonight!"

We were almost to the door when Mrs. Peebles called out to us. "Wait a minute! Did you bring your cats with you?"

Our Mom turned around. "I'm sorry, Penelope. But the boys were at the store with us today. And with all the excitement, we didn't have time to drop them off at home."

"Well! That simply won't do!" Mrs. Peebles said. "You'll have to leave them in their pet carriers out here. Under the front desk."

"They won't be any trouble," our Mom told her. "We'd rather keep them with us."

Now Gracie piped up. "There used to be cats in this library. Mrs. Fartheringston had three cats who lived here."

Mrs. Peebles stood up straight with her chin in the air. "You don't need to lecture me on the history of this place, young lady. Besides, the auditorium was added on later. There are no food or drinks in the auditorium! And certainly no cats!"

Right about then, my jaw practically hit the bottom of my pet carrier. If we weren't allowed in the auditorium, how could we watch Gracie read her essay?

"What will we do?" I meowed to my brother.

But he just grinned back. "Don't sweat it, kid. Time to put on your 'cute' routine."

"My 'cute' routine?" I asked him.

"Yup, kid. You know the drill. Remember what Lil Bits showed you about being cute. Then put it into high gear."

"Huh?" I asked, right before I remembered what Bogey was talking about.

We had once gone undercover at a cat show. And part of solving our case depended on me being cute. So one of the older, formerly retired cat detectives at our house, Lil Bits, taught me how to act cute. And let me tell you, she sure knew what she was doing. Because it worked like a charm.

But I didn't exactly enjoy acting cute or even being called cute. Big, tough cat detectives weren't supposed to be cute or adorable. And I sure didn't see Bogey acting that way. Still, the job of being a cat detective wasn't all tuna fish and cat treats. Sometimes a guy just had to do his part. Even if he wasn't happy about it.

So as our Mom and Gracie carried us to the desk just like they'd been told, I did just as I'd been told. I tilted my head to the right. Then to the left. And I looked right at Gracie when I did. I kept it up until she couldn't stop staring at me.

Our Mom scooted Bogey's pet carrier under the desk and then Gracie started to scoot mine beside his.

"*Ooooh*, Buckley," she sighed. "You are *soooooo* cute. I sure wish you boys could be there when I read my essay."

I meowed and kept on acting as cute as I could be.

"Okay," Gracie finally whispered. "If I leave your pet carriers unzipped, do you promise to come watch me in the contest? And be back here before we're ready to leave? And not let anyone see you?"

I put my paw up against the front of my carrier.

"All right," she whispered even softer.

I could see our Mom and Mrs. Peebles heading into the auditorium.

Gracie quietly unzipped my pet carrier. "Now, you boys be good and don't get into trouble. I'll look for you while I'm reading my essay."

I reached up and gave her a kiss on the nose.

She smiled before she unzipped Bogey's pet carrier, too. Then she jumped up and skipped off to follow our Mom and Mrs. Peebles. She looked back at us once before she went into the auditorium.

Bogey and I waited a few minutes before we stepped out of our carriers.

Bogey gave me a paw bump. "See, kid. I told you. Cute gets 'em every time."

"Um . . . I guess so," was all I could say.

He nodded toward the ceiling. "Now, let's go investigate this library. And find out why Gracie likes it so much."

Without waiting for a response, he took off running. Straight for that curved staircase with the pretty banister.

And all I could do was run after him and try to keep up.

Holy Catnip!

CHAPTER 6

Holy Mackerel!

I could hardly believe it. There we were, running through that huge four-story library just as fast as we could go. Bogey had dashed across that red carpet in a black blur as he made a beeline for the big staircase. And I had raced right after him. Before I knew it, we were running right up those stairs. We took the steps two at a time, and let me tell you, we were zooming! At some point, I'm pretty sure Bogey was actually flying. I dug in my claws and pushed off with all my strength to keep up with him. It was a lot of fun, especially since the whole staircase went around in a gigantic circle.

But it straightened out after we reached the second floor. That's when the stairs went up and down, just like regular stairs. And the wooden banister wasn't nearly as fancy, even though it was still really pretty.

Thankfully, we didn't run up the next set of stairs right away. Instead we paused for a moment on the second floor landing. I was breathing really hard and it took me a few seconds to catch my breath. But Bogey was breathing just like he normally did. He sat and licked the bottom of his right front paw while my heart slowed down a little.

Then he nodded at the stairs. "Let's start at the top and work our way down. Sound good, kid?"

I glanced over at a big rock in a glass display case not far from us. "Um . . . sure. Okay."

With that, we were on our way again. We raced up the next staircase and just kept on going. Luckily, there weren't any people around. That's because the library was closed except to the people going to the essay contest on the first floor. It was the perfect time for Bogey and me to run around without anyone seeing us.

We finally stopped when we reached the fourth floor. Right away, I could tell there was something very different about this floor. Somehow, everything looked a lot older up here. Gracie had told us this was where Emily Fartheringston had lived when she turned the rest of the mansion into a library. It had been her apartment back then.

But it sure didn't look like someone's apartment now. Instead it was kind of dark, and some of the lights didn't even work at all. Plus there was a light in the back corner that sort of blinked on and off. Not that it mattered so much to us cats, since we can see in the dark anyway. But I was pretty sure humans wouldn't be able to see up here so well. Maybe that was why it looked like people didn't come up to this floor very often.

Bogey sniffed the musty air and started walking slowly. I could tell his senses were on full alert.

So I figured I'd better have my senses on full alert, too. Especially since I wanted to be as good a cat detective as my brother was. And well, if he had his eyes peeled and his ears tilted forward, then I figured I should probably do the same.

Together we walked softly up one row and then down another. And up and down, from row to row. The old wooden bookshelves were so tall that they nearly blocked out what little light there was in that huge room. Especially since each one of those big, giant bookcases was absolutely crammed full of books. Very, very old books, as near as I could tell. With lots of dust on them.

For some reason, we started tiptoeing around very quietly. Though to tell you the truth, I wasn't sure why we were being so careful.

Finally, Bogey paused and nodded toward a set of books near the floor of one bookcase. "Take a look at these, kid. Notice anything unusual about these books?"

I took a good look and tried to figure out what he was getting at. "Um . . . well . . ."

I leaned in closer and sniffed. Before I knew it, I sneezed louder than I'd ever sneezed before. A few seconds later I sneezed again. Then I looked around to see if anyone had heard me. Funny, but my heart started to pound like we were about to get caught or something.

Bogey grinned at me. "I'd say you picked up on something, kid."

I did?

I shook my head and blinked a couple of times. "There sure is a lot of dust around these books. And they smell funny."

Bogey nodded at the books. "You got it, kid. That's mold you're smelling. These books are really old. Probably some of the first ones brought into this place."

I leaned in again. "These books are a lot like the books our Mom sells in her store."

Bogey nodded. "They're old enough to be antiques, all right."

He ran his paw along the edge of the bookshelf, and his black toes turned gray with dust. I could see the place on the shelf where he had swiped it clean. In fact, that clean spot stood out from the rest of the dust on the shelf. Bogey had once told me that cat detectives call marks in the dust a "disturbance." He said he'd seen footprints and fingerprints and all kinds of things in dust or a layer of dirt. Sometimes a disturbance could even be a big clue in a case.

But not this time. Not when Bogey had been the one to do the disturbing. I watched as he grinned and wrote the letters "BBCDA" in the dust, too. For the Buckley and Bogey Cat Detective Agency. Then he blew the dust off his paw.

He stood back and admired his paw-work. "I'd say no one has checked these books out in a while, kid."

I looked closer at them. "That's weird. I wonder why not."

Bogey shook his head. "Don't know, kid. Guess people only want to read new books."

I crinkled my brow. "But if they only read new books, won't they sort of miss out on things people knew a long time ago?"

Bogey moved down the row a little way. "That would be my guess, kid. Seems like old stuff might be important to know, too."

I suddenly thought of the oldest cat who lived at our house. She was so old you might even say she was ancient. But because she was so old, she'd seen all kinds of things and been all kinds of places. As a result, she was very, very wise. That's why we called her the "Wise One." Even though her real name was Miss Mokie.

Now Bogey pointed to a set of books that were extra tall and more narrow than the other books around them. There was an entire collection of them. He wiped the spines off with his paw, so we could read the titles. It turned out they all had the same title but different volume numbers.

So I read that title out loud. "The Complete Works and Diaries of . . . Arthur J. Father . . . Farther . . . Farthering . . . ston . . . Fartheringston."

Let me tell you, a name like Fartheringston wasn't exactly the easiest name for a guy like me to say!

I raised my brows. "This guy must have been pretty important to St. Gertrude."

Bogey nodded his head. "Sounds like it, kid. But I never heard of him before today."

I looked closer at the collection. "Well, whoever he was, he sure wrote a lot of books."

Bogey sniffed around and then tilted his ears forward. "You got that right, kid. But we'd better get a move on. We've gotta be there when Gracie reads her essay."

"Aye, aye," I told him.

I tried to salute him but I only ended up poking myself in the nose. Luckily he didn't see me since he was already headed for the stairs. So I chased behind him and together we raced down to the third floor.

This floor looked a lot different from the last floor. I could hardly believe they were even part of the same building.

The lights on this floor were nice and bright, and I didn't see any dust anywhere. In fact, the whole place looked pretty clean. And the books here looked like they were new. Or at least, they weren't as old as the ones we'd seen on the last floor.

Bogey and I zoomed up and down the aisles. The bookshelves here weren't as tall as the floor before, and they were made from metal. But each one was still packed with books.

It didn't take us long to run around all the rows. Then we headed down to the second floor right away. This floor looked a lot like the last floor. Again, we ran through all the aisles and came out near the staircase.

That's when I stopped and sat in front of the display case with the big rock. I stared at it for a few seconds and tried to make sense of it. There were lots of marks and lines that looked like they had been carved into that rock. And at first, I just thought it was some kind of artwork. But after I tilted my head from side to side and kept on staring at it, I could finally make out some letters. Then the more I looked at it, the more clearly I could see those letters. They were in groups, like words. But the only thing was, those letters didn't exactly spell out any words that I recognized.

Bogey loped over and sat beside me. Then he gazed at the big rock, too.

"What do you make of this, kid?" he asked me.

I squinted my eyes and stared at it some more. "I'm not sure. It's like somebody was trying to write words on this rock, but those words just don't make any sense."

Bogey shook his head. "It doesn't look like English, kid. Or Spanish or French."

He pointed to the label on one corner of the rock. It read, "Found in library basement, after the passing of Emily Fartheringston, when the entire building was willed to the City of St. Gertrude. Message carved into stone is of an unknown tongue, possibly ancient Native American."

"Tongue?" I repeated. "It doesn't look like a tongue to me. It looks more like the kind of rock we have in our front yard."

Bogey put his paw on my shoulder. "Just an expression, kid. Tongue is a word they use for language."

I tilted my head. "Oh . . . okay. Sometimes I don't understand why there are so many expressions for things."

Bogey nodded. "I hear ya, kid."

Then I remembered Gracie and her essay. "Um . . . Bogey. We probably better hurry up and get to the auditorium."

But Bogey didn't answer. Instead he just stayed put and kept his eyes glued to that rock.

I got up and slowly trotted toward the stairs. "C'mon, Bogey. We'd better get going."

Bogey turned his body my way but his gaze didn't follow. It stayed right on that stone.

"Sure. Right, kid," he sort of mumbled. "Let's go."

This time I was the first one to make it to the stairs. Finally, Bogey got up and loped in behind me. And though his feet were moving, his mind seemed to be somewhere else.

So I ran on ahead, down that circular staircase to the first floor. I had to say, it was as much fun to race down those stairs as it was to race up them. I sure hoped we could come back to the library another time. So we could run those stairs again!

I was almost to the bottom when I looked back at Bogey. And I could hardly believe it! Once again, I'd gotten somewhere before he did! That had never even happened *once* before, let alone twice in one day. I waited until Bogey joined me and we trotted toward the auditorium. All the while, we kept an eye out for any people who might be around.

We were almost to the door when Bogey said. "What if it's not really a language at all, kid?"

I glanced back at my brother. "What if what isn't a language?"

Bogey stopped and stared up at the tall ceiling. "The letters on that stone, kid. What if they're not written in any kind of a language?"

I tried to keep him moving toward the door of the auditorium. "Um, I don't know. If it's not a language, then what would it be?"

Bogey grinned. "Think about it, kid. If you wanted to leave a secret message for someone, how would you write it?"

By now, we were just a few feet from the door. It had been propped open with a doorstop.

"Um . . . I don't know," I whispered.

Bogey glanced back at the stairs. "In a code, kid. You'd put it in a secret code."

Right then, I think my eyes went about as wide as my food dish. "A secret code?"

Bogey nodded, just as we reached the side of the open door. "That's right, kid."

"But-but-but . . ." I sort of sputtered. "Why would somebody write something in a secret code?"

Bogey grinned again. "So everyone else can't read it. It's meant for a certain someone's eyes only. Because secret codes usually lead to something hidden, kid. Something big. Something important."

I gasped. "They do? You mean, something like hidden treasure?"

"Could be, kid," Bogey said.

"Wow . . ." I breathed. "But if something is written in a secret code, how can anyone ever figure out what it says? Like the one who is supposed to read it?"

Bogey ran toward the wall next to the open door, and he motioned for me to do the same. Together we hid behind the wall and peeked into the huge room.

"There's usually two parts to a code, kid," he said quietly. "There's the code and then there's the thing that decodes it. The part that decodes the secret code is called the key."

"A key? Like a door key?" I asked.

Bogey shook his head. "Nope, kid. It's different. A key for decoding a code is usually something like a document. Or a page in a book. Or a letter."

I blinked my eyes a few times. "Sounds like a lot of work to me."

Bogey shrugged. "Back in the olden days, people used secret codes all the time. It's how they kept other people from getting their personal info, kid. Or from finding something they'd hidden for a certain person to find."

"Oh . . ." was about all I could say.

A secret code. I'd never seen a secret code before.

"Too bad we didn't memorize it, kid," Bogey said. "So we could take a shot at decoding it ourselves."

Suddenly my heart started to pound really loud. "We could?"

Bogey nodded. "Absolutely, kid. In the biz we call it 'cracking the code.'"

Holy Mackerel! That was a new one for me. In all my training as a cat detective, I hadn't learned how to crack any codes yet. It sounded like it might be really hard, and, well, kind of exciting at the same time.

"We'd better go back," I whispered to my brother. "We'd better go take another look at that stone. Maybe we can each remember part of what was written there."

Bogey shook his head. "No can do, kid. Take a gander inside."

I crinkled up my forehead. "A gander? Isn't that some kind of a bird?"

Bogey tilted his head toward the door opening. "Nope, kid. Just another expression. For looking at something."

So I did just that. I looked inside that auditorium. Mrs. Peebles had just walked onto the stage in front. She picked up the microphone and starting speaking into it.

The ten kids who were in the essay contest all sat side by side in the front row. And they were the only ones sitting in the front. I spotted the back of Gracie's head and I couldn't help but smile. I really hoped she was going to win the contest tonight!

There were a whole, big bunch of people sitting in the audience, so I knew Gracie was probably going to be pretty nervous. That meant it was even more important than ever for Bogey and me to be there for her.

Bogey nodded toward the row of seats in the back. "C'mon, kid. It's show time. Let's run in now. While all the eyes are to the front."

With that, I followed Bogey as we zoomed into the auditorium. Single file and low to the ground. And even though I was dying to go back and look at that big stone again, I knew it was too late. We'd just have to figure out another time to see it, so we might have a chance to crack that code.

But right now, the essay contest had begun.

Holy Catnip!

CHAPTER 7

Holy Catnip!

I had so much on my mind as Bogey and I raced into the auditorium that I could hardly think straight. Not only was I worried about Gracie, but I couldn't stop thinking about that stone. If Bogey was right — just like he almost always was — the letters on that rock were a secret code. And the more I thought about it, the more I was dying to figure out the message in that code. And best of all, what it might lead to.

Would it be treasure? Or a map to a secret hideout? Or something else?

My heart must have been beating about a million miles an hour as I followed Bogey. It sounded so loud in my ears that I was afraid someone might hear it as we zoomed to the left side of the room. We paused when we reached the back row of folded, padded seats. That's when I took some deep breaths and tried to settle down.

"Okay, kid, stay low and follow me," Bogey whispered. "I see the perfect spot for us down there. We'll have a front row view."

"Okay, got it," I told him.

Then we stayed single file as we slunk past row after row of seats. We had to be careful not to be spotted, because lots of those seats had people sitting in them. So we ran nice and smooth and didn't make any sudden movements that might get someone's attention. We kept our tails down and stuck close to the side of each row.

We continued slinking along until we were almost all the way down the slope of the auditorium floor. That's when Bogey nodded toward an empty section on the end of a row. He slipped into that row and I followed right behind him. Then we started to sneak down under the folded chairs. From one level to the next. Row after row. Until finally, we made it to the front row where the contestants were seated. Gracie was sitting on the left of all the kids and closest to us. We moved over so we were just a few seats away from her.

I peeked out and caught her eye. She started to giggle but she quickly put her hand over her mouth.

I knew that she knew we'd made it. She knew that Bogey and I were there to watch her and support her.

Then Bogey and I scooted into the shadows under the chair. Sometimes there are real advantages to being black cats. We can hide in the shadows a whole lot better than cats of other colors. That meant we could see out, but no one could see us.

Now Mrs. Peebles announced, "Would everyone please rise for the presentation of the colors followed by our National Anthem? Please remain standing until the color guard exits the hall."

I turned to my brother. "Huh? The what? Do we have to rise?"

Bogey shook his head. "Nope, kid. We just stay hidden. This is where they bring out the flag and play the National Anthem."

I crinkled my forehead. "The what?"

Bogey flexed a paw. "The National Anthem, kid. Every country's got one. And this is ours. The Star Spangled Banner."

Before I could say another word, everyone in the audience stood up all at once. Then three men and one woman marched single file onto the stage. They wore really nice uniforms, and I had to say, they looked pretty sharp. They stepped around so they stood side by side and formed a perfect line. The two people on the outside had long rifles resting on their shoulders, while the two people in the middle carried flags. One was the American flag, just like our Mom had in her store. Suddenly the man holding the American flag shouted some commands. Then the group did some pretty fancy marching for a few minutes.

Holy Catnip! I could hardly believe it! Here I was, a guy who could never get his paws to go where he wanted them to go. And now I was watching those people march around without even bumping into each other. Or tripping over their own feet. I was so amazed that I closed my eyes and shook my head a couple of times. Just to make sure it was all real.

Finally, some music started to play and everyone stood up and sang. I saw Gracie stand up, too, and she started to sing just as loud as she could.

"Oh say can you see? By the dawn's early light . . ." everyone sang.

I leaned over to Bogey. "Do you think we should get uniforms? Those people sure do look nice in theirs."

Bogey nodded. "They look spiffy, all right, kid. But we do so much undercover work, they might make us stand out."

Well, Bogey had a point about that.

When the song was over, the man with the flag shouted a few more commands. Then the whole group marched off the stage. Again, they all stepped together perfectly. They went up the right side of the room and out the back door. I'd never seen anything like it in my life!

Now Mrs. Peebles climbed the stairs onto the stage and went back to the microphone. Then she introduced all ten of the essay contestants. When she did, each contestant stood up and the people in the audience clapped. She called Gracie's name last, and I could hear our Mom cheering for her. Bogey and I sat there and grinned. I was so proud of Gracie, I could hardly stand it!

Next Mrs. Peebles introduced the three judges who were sitting at a table near the stage. There were two men and one lady. One of the men was the mayor of St. Gertrude, a man with bushy, gray hair named Phineas Bobb. The other man and lady worked for businesses downtown. The man was about the same age as our Dad and had a baldhead. And the lady was probably a little younger than our Mom and had puffy, blonde hair.

After everyone had been introduced, Mrs. Peebles called the first contestant onto the stage. A red-haired girl named Lizzie Smith.

But poor Lizzie was shaking so hard that she could barely even read. That was, until I saw Gracie wave and smile at her. And suddenly Lizzie's voice started to sound a whole lot stronger.

I thought that was awfully nice of Gracie to help Lizzie. Especially since Lizzie might even win the contest now, thanks to Gracie's help. But I guess Gracie knew what it felt like to be nervous, and she didn't want Lizzie to feel that way.

When Lizzie had finished her essay, the audience clapped again. Then Mrs. Peebles called the next contestant, Billy Canton. And it went on and on like that. Each one of the contestants had good essays. But I didn't think they were as good as Gracie's.

That was, until Mrs. Peebles called the contestant right before Gracie, Dylan Federov. When Dylan came to the stage, it was almost like someone had turned on some extra lights. I guess you could say he sort of had a glow about him. He had light brown hair and light blue eyes. And to tell you the truth, he was probably a kid who wouldn't normally stand out much. But when he smiled up there on stage, well, he stood out, all right. He walked up to the microphone with one hand behind his back and his essay in his other hand.

"It is my sincere pleasure to be here, today," he told the audience. "Because nothing makes me happier than talking about America."

"And when I think of America, I think of the American flag," he went on without looking at his essay. "A flag known as 'Old Glory.' A flag with white stars on a blue background, and red and white stripes. The red, white, and blue. I'd like to show you an American flag that I own."

He took his hand from behind his back. Now I could see he was holding a little American flag on a small stand.

Dylan smiled even brighter. "My flag is probably not the biggest flag you've ever seen. And well, it's a little bit tattered around the edges. It's faded some, too. But in my eyes, it's one of the most beautiful flags ever. You see, this flag once belonged to my grandfather. He gave it to me before he passed away when he was very, very old. I miss my grandfather. Not only was he a great man, but he taught me a lot of important things."

I noticed Dylan still hadn't looked at his paper. Holy Catnip!

Now he took on a more serious expression. "My grandfather taught me that freedom is one of the most important things of all. Being free makes people happy. In the United States, we have something called the Constitution. It guarantees us things like freedom of speech and freedom of religion and lots of other things. These things were important to my grandfather, because he didn't grow up with any freedoms at all. That's because he grew up in Russia, when it was a Communist country. Under Communist rule, my grandfather's family was very, very poor. They had to stand in line for hours to get things like a loaf of bread. Or some coffee. Or even a roll of toilet paper."

A couple of the contestants giggled at that.

Dylan smiled before he became serious again. "A lot of people starved in his country, because they couldn't get enough food. But they weren't allowed to work harder and make more money, so they could buy more food, either. No, they were forced to live a life of poverty, and they had no way out. Especially since my grandfather's family was not allowed to travel more than twenty-five miles away from home. And speaking of homes, his family wasn't even allowed to own their own home. No, his family was forced to live in an apartment owned by the government, and, well, the government didn't take very good care of it. So it was not a very nice place to live."

Right about then, I sat up and leaned closer. Dylan's essay was so good it had me on the edge of my seat. Well, except that I was *actually* sitting on the floor . . . But either way, Dylan's words really made me think about things. Our Mom and Dad got to choose what home they wanted to live in, and they worked to pay for it. Plus, they worked to buy all the food that we needed. And, I had to say, I sure was glad I was free to work as a cat detective. I would be awfully sad if I couldn't.

"When my grandfather became a young man," Dylan went

on, "he defected to the United States. America. Where he had freedom. He soon learned that he could work hard and make money to pay for the things he wanted. Here in the 'Land of the Free,' he finally owned a house of his own. Plus he had enough food to eat, and he could travel wherever he wanted to go. Whenever he wanted to. My grandfather was so much happier living here."

Dylan paused for a moment and his voice became a little softer. "But my grandfather never forgot what his life was like when he was little. And he wanted to make sure I understood what it was like, too, and how important it is to be free. That's why he gave me his flag, the flag I wave before you here today. Because this flag was very important to him."

Now Dylan paused and looked around the room. "So why, you must wonder, was this flag so special to him?"

He held the flag up and waved it slowly back and forth. "Because this is the flag that was given to him on the day he became a citizen of the United States. In a ceremony before a judge. It was one of the happiest days of his life. He wanted to pass on the story of freedom to me, so that I would never take freedom for granted."

By now the whole audience sat like they were in a trance, and all eyes were on Dylan.

"Freedom," he went on, still without looking at his essay. "Such a simple word. But yet it means so much. And it was exactly what George Washington, the man called the 'Father of our Country,' was fighting for. He and the rest of the soldiers in the Continental Army, who fought in the Revolutionary War . . . Thanks to all those who fought for freedom, I am lucky enough to stand here before you today, telling you the story of my grandfather. So you will know just how precious freedom really is."

Then he simply smiled and said, "Thank you very much. God Bless America!"

When Dylan finished his essay, I was sort of sad it was over. Because I really liked listening to him.

Then all of a sudden, the people in the audience started clapping like crazy. Some people even cheered and whistled. Before long, all that clapping and cheering got to be pretty loud. Lots of people stood up and gave him a standing ovation.

One thing was for sure, everyone really liked what he had to say. They really liked his essay.

I glanced over at Gracie. She was even standing and clapping for him, too. When the audience had quieted down, I saw her glance at us. She was going to be the last one to read her essay.

And let me tell you, I sure wouldn't want to read an essay after Dylan had just given his.

Beside me, Bogey shook his head. "Tough act to follow, kid."

"You can say that again," I murmured.

Now I saw our Mom stand up and move down to the chair behind Gracie's.

Gracie turned and frowned. "Mom, I'll never beat Dylan. His essay was the best. Better than any essay I've ever heard. Better than my essay."

Our Mom touched Gracie's arm. "It doesn't matter if you win or lose. I'm proud of you for entering this. You've done a great job with your essay."

But Gracie just gave our Mom kind of a wobbly smile.

The next thing I knew, Mrs. Peebles was calling her name. Gracie walked over to the right side of the stage and climbed the stairs. She held her essay in front of her and she kept turning the pages in one direction and then the other. Her bright flowered sundress swirled around her legs.

Bogey nodded toward her. "I don't like the looks of this, kid. She's having a hard time reading all that junk Frank wrote on her pages."

I suddenly started to shake in my paws. What if Gracie couldn't read what Frank wrote?

Gracie took big, lumbering steps toward the microphone. She kept on trying to read her papers all the way to the stand.

Once she got there, she looked up at the audience and smiled. Then she started to read.

"My name is Gracie Abernathy and I am proud to be an American. It makes me smile every time I see the red, white, and blue — the flag that is the un-de-niable and ir-re-fut . . . ir-re-fut-able . . ."

She paused for a moment and stared at her essay, before she kept on reading. "Ir-re-fu-table symbol of our country, one of the great, super powers of the world. When I set my eyes upon our flag, I am so happy that the likes of Benjamin Franklin and Patrick Henry and Abigail Adams put their fortunes and their lives on the line to create a country born of an idea. And that idea was freedom. Pure and simple. Freedom."

"Wow," I whispered to my brother. "That doesn't even sound like her essay at all."

Bogey shook his head and frowned. "Don't I know it, kid. Don't I know it."

Gracie took a deep breath and kept on reading, but very slowly. "While many European countries are very old, the United States is but a . . . a merry . . . I mean, a mere . . . babe in diapers compared to the likes of France or England. And like a baby, we started out small, with only thirteen colonies — Massachusetts, New Hampshire, Connecticut, Rhode Island, New York, New Jersey, Delaware, Pennsylvania, Virginia, Maryland, North Carolina, South Carolina, and Georgia."

She finished reading the paragraph and I could tell she let out a sigh. Though at least she'd stepped away from the microphone before she did.

I waved at Gracie and tried to get her attention. Just so she would know we were there for her. Especially since she was having such a hard time reading her essay. Or, maybe I should say, the new version of her essay that Frank Jefferson had written.

She took another breath and kept on reading in a shaky voice. "Let me take you back, way back . . . Back to colon-ial America. Men wore triangle . . . I mean, tri-cornered hats. And women wore long dresses with petti-coats. Somewhere in the distance, a fife and drum were playing. At first life was peaceful in the colonies. But then King George III became a merci-less . . . ty . . . a merci-less ty-rani-cal ruler, an absolute des-pot, and a page in history was turned forever. And the colonists were set on a col-lision course with destiny . . ."

By now I felt kind of a pain in my chest. Poor Gracie was having so much trouble reading the words on her paper. Partly because she hadn't practiced this new version of her essay. And partly because she probably couldn't read Frank's writing. I only wished the audience could've seen her earlier, when she read the essay that *she* wrote. Because she had done such a wonderful job then.

I saw her take another breath and I could tell she was fighting back tears.

"I can't bear to watch," I whispered to my brother. "I sure wish this was over."

Bogey blinked and lowered his head. "You and me both, kid."

I tried to cover my eyes with my paws, but one paw went straight into my ear and the other paw bonked me in the nose.

Gracie started to read on and then she paused again. That's when the whole audience gasped.

Right at that moment, I sure wished I could make my paws go exactly where I wanted them to go. Because, more than anything, I wanted to cover my eyes and ears and anything else. I just didn't want to see and hear poor Gracie suffer like this. It was bad enough that she couldn't read what that writer had written on her paper. But it was even worse that everyone in the audience had gasped!

But then I saw the reason why everyone had gasped. For racing down the aisle and onto the stage was none other than Steele Bronson! His golden hair glinted in the overhead lights, just like the trophy he was still carrying with him.

Gracie's mouth fell open wide when he grabbed the microphone from her. He raised his arms up and announced, "It's me, Steele Bronson! And I declare this little girl to be the winner of this . . ."

He paused for a moment and glanced at Nadia, who came running up to the side of the stage. She mouthed some words to him and he turned back to the audience.

"Yes, that's right!" he went on. "I declare this little girl to be the winner of this Fourth of July essay contest!"

Suddenly applause rang throughout the auditorium. And people started to cheer.

My own mouth fell open wide and I think my chin practically hit the floor.

I turned to Bogey. "You mean, Gracie won the contest?"

Bogey blinked a few times and shook his head. "I dunno, kid. Doesn't add up to me."

I started to choke and coughed a couple of times. "But she

didn't even finish reading her essay."

"I hear ya, kid," Bogey said.

I looked back to the stage to see Steele Bronson taking a bow. All the while, Gracie just stood there with wide eyes, staring at him.

Holy Catnip!

CHAPTER 8

Holy Mackerel!

I could hardly believe it. Steele Bronson stayed on the stage with Gracie while the judges all came up and congratulated her. But to tell you the truth, they really didn't seem to be paying much attention to her at all. They barely shook hands with her before they each turned to Steele Bronson. The female judge blushed and put her hand to her throat and laughed a tinkling little laugh. The Mayor grabbed Steele Bronson's hand and started pumping it up and down. The other male judge slapped the movie star on the back.

The whole audience seemed to be going *ooooh* and *aaaah*. Plus people were laughing and talking. Really, really fast.

And really, really loud.

Everyone was as excited now as the people were at our Mom's store earlier today.

Mrs. Peebles tripped up the stage stairs with the winner's trophy. But the Librarian barely took her eyes off Steele Bronson as she walked toward Gracie.

Mrs. Peebles passed the trophy to Gracie and spoke into the microphone. "Gracie will be riding on our float in the parade on Saturday morning. Then she'll be reading her essay after the town picnic on Saturday night." She paused and frowned at Gracie. "Hopefully she'll get a little more practice in before Saturday."

All the while, Gracie stood there looking more unhappy than I've ever seen her.

Suddenly a red-haired young man with a camera stepped in front of the stage and started taking pictures. He wore a name badge that read "Press." I guess that meant he was a reporter.

I peeked out from our hiding spot and glanced over at the other essay contestants. They all sat silently with wide eyes. Some were frowning and some had their mouths hanging open. I couldn't tell if they were unhappy or just plain shocked.

"I don't understand," I told Bogey. "How did Gracie win if she didn't even finish reading her essay? And how did she win when she didn't do . . ." I paused for a moment. Because I wanted to pick the right words so I didn't sound like I was being critical of her.

But I finally just blurted it out. "How did she win when she didn't do such a great job reading her essay? I don't think she'd seen a lot of those words before. Or she couldn't read Frank's handwriting. Which is really rotten because Gracie is a very good reader!"

"Doesn't add up to me either, kid," Bogey kind of murmured. "And I don't like it one bit. This is a cheat. Gracie's getting the short end of the stick here."

Funny, but I didn't know there were any sticks involved in this contest. But apparently getting the short end was a bad thing.

Still, there was one thing I did know — that Gracie was looking more upset by the minute! And I had to say, I wasn't exactly sure what to make of it all. She had wanted to win the contest so badly. She wanted that trophy and she wanted to ride on the float. But now that she'd won, something sure didn't seem right about it all.

I twitched my whiskers. "I didn't know Steele Bronson was a judge. He wasn't here for the whole contest. How did he decide to pick her essay?"

Bogey let out a long sigh. "You got me on that one, kid. None of this adds up."

By now I could tell that Gracie was about to start crying.

She just stood there hanging her head and holding her big trophy.

Holy Catnip! That's when I'd had about all I could take.

I stood up, ready to make a leaping run onto that stage. "I'm going to go give Gracie a hug."

But Bogey put out an arm. "Sorry, kid. You'll have to save it for later. Remember, we're undercover. We're not even supposed to be here."

I gulped. It took everything I had not to go running up to poor Gracie. I knew a good hug would make her feel a whole lot better.

Then I heard the reporter hollering, "Let's get a picture of the winner with Steele Bronson!"

Steele Bronson must have heard the man, because he made a beeline for Gracie and put his arm around her shoulders. He smiled his blinding smile while Gracie stood there looking sad. Then the reporter took a couple of pictures.

When he was finished, Steele Bronson picked up the microphone again. "I know my unexpected arrival is probably the biggest thing that's ever happened to this town. And a lot of you have been asking why I'm here. Well, I'm going to be filming my newest movie right here in . . ."

He glanced Nadia. I could see her roll her eyes before she mouthed something up to him again.

He turned back to the audience, smiled brightly, and finished with, " . . . right here in St. Gertrude. And, I will be using this library for some scenes in my movie."

Murmurs and applause rose from the audience.

He put his arm around Gracie's shoulders again. "Plus, as part of the prize for winning this essay contest, I will be having dinner at the home of this lucky little girl tomorrow night. How many kids can say they got to have dinner with Steele Bronson?"

While the entire audience cheered and clapped some more, I gasped and tilted my head toward Bogey. "He will? He's coming to dinner at our house? Do our Mom and Dad know about this?"

Bogey squinted his eyes and stared in the direction of Steele Bronson. "I don't think so, kid. It will be news to them. It's a lousy deal, if you ask me. I think I smell a rat. A very big rat."

I crinkled my brow. "A rat? Do you think that's what our Mom and Dad will be serving for dinner?"

Bogey shook his head. "Nope, kid. Just an expression. It means something seems wrong here."

Well, I had to say, he sure had that right. Something did seem wrong. Very wrong.

Bogey nodded toward the aisle. "We'd better get a move on, kid. We're supposed to be in our pet carriers when this shindig is over."

With that, we stayed low to the ground and carefully wound our way around all the people. Not too many were sitting in their seats anymore. Now they were mostly standing and talking excitedly in the aisles. They were all too busy chatting and looking up at Steele Bronson to notice us. It was only a matter of minutes before we were back in our pet carriers.

And not a moment too soon. Because our Mom and Gracie showed up to take us home. Gracie still carried her trophy and kept her eyes to the floor. Neither one of them were smiling.

Our Mom crinkled her eyebrows when she noticed our pet carriers were unzipped. But she quickly zipped them up again without saying a word.

She had just started to carry us out of the library when I remembered the stone on the second floor. If only we'd had time to go back and memorize the letters carved into that big rock. Letters that we thought were a secret code. But I guess the night hadn't turned out the way any of us had hoped.

The sun was still bright in the sky and slowly starting to sink toward the horizon. And even though the sun was setting, it still felt like it was a thousand degrees outside. It wasn't fun having long, fuzzy, black fur on a hot summer day like this.

But once we were in the car, our Mom turned the air conditioning on full blast. Gracie plopped down and stared out the window. I could tell she was still feeling bad. Really bad.

But I knew exactly how to make her feel better. I only had to get out of my pet carrier first. So I started making a gigantic fuss. So she'd have no choice but to turn around and look at me in my pet carrier in the backseat.

Bogey grinned and gave me a "paws up." "I gotta hand it to

you, kid. You're working it like a pro. You've got this covered."

I kept on meowing and hollering and scratching at my pet carrier. I made so much noise that Gracie finally turned around while our Mom glanced into the rearview mirror.

"What is it, Buckley?" Gracie asked in a shaky voice.

And that's when I meowed at the top of my lungs.

"I don't know what's gotten into Buckley," our Mom said. "Maybe you should hold him."

Gracie had barely unzipped my pet carrier when I practically leaped into the front seat. Right into her lap. Then I climbed up and put my arms around her neck. I tucked my head under her chin and started to purr just as loud as I could.

She wrapped her arms around me and held me tight. "Oh Buckley, I love you so much. I needed one of your hugs. I feel so awful and I don't know why. I won the contest."

"I know you're feeling bad," our Mom said softly. "But let's talk about it later. We're both hot and tired, and we'll be thinking straighter in the morning."

"Okay," Gracie sort of whimpered. "I never thought I'd feel bad about winning something."

"I know," our Mom said. "It's sort of complicated, isn't it?"

Boy, she had that right. Sometimes things really were complicated. It was hard to imagine that you could get something you really, really wanted and not be happy about it.

Gracie leaned her head on top of mine and I could feel a tear or two touch my forehead. I knew she was trying hard not to cry, but it didn't seem to be working.

A few minutes later, we arrived home and pulled into the garage.

Our house is over a hundred years old and has a big porch that wraps around the front. It has an upstairs and a downstairs, and well, I know every single inch of the place. That's because my brother and I run surveillance on it each and every night. It's part of our job as cat detectives. And if you don't know what the word "surveillance" means — as my brother would say — don't sweat it. I didn't know what it meant either, until I got adopted into our home. Bogey told me that running surveillance just means we check the place out and make sure everything is okay. We make sure the doors and windows are all shut and locked. And that everything is just the way it's supposed to be. To keep our family safe and sound.

Our Mom opened the car door just as our Dad walked into the garage to greet us. That's when I realized that, even though our Dad has shiny blonde hair, it didn't look a thing like Steele Bronson's hair.

He kissed our Mom hello and then came over to Gracie's side of the car. He took me from Gracie and held me in his big arms. I reached up and gave him a kiss on the nose.

He laughed. "Buckley seems pretty happy. What's going on, boy?"

Then he must have spotted Gracie's trophy. "Oh wow, kiddo! Good job! You won!"

Gracie sniffed and wiped her eyes. "I guess."

She got out of the car and headed straight into the house. I noticed she'd left her trophy in the car.

Our Dad's eyebrows shot up, and he and our Mom looked at each other.

She shook her head and said, "It's a long story. A very long story."

"I've got some iced tea made," he told her. "We can sit and relax, and you can tell me all about it."

Our Mom picked up Bogey in his pet carrier. "Sounds wonderful. This has been such a crazy day."

Our Dad leaned over and grabbed Gracie's trophy, while he still hung onto me. He shut the car door and we all went into the family room. Gracie was nowhere to be seen. But two of the other cats who live at our house, Lil Bits and the Princess, were there waiting for us.

Our Mom let Bogey out of his pet carrier and our Dad put me on the hardwood floor. Then they went into the kitchen next to the family room to get some iced tea.

Lil Bits and the Princess had lots and lots of questions for Bogey and me. And believe me, we had lots and lots to tell them.

Lil Bits is years older than us, and she's a big, white cat with black spots. Bogey told me she's a kind of cat called a British Shorthair. But to me, she looks more like a linebacker than she does a cat. I sure wouldn't want to be tackled by her! Lil was once known as being one of the best cat detectives in the business. Then all of a sudden, she quit and went into retirement one day, though no one knows why. But she came out of retirement just recently to help Bogey and me with some of our cases.

The Princess, or Princess Alexandra, is kind of the opposite of Lil. She's a small, white cat with big, green eyes, and she's a kind of cat called a Turkish Angora. The Princess is a former cat show cat who used to be prim and perfect. That was, until we rescued her from her abusive owners. While they went to jail, we brought her home to live with us. In fact, she's still sort of hiding out at our house, and we kind of keep hush-hush about her living with us. So her old owners would never be able to find her if they ever got out of prison. And since she's come to live with us, well, she acts a whole lot more free. She spends her time running around the house and climbing on the tallest things she can find. And though we always call her the Princess, the humans in the family call her Lexie.

"What happened today, Buckley?" the Princess asked in her soft voice. "Gracie ran through here in tears!"

She stared at me with her big, green eyes.

And that's when I pretty much couldn't tell anyone anything. That's because my heart started to pound really hard inside my chest. The room started to spin, and well, my mouth didn't seem to work either. I had the same reaction every time the Princess looked at me like that.

I could barely make out Bogey as he passed me a cat treat. "Here you go, kid. This'll get you going again."

So I munched on the treat while Bogey passed out cat treats for everyone. It looked like he'd already pulled out the bag he kept stashed in the kitchen.

He handed me a second treat and I started to feel better. In the meantime, Bogey began to tell the other cats everything that had happened today. He started with the limo and how Steele Bronson had shown up. In the background, I could hear our Mom telling our Dad some of the same stuff.

At one point, I heard our Dad say, "Steele Bronson? *The* Steele Bronson? What in the world is he doing here?"

Gracie still wasn't around. I figured she must have gone up to her room.

Bogey had barely finished telling the story of the essay

contest when the doorbell rang.

And when I say it rang, I mean it rang and rang again.

Our Mom and Dad looked at each other, and us cats did, too.

"Who could it be at this hour?" our Dad asked. "It's time for us to go to bed."

Our Mom shook her head. "Who knows? But somehow this doesn't surprise me. After all the weird things that have happened today, this is just one more link in the chain."

Together, they left the kitchen and headed for the front door.

Bogey glanced at me. "We'd better check this out, kid. We don't usually get visitors this time of night."

"I'm on it," I told him.

Lil looked from me to Bogey. "I'll take the Princess and we'll head upstairs. So nobody will spot her. Plus, it sounds like Gracie could use some extra TLC tonight."

Bogey nodded. "Good plan, Lil. As always."

Then we all ran off together. Bogey and I zoomed to the front entry while Lil and the Princess raced on up the stairs. My brother and I had just put on the brakes when our Dad glanced out the peephole in our front door.

"What in the world . . ." he said before he turned to our Mom. "There's two huge guys on our front porch. Maybe we'd better call the police."

He stepped aside to let our Mom glance out.

She sighed. "They're Steele Bronson's bodyguards."

I turned to my brother. "Huh? Why would they be here tonight?"

Bogey didn't take his eyes off the front door. "I think we're about to find out, kid."

Our Dad opened the door and, sure enough, there stood Bravo and Tango. Together they were holding onto a big, giant open wheel. The wheel was probably was as tall as their shoulders. Nadia was standing behind them.

Our Mom blinked a couple of times. "What are you guys doing here at this time of night?"

Tango smiled. "Special Delivery. Where would you like this?"

Our Dad sort of laughed. "What in the world *is* it?"

"Exercise wheel for Buckley and Bogey," Bravo told him.

Now Nadia stepped forward and introduced herself to our Dad. "Steele sent it over. He wants Buckley and Bogey to be in prime shape for their scenes in the movie. Especially since they'll have starring roles. A camera adds ten to twenty pounds, you know. And we want those boys to look svelte."

I turned to my brother. "Svelte?"

I didn't even know what that word meant. How could I be svelte when I didn't even understand what svelte was!

Holy Catnip!

CHAPTER 9

Holy Mackerel!

Bravo and Tango just stood there on our front porch, hanging onto that gigantic wheel. I was pretty sure if they let go of it, it would go rolling right off the porch and straight down into the street.

"Where would you like it?" Tango asked our Mom.

She sputtered a few times and finally said, "I have no idea. I didn't even know it was coming. How did you even get our address?"

All the while our Dad just kept saying, over and over, "Buckley and Bogey are going to be in a movie?"

Nadia stepped inside our house. "Our writer, Frank, is really good at research. He found your address without any problem."

Our Mom stared at Nadia. "We haven't even agreed to let our cats be in this movie, yet. I want to know exactly what their roles will be. And what kind of conditions they'll be working under."

"Oh don't worry," Nadia said. "Everything's on the up and up. And Frank just finished writing the script tonight, so you can't back out now."

I leaned into my brother. "He already wrote the script? How long does it usually take to write a movie script?"

Bogey shook his head. "A lot longer than one evening, kid. Let's add this to our 'something's fishy here' pile."

Nadia pointed down the hallway to our living room. "How about if we put the exercise wheel in there? Right next to the baby grand piano?"

"Well . . ." Our Mom looked at our Dad.

But he seemed to be in a daze.

"I guess that would be fine," our Mom finally said.

And without another word, Tango and Bravo slowly rolled that wheel right across the hardwood floor and toward the living room. The wheel was made from wood that had been painted black. It was about a foot wide, and the entire inside was lined with short, gray carpet. From the noise it made as it lumbered across the floor, it sounded like it weighed a ton.

Bogey and I followed the security guards while our Mom and Dad talked to Nadia at the front door. But let me tell you, we stayed a nice safe distance from that wheel as the men rolled it in. And I do mean a safe! Because I sure wanted enough room to run out of there if that wheel suddenly switched directions and came our way. It was so heavy it probably would've flattened us if it ran us over.

"Do you know what 'svelte' means?" I asked my brother.

Bogey raised his brows. "It means this Steele Bronson guy wants us to be in shape, kid."

I glanced toward the back of the huge wheel. "In shape? Aren't we already in a shape? I'm big and fuzzy. That's a shape."

Bogey grinned. "I hear ya, kid. But he sent the wheel over so we'll get plenty of exercise."

I could hardly believe my ears. "Exercise? We get tons of exercise just by running surveillance every night."

Bogey kept on grinning and nodded at the wheel. "I wouldn't sweat it, kid . . . Especially not in that contraption."

We followed Bravo and Tango until they stopped right beside the piano. That's when I noticed Bravo had been carrying some kind of a stand under his arm. He put it on the floor and I saw it had some little black wheels sticking up. Then together, both men lifted that huge wheel and put it on top of the stand.

Bogey turned to me. "This thing doesn't even look safe,

kid. It wouldn't take much to derail it."

Holy Catnip! I sure hoped not. I wouldn't want to see that huge wheel go barreling right straight for the front door sometime. It would probably break the door! And run over anyone in the way.

Now Bravo and Tango checked to make sure the wheel was in place. Then they turned it around and around a couple of times, just to make sure it worked. They seemed to be satisfied, and they headed back to the front door. We followed them again, but we still kept our distance.

Nadia gave them a quick glance before she turned back to our Mom. "What will you be serving tomorrow night for the dinner with Steele?"

Our Mom folded her arms across her chest. "I have no idea. I wasn't even consulted on this dinner. And I certainly hadn't been planning on it. It would have been nice if you had asked me ahead of time."

Nadia let out a little laugh. "Yeah, right. This is Steele Bronson we're talking about. Nobody asks if it's okay for him to come over to dinner. Most people would jump at a chance like this."

"Most people would have the courtesy not to invite themselves to dinner at a moment's notice." Our Mom spoke very slowly and pronounced every word very firmly. "Even the president of the United States would make sure someone checked with the host and hostess first. Before setting up a dinner."

Nadia shrugged and held up her hands. "But lady, this is a done deal. We've already told the press."

Our Mom raised one eyebrow. "Then Mr. Bronson will eat what we're serving. It'll probably be macaroni and cheese."

Nadia's eyes went wide. "Okay, okay, I get it. We can't have Steele eating something like mac and cheese. I'm sure it's not even organic or gluten-free or anything. I'll have something catered then."

With those words, she turned and walked out the door. Tango and Bravo followed her. At least they smiled and said goodnight to our Mom and Dad before they pulled the door closed behind them.

Our Dad's eyes were really wide. "Steele Bronson is

coming to our house for dinner tomorrow? Are you serious?
I'm going to invite some of the guys from work. And my boss.
They will love this."

But our Mom shook her head. "Maybe I'd better explain it
all to you. You might not be so happy when you hear the rest
of the story."

Our Dad tilted his head to the side. "Including why Gracie
was so upset?"

Our Mom nodded. "Uh-huh. And speaking of Gracie, we'd
better go check on her."

Our Dad took her hand and they quietly went upstairs to
Gracie's room. Bogey and I tiptoed behind them.

We found Gracie sound asleep in her bed. She had her
favorite pajamas on, and Lil was sitting at the end of the bed.
She was watching over Gracie, just like she does every night.

I figured the Princess had probably gone on into the
sunroom, to stay with the Wise One. Just like Lil watched over
Gracie, the Princess liked to watch over Miss Mokie. And I
think Miss Mokie really appreciated the company, since she
didn't wander far from the sunroom these days.

Our Mom and Dad looked down at Gracie and then they
looked up at each other. I could tell by the way our Mom's
mouth was set that she was worried. I'm sure she didn't like
the way the essay contest had upset Gracie so much. And I
sure didn't like it either. Especially since Gracie must have
been so upset that she just went to bed without even saying
goodnight to her family.

That wasn't like her at all.

I let out a loud sigh. There was so much about that contest
tonight that I just didn't understand. And I sure wished I
knew what to do to make Gracie feel better.

"We'll have to talk with her in the morning," our Mom
whispered to our Dad. "I've never seen Gracie so shook up.
And I don't blame her for being upset."

Our Dad just nodded and pointed to the hallway. I was
pretty sure he wanted to talk to our Mom out there. So our
Mom gave us each a quick kiss on the head before she and our
Dad left the room.

A few seconds later, Bogey and I left, too.

"Our Mom and Dad will be headed for bed," Bogey told me

when we were in the upstairs hallway. "Soon as they're asleep, I'll get on the computer. I've got a few things I need to check out. Then we'd better start our surveillance rounds, kid."

"Aye, aye," I told him. I tried to salute him, but I only ended up bonking myself in the mouth.

Thankfully he'd already headed for the stairs and he didn't even see me.

But to tell you the truth, I was kind of glad to have some time to myself. That's because I really needed some advice. And I needed it right away.

There was only one place where I knew I could get the kind of advice that I needed.

The Wise One.

And Miss Mokie was only a few rooms away. So I turned and walked toward the sunroom. Slowly. Very slowly. For some reason, I always felt a little nervous when I was around Miss Mokie. Maybe it was because she was so smart that it almost seemed like she could read my mind.

Or maybe it was because she was absolutely revered in our house. It was said that she once ruled the roost with an iron paw. And other cats learned pretty quickly to show her respect and not to talk back to her. I only hoped I would be as old and wise as she was one day.

Then again, Miss Mokie was so old that nobody even knew exactly how old she was anymore. I guess she had lived a lot longer than most cats ever did. I remembered Gracie once saying that Miss Mokie was over a hundred in human years. I wasn't sure how old that made her in cat years, though. But it still sounded really, really old to me! I did know that she'd been to lots of different places and seen lots of different things in her life. Some said she'd even flown on an airplane once. Bogey told me she'd lived in five different states and two different countries.

I guess that's what happens when you get to be so old. It seems like the more candles you count on your birthday cake, the more stuff you've done and learned in life. So by the time you get to be really, really, really old, you have all kinds of wisdom.

Yet even though Miss Mokie had become very wise, her joints were kind of stiff and achy. That meant she had a hard time getting around the house. So she mostly just stayed in the sunroom. Because she liked to feel the warmth of the sun as soon as it came up in the morning. The heat made her aching joints feel better.

I finally made it to the sunroom door and I peeked inside. Then I paused to take a deep breath. Sure, I had to run surveillance on this room every night. But that was a whole different ballgame from going inside and asking for advice. Running surveillance was just part of my job.

But asking for advice? Well, sometimes that took a little more courage than I really had.

So I closed my eyes and took another deep breath. I tried to remember all the brave things I'd already done in my life. For some reason, I couldn't seem to think of a one. And it didn't help that I knew *even* Bogey felt a little nervous around the Wise One.

Still, I wanted to know what she thought about Gracie's situation. Especially since I didn't want to see Gracie feel so sad. And sometimes a guy just has to be brave for the ones he loves. So I opened my eyes and stood up nice and tall. Then I stepped into the room.

Miss Mokie noticed me the second I walked in. Just like always. She is a huge, gray cat with long fur. Her fur sticks out in a ruff around her neck that kind of makes her look like a lion. Bogey said she was a kind of cat called a Norwegian Forest cat. And even though she's a little shaky these days, her green eyes are still bright and full of life.

She was lounging on her purple velvet couch, like she always did. She raised a paw just as I stepped inside the room, letting me know that I should halt.

"Please identity yourself," she commanded.

I bowed, just like Bogey had taught me to do. "It's me, Miss Mokie. Detective Buckley Bergdorf."

She nodded to me, like a queen nodding to her subject. "Ah yes, young Detective. Please enter and partake of a drink." She pointed a paw in the direction of her private water dish.

I noticed the Princess was also in the room. She was stretched out on a flowered chair with her front feet crossed. She waved to me.

Of course, seeing the Princess with her big, green eyes

didn't exactly help matters. My heart started to pound, but I quickly leaned over the water dish and took a nice sip. Luckily the cool water helped me to keep my cool. Besides that, it would have been rude not to take a drink. And us cats always used our very best manners around Miss Mokie.

When I'd finished, I stood up straight and turned to face her. Before I'd walked in, I had a pretty good idea what I wanted to say. But now all of a sudden, my mind went blank. And I do mean blank. It was like all my thoughts had just completely disappeared. Like someone had wiped them away. And I had no idea what to say.

But the Wise One knew exactly what to say. I guess that's the way it goes when you're so old and wise.

She nodded to me. "Ah, young one. I see that you are terribly troubled and something is weighing heavily on your mind. Perhaps some event has distressed you. Perhaps it has something to do with the very kind daughter of our human parents."

Right about then, my eyes flew wide open. How in the world did she know that?

Wow, this cat *really* was wise. That, or she really could read my mind.

Holy Catnip!

"How did you . . .?" I sort of stammered.

But she just waved her paw in front of her face. "After so many, many years of dispensing advice, I have come to read the signs. I know when someone is troubled. And I can often pinpoint the cause simply by looking into their eyes."

"Wow . . ." I breathed. "That's amazing."

Miss Mokie smiled one of her rare smiles. "Of course, it didn't hurt that the young Princess Alexandra filled me in before you got here."

I crinkled my brow. "Um . . . Oh okay . . ."

She sat up straight. "So tell me, young Detective, exactly what happened today? What is weighing on you?"

So I told her everything. From when Gracie practiced reading her essay, to the writer who grabbed her paper and made a whole bunch of changes. Then I told her about everything that happened at the essay contest. Exactly as it happened."

The whole time, the Wise One merely nodded her head and said, "I see. I see."

I finished by saying, "So now I don't understand. Gracie won the contest and the trophy. But she's upset. And well, now I'm upset, too. But none of that makes any sense. Because she won, and that's what we wanted for her. So why aren't we all happy?"

The Wise One raised a paw. "Ah yes, it certainly is a complex situation. To get what one wants, but yet not get what one wants at the same time."

I crinkled my brows. "Huh?"

The Wise One shook her head slowly. "It sounds as though Gracie was only proclaimed to be the winner. The only problem is, she didn't *actually* win anything."

I tilted my head to the side. "I don't understand."

Miss Mokie closed her eyes and nodded. "The word 'win' implies some sort of action. It says that *someone* has done *something* in order to achieve a prize. For instance, those who run races, or compete in other competitions, want the feeling of having earned their prize. To have the prize merely handed to you, well, that does nothing but make one feel unworthy. And without the sense of having achieved something, what good is the trophy? Humans and cats, too, feel a sense of pride when they've won something they worked hard for. They grow in their confidence in such a situation. But if the prize is awarded without a sense of having earned it, it hurts one's pride. As well as their confidence."

"*Oooh* . . ." I said.

Miss Mokie flexed her right front paw and studied her long nails. "You must be careful in simply giving people and cats various things. While gifts and other tokens of affection can be wonderful, handouts are another matter. Giving a handout can cause a problem. It can take away the receiver's sense of independence and pride. It can hurt their confidence. It can actually make a person feel rather small and miserable."

I thought back to the time when Bogey and I went undercover at a cat show. We earned all the prizes we had won. And to tell you the truth, I was proud of those ribbons that were hanging on the wall in our Mom's office. But I'm not sure I would have been so proud of them if someone had just handed them to me.

And that's when I understood — it must have been exactly how Gracie was feeling now. That's why she was so miserable.

I sat up straight and the words just started spilling out of me. "Now I get it! Gracie feels bad because she was just handed that prize. She didn't feel like she deserved it. Or earned it. Especially since she wasn't doing a very good job of reading that essay. And, she didn't even get a chance to finish reading it."

Miss Mokie held her paw above me in the air. "That is correct. You have done well, Grasshopper."

"Um, thank you," I told her.

Funny, but neither Bogey nor I ever really understood why she called us that sometimes. Like Bogey once told me, it's just something she does.

I scooted forward a little bit. "But what can Gracie do? What will it take for her to feel better?"

The Wise One closed her eyes for a moment. "Ah, that is the difficult part. She must give up the trophy. Otherwise she will feel bad every time she looks at it."

Holy Mackerel! I sure didn't want Gracie to feel bad just by looking at a trophy. But what could I do about it?

"And now you must leave me," Miss Mokie said. "For I must rest."

I bowed to her again. "Um, thank you, Miss Mokie."

Then I scooted backwards out of the room. I nodded to the Princess on my way out. She smiled back at me.

Yet all the while, I kept wondering what Gracie could do about her situation. Especially since there was a lot more to being the winner of that contest than just getting a trophy. She was supposed to read her essay on Saturday night. And she was supposed to ride on the float that morning, too. People were expecting her to do those things.

But what could she do about all that? And what could us cats do to help her?

Holy Catnip!

CHAPTER 10

Holy Mackerel!

The words the Wise One had spoken stayed with me as I trotted through the upstairs hallway. The whole house was dark and all the humans had gone to bed. But that didn't bother me one bit, since us cats can pretty much see in the dark anyway. So I could still see really well when I made a beeline down the stairs to our Mom's home office. I knew I'd find Bogey there, since he'd told me he'd be working on the computer. Most humans have no idea how good cats are with computers. Lots of us learn to work on them as shelter cats. When I was at the shelter, we'd get on the computer every night. Right after the humans had gone home for the day.

Bogey and I even opened our Buckley and Bogey Cat Detective Agency on the Internet. The BBCDA. We got our very first case from an email.

My paws touched the bottom stair and then I jumped down to the first floor. I took a right and went through the open French doors to our Mom's office. I spotted Bogey in the light from the computer right away. He was on top of our Mom's huge, antique mahogany desk. It had a wide wooden top that was covered with a thick piece of glass. The legs were round and carved so they went from thin to wide to thin again. Then there was a piece of wood at the bottom that connected all the legs. It was sort of like a curved "X."

Bogey was typing away when I jumped up onto the desk to join him.

"Be with you in a minute, kid," he told me. "I'm just finishing up an email to my agent."

I crinkled up my brow. "You have an agent?"

Bogey grinned. "Yup, kid. Had her since the days when I did cat food commercials."

Bogey had told me he'd been in commercials once. But it was long before I knew him, and long before he'd even come to live at our house. And even before he'd become a cat detective, too. In fact, he still had some money from his commercials stashed away in a secret, private bank account. We used the money for our emergency fund.

Bogey passed me an open bag of cat treats. "Here you go, kid. Help yourself while you're waiting."

And so I did. This bunch was turkey flavored. Some of my favorites.

Bogey finally finished what he was doing and waved me over to the computer. "You'll never guess what I found on the Internet, kid."

Well, he sure had that right. I didn't even know where to begin when it came to guessing.

Luckily, I didn't have to. Bogey called up a big picture on the computer screen just as I slid on over. There before me was a photo of the same stone that we had seen at the library.

Holy Mackerel!

I gasped. "I can even see all those carved letters!"

Bogey grabbed a couple of treats from the bag. "Me, too, kid. But I'm going to enhance it. To give us a clearer picture. And see if there's anything we're missing."

I tilted my head back and forth, and looked at that picture from a bunch of different angles. Maybe I could make sense of it if I found the right view of that stone. But no matter how I looked at it, I still couldn't figure out what it was supposed to say.

Instead, I just read the article attached to the photo. It was an old news story from the *St. Gertrude Times*. And the title read, "Famous Fartheringston Stone Remains a Mystery to This Day."

Then it went on to talk about how no one else had been able to figure out what that stone was supposed to say, either. Apparently experts had been coming from all over the world to look at it. And they'd been doing that for decades.

I pointed to the picture. "Look, Bogey. Maybe no one figured this out because no one thought it might really be a secret code."

Bogey nodded. "Maybe not so far, kid. But maybe they have now."

I looked at my brother. "What do you mean?"

Bogey handed me another cat treat and took one for himself. "Think about it, kid. We've had some pretty weird things happen today."

I let out a long sigh. "Boy, you can say that again. First that limo showed up. Then Steele Bronson showed up. Then he stayed and stayed and stayed. Right after he bought tons of furniture from our Mom's store."

Bogey stretched out his right front paw. "Furniture he couldn't afford."

I stared at my brother. "He couldn't?"

Bogey shook his head. "Nope, kid. Remember, his credit card didn't go through."

I gasped. "Oh yeah . . . I forgot about that. But he's a famous movie star, and I guess they have tons of money. He should be able to pay for all that furniture. Maybe there was just something wrong with his credit card."

Bogey passed us each another round of treats. "Sometimes people who make tons of money get into some pretty bad spending habits, kid."

"Oh . . ." I sort of breathed. "Do you think Steele Bronson might be . . .?"

"Flat broke?" Bogey finished for me. "I dunno, kid. But there's more here that doesn't add up."

I'm sure my eyes went about as wide as my food dish. "There is?"

Bogey stashed the bag of cat treats into a vase on our Mom's desk, the place where he always hid them. "Don't you think it's a little strange that he showed up like he did? Right here in St. Gertrude?"

I licked my paw to get rid of the crumbs from the cat treats.

"Um . . . well, I don't know. I guess so."

Bogey shook his head. "Rich, famous movie stars don't usually do their own shopping, kid. And they don't go riding around small towns in a big limo."

I had to think about that for a second. "Oh . . . okay. Then what was he doing at Gracie's essay contest? And why did he tell everyone that she was the winner before she even finished reading her essay? Especially when he didn't even hear all the other essays?"

Bogey nodded. "Great questions, kid. You're really thinking like a cat detective. The same things have been crossing my mind. I'll say it again — I smell a very big rat."

I was about to ask Bogey more about this rat. But then I remembered it was just an expression. And I also remembered what had started us talking about this stuff.

I pointed to the computer screen. "So what's all that got to do with a secret code?"

Bogey tilted his ears toward the picture. "What if Steele Bronson caught wind of this, kid? Maybe he thinks the writing on that stone is a secret code, too."

I crinkled my nose. "So he came to St. Gertrude because he likes solving secret codes?"

Bogey shook his head. "Nope, kid. Do the math. If Steele Bronson needs money . . ."

And that's when it seemed like a light bulb went on inside my head. "Maybe he's here because he wants to crack the secret code. Because he thinks it leads to something that is worth a lot of money. So then he won't be flat broke anymore."

Bogey reached over and gave me a paw bump. "You got it, kid. Good job. But if it's true, it's also a pretty shady deal. And I don't much care for it."

I crinkled my brow. "It is?"

Bogey pointed to the computer screen. "Think about it, kid. Arthur Fartheringston went to a lot of work to carve that code into a rock. You can bet he meant if for somebody special."

I stood up and stretched. "But who?"

Bogey shook his head. "I've been wondering the same thing, kid. It would help if we knew what that secret code led to."

That got my attention. "You mean like hidden treasure?"

Bogey flexed his right front paw. "Who knows? Could be something even more valuable, kid."

I started to pace back and forth across the desk. "But if Steele Bronson cracks the code, and then he finds whatever that code leads to, we might not even know about it. He could just take it and keep it secret. And leave town with it."

Bogey nodded. "Exactly, kid. And that's the part that ruffles my fur."

I stopped pacing and looked at my brother. "Maybe it really belongs to someone else. And they just might like to have it."

Now Bogey got up and moved to the edge of the desk. "Couldn't have said it better myself, kid."

I shook my head. "I sure wish there was something we could do."

Bogey grinned. "There is, kid. We could crack that code before Steele Bronson does."

Right about then, I'm sure my eyes went pretty wide. "We could?"

Bogey glanced into the hallway. "Seems like it would be the smart thing to do."

I'm sure my eyes went even wider right then. "Is this the new case for the Buckley and Bogey Cat Detective Agency? The one you were talking about earlier?"

Bogey grinned again. "Bingo, kid."

"Wow . . ." I just sort of breathed.

A whole new case for the BBCDA. And probably our toughest case ever. Because, to solve this case, we had to crack a secret code that had been around for a long, long time. Then we had to figure out what it led to. And, we might even have to figure out who owned what it led to.

Holy Catnip! That was quite a trail to follow!

Now the question was, were we smart enough to figure out that secret code? People had come from all over the place, for decades and decades, trying to figure out what those letters meant. But they had failed. So how were Bogey and I ever going to figure it out?

In any case, one thing was for sure — we could use one of Bogey's hunches right about now. Or better yet, it sure would be nice if I got a hunch for a change.

Bogey pointed at the floor. "Let's chew on this while we run our rounds, kid. We're already late."

"Aye, aye," I told him. I tried to salute him, but I only poked myself in the ear.

Thankfully, he'd already jumped off our Mom's desk and was headed for the hallway. So I jumped off the desk and joined him. Then together we zoomed out of the room and into the dark house. We trotted side by side as we ran our first surveillance rounds of the night. We started on the first floor and checked out doors and windows to make sure everything was secure.

After we finished the downstairs, we headed upstairs. Along the way, I told Bogey what I'd learned from the Wise One.

Bogey shook his head. "Gracie's getting a raw deal on this contest, kid. Especially since the other kids will probably be mad at her. You can bet they don't think it was a fair contest, either.

I followed Bogey as we turned a corner. "So Gracie ends up looking like the bad guy. And she didn't even do anything wrong."

Bogey sniffed at a window. "I hear ya, kid."

I looked out a second-floor window and noticed the moon was big and shiny tonight. "But what can Gracie do?"

Bogey shrugged. "Wish I knew, kid. But I don't have a clue. Maybe the Princess or Lil will have some ideas."

Maybe they would. In fact, maybe a family meeting was in order the next day. Just to see if we could figure something out.

I suggested the idea to both Lil and the Princess when we saw them on our second surveillance run. They were both more than happy to help. Then we made plans to meet around lunchtime the next day. I only hoped we could come up with some good ideas to help Gracie.

After we finished our second rounds, we stopped back at our Mom's office. Bogey did some more work on the computer while I took a nice, long nap.

Later, we finished our final rounds just before our Dad got out of bed. He was half asleep when he picked up the morning paper from the front porch.

I could see the picture on the front of the paper from halfway across the room. There was Gracie, looking so sad and standing next to Steele Bronson. He had a big smile on his face, and his teeth were blinding even in the photo.

I sort of choked and then my chin practically hit the floor. What happened to Gracie last night was bad enough. But now she was going to have to live it all over again. And again and again. Every time she looked at that picture! If I thought she was upset before, well, I could only imagine how upset she would be now.

I glanced over at Bogey. He was shaking his head and I knew that he'd seen it, too. Now it was more important than ever for us cats figure out a way to help Gracie.

Except that brought up another question in my mind. Something the Wise One had said. She talked about how we had to earn things and how we would feel bad if someone just handed something to us. And that's where things got tricky. We had to help Gracie, but not fix things for her. That meant we had to help her to help herself.

And let me tell you, that wasn't going to be easy. I could sure see how it would be a whole lot easier just to take care of things for someone. And be done with it.

It seemed like I had so many things to think about. Steele Bronson. Secret codes. And helping Gracie. It was almost more than a guy like me could handle.

I flopped down in my cat bed in the family room. My eyes were barely starting to close when our Mom came down for breakfast. That's when our Dad pointed to the picture in the paper.

"What can we do about this?" our Mom sighed.

"I don't know," our Dad told her. "It doesn't sound like any of it was fair. For any of those kids. And if Gracie stays the winner, she won't feel right."

Our Mom got some coffee started. "And if Gracie doesn't go through with reading her essay on Saturday night, she's going to look like she's not being responsible. Or grateful for winning. She would look completely selfish if she quit now. And Gracie is very responsible and she's not a selfish girl."

Boy, our Mom could sure say that again! Gracie was one of

the nicest girls around.

Finally, Gracie herself came downstairs and plopped into one of the kitchen chairs. She was still wearing her pajamas and she was wrapped up in her bed comforter. She coughed a couple of times, but I could tell it wasn't a very bad cough.

Then she started to talk in a whisper. "Mom, Dad. You'll have to call Mrs. Peebles. I'm really, really sick. I took my temperature and it's a hundred and twenty-five degrees. I've got the worst sore throat ever and a really bad cough. I won't be able to read my essay on Saturday night."

Our Dad shook his head. "Wow, a hundred and twenty-five, huh? That's quite a temperature. I guess we'd better take you to the Emergency Room then."

He looked at our Mom. "Don't you think so, Abby? But she probably won't like all the shots they'll give her."

Now our Mom nodded. "You're right, Mike. But since she has a fever of one hundred and twenty-five, we don't have much choice."

Gracie's eyes went wide and she gulped. "The Emergency Room? Really? I have to go there?"

I glanced at my brother. "Oh no! Gracie is really sick. She has to go to the hospital. Maybe our Mom should call an ambulance to come pick her up."

I suddenly started to shake in my paws. I didn't know what I'd do if something ever happened to Gracie! I loved her so much! But we had to do something. Funny, but I no longer cared about helping her to help herself. I just wanted to make sure Gracie was okay!

Holy Catnip!

CHAPTER 11

Holy Mackerel!

I turned to my brother. "Oh no! Gracie must be really, really sick!"

Bogey glanced up at her sideways. "Something's wrong, all right, kid. But I don't think she's sick."

How could he say that? Not when she'd just told us she had a fever of a hundred and twenty-five. And our Mom and Dad were about to take her to the Emergency Room. So how could Bogey be so calm about it all?

"I'm going to go give her a hug," I told him.

He nodded. "Knock yourself out, kid. That's probably what she really needs, anyway."

I jumped up and ran over to Gracie. I was so worried about her. I rubbed around her legs and then I stretched up her side so she would pick me up.

She grabbed me and pulled me up to her. Right away I wrapped my arms around her neck and gave her a kiss on the nose. Funny, but she didn't feel like she had a really bad fever.

Gracie coughed a few more times. "Um, Mom and Dad, I probably don't really need to go the Emergency Room. I'm sure it's just some kind of flu or something. I'll probably be better by Sunday. Maybe if you could just tell Mrs. Peebles that I won't be able to make it, then I can go to bed."

"Maybe we should talk about this first," our Mom said.

Gracie leaned her head onto my head. I kept my arms around her neck and she kept her arms around me.

"I don't think you really have a fever quite that high," our Dad said softly.

Gracie turned to him. "You don't?"

Our Dad shook his head and smiled. "You probably wouldn't be sitting there if you did. Anything over one hundred and five is usually fatal for a person."

"Oh," Gracie said. Then she tucked her face into my long, fuzzy fur.

Our Mom put her hand on Gracie's arm. "I'm guessing you're not really sick. I think you're mostly just shook up about the way the contest went last night. I am right?"

Gracie nodded her head yes. Then I could feel her hot tears falling into my fur.

"I don't blame you for being upset," our Dad said. "It sounds like a rotten situation. But I'm still very proud of you for entering that contest."

Now tears flowed freely down Gracie's face and I licked them off just as fast as I could.

All of a sudden, words just started pouring out of her. "It was all so horrible and now I don't know what to do! I got so distracted yesterday when Steele Bronson showed up. It was like I was dizzy and couldn't even think straight or anything. Then that writer made all those changes on my essay. I know I should have practiced reading it, and I'm not sure why I didn't."

Her tears flowed as fast as her words. "I guess I just couldn't stop being excited about Steele Bronson. Then when I got on that stage, I couldn't even read what that writer had written on my pages. And he marked out some of the sentences and words I already had on my essay, so I couldn't even read those, either. I was so embarrassed I wanted to die. I just wanted to finish my essay and get off that stage and out of there. Then Steele Bronson showed up again, and he was being so nice and he made me the winner."

She paused and hiccupped a couple of times. "But I sure didn't feel like a winner. Instead I just felt like a big, giant loser. Because I didn't really win that contest. I knew it and all the other kids knew it, too. So did everyone in the audience. Except, for some reason, they all listened to what Steele Bronson said. But that wasn't right, because Dylan's essay was way better than mine."

Now she hugged me extra tight. "I don't know how I'm going to face all those kids. They probably think I cheated. And I don't know how I'm going to read that essay on Saturday night. It's going to be so embarrassing. I just want to crawl under a rock."

Our Dad put his hand on her head. "I understand what you're saying, honey. But here's the thing, together we will face this. One way or another."

And that's when Gracie saw her picture on the front page of the paper. She squealed and I almost jumped to the ceiling. Then she started to cry even harder.

Finally she said, "I just don't know what to do. I don't know how to make this right. And I didn't even do anything wrong. All those kids are going to hate me."

So I gave her a kiss on the nose, to let her know that I didn't hate her.

Our Mom stroked Gracie's long, dark hair. "I know this looks awful right now. But together we'll figure this out somehow. We'll just have to think about it, and then we'll come up with the best solution."

"I only want to do what's right," Gracie sobbed. "But I'm not even sure what that is."

Our Dad shook his head. "I know, honey. This is very complicated. But first we have to pull ourselves together. We can't think up any ideas if we don't have clear heads."

Our Mom smiled. "That's right. We need to have some faith that we'll come up with an answer. But let's give it a little time so we can calm down. Then our brains will work better."

With those words, I gave Gracie another kiss on the nose. This time she giggled.

"And it looks like Buckley wants to help, too," our Dad said with a smile.

Boy, he sure had that right. Little did he know, but us cats had a family meeting planned for later. To come up with some ideas to help Gracie.

To help Gracie to help herself, that was.

"Why don't you go have a shower," our Mom suggested. "It'll make you feel better."

Gracie stood up with me. "Okay, Mom."

Then she leaned over and kissed our Mom on the forehead. She did the same thing to our Dad, too. Each time she did, I put my paw on their cheeks.

She put me back on the floor before she grabbed her comforter and raced off.

I glanced over at my brother.

"We'd better get some shut-eye, kid," he told me. "So we'll have clear heads, too."

Well, let me tell you, he didn't have to tell me twice. I ran over to my bed that was right next to his. I flopped down and suddenly my eyes felt like they weighed about a thousand pounds each. I barely remember our Dad leaving for work. And then later, our Mom and Gracie left, too. Gracie leaned over and kissed us both good-bye.

"You won't be coming to work with us today, Buckley and Bogey," she whispered. "But we'll be home early. Since Steele Bronson is coming for dinner."

I had forgotten all about him coming to dinner tonight. Funny, but Gracie didn't sound too excited about it, and she sure didn't sound excited when she said his name this time. Not like she had yesterday. In fact, she almost sounded sort of hesitant.

"I love you, boys," she said. "Thanks so much for all the hugs, Buckley."

I really wanted to tell her that I loved her, too. But for some reason, my eyes wouldn't open and my mouth wouldn't work.

The next thing I knew, Bogey was shaking my shoulder. "Look alive, kid. Time for our family meeting."

It took me a minute or two, and lots of yawning, but I finally managed to drag my big, furry body out of bed. I stopped at our food dish for a quick bite before I made a beeline for the living room. Lil and the Princess were already there, sitting up nice and straight. And Bogey was leaning over with one arm reaching into the base of the exercise wheel. He pulled out a bag of cat treats and brought it over to our group.

He raised his brows. "I suggest we skip the small talk and

get right to the point."

I nodded. "We need to figure out a way to help Gracie. And the hard part is, we have to help Gracie to help herself."

The Princess smiled. "It sounds like you learned a lot from the Wise One last night. Didn't you, Buckley?"

"Uh-huh . . ." I managed to say, right before I made the mistake of looking into the Princess' big, green eyes. That's when the room started to spin. And then I couldn't remember what I wanted to say next.

Bogey tugged the treat bag open and passed me a treat right away. "Here you go, kid," he murmured to me just under his breath. "Eat this. It'll get you going again."

I ate my treat while he passed out treats for everyone else.

A few seconds later, I remembered exactly what I wanted to say. "We have to be careful that we don't just fix the problem for Gracie. Otherwise she might end up feeling bad all over again. So . . . does anybody have any ideas?"

Lil put a paw to her head and thought for a moment. "Maybe we could send a secret email to the *St. Gertrude Times*. We could tell them the whole story. The *real* story. And maybe they would print an article about it."

Bogey put his paw to his chin. "Hmmm . . . It's a good idea, all right. One we could probably pull off. But I wonder if the paper would print it. Not after they made such a big fuss with the picture of Gracie and Bronson. They might not be willing to change their tune. And print the truth."

"Very true," Lil said with a nod.

That's when an idea hit me. I tried to put my paw to my forehead, but I only ended up sticking it right straight into my ear. I noticed Lil didn't have any problem getting her paw to go where she wanted it to go. Neither did Bogey. Why did I have that trouble?

Lil glanced at Bogey and then back to me. "You'll grow into those paws someday, Detective Buckley. It just takes some time."

I shook my head. "It seems like every time I grow into them they just grow some more."

Bogey kept on grinning. "Don't sweat it, kid. We've all been there."

I'm sure my eyes went pretty wide. "You have?"

"You'd better believe it," Lil laughed. "I went through a very rough stage when I was growing up. I was all legs and arms and ears."

"Ditto to that, kid," Bogey added. "But I grew out of it."

Well, I sure was looking forward to the day when I grew out of it, too. If that day would ever come.

The Princess leaned her little head onto my shoulder. "I think you have very nice paws, Buckley. Now what did you want to tell us?"

This time I just kept my paws on the floor. "Maybe we could send out announcements that say the Fourth of July celebration has been called off. Maybe because of mosquitoes. Everyone hates mosquitoes. Or maybe we could say a bad storm is on the way."

"Interesting idea," Bogey said and passed out another round of treats.

"It is interesting," Lil added. "But I'm afraid it won't work. Fourth of July is too big of a celebration. It's the birthday party for our country. Nobody will want to call it off. Rain or shine."

Then we all sat silently chewing our treats for a moment.

All of a sudden, the Princess smiled and waved her paw in the air. "I know! I know!"

This time I was careful not to look into her big, green eyes. "Yes, Princess? Do you have an idea?"

She smiled bigger than I've ever seen her smile. "Gracie should have a party."

The rest of us crinkled up our brows and said, "A party?"

She nodded her little head up and down really fast. "Yes. A party!"

"Um . . . okay," I said. "But how will that help her solve her problem?"

The Princess stood up and began to prance around like a ballerina. "It's easy. Gracie can host a party and invite all the kids who were in the contest. She can make cupcakes and hang decorations. It'll all be so pretty."

"That sounds nice," Lil told her. "But I'm not sure it will help her situation."

"Sure it will," the Princess said and flicked her fluffy white tail. "She can invite the judges, too. Then she can have a little award ceremony and hand off her trophy to the boy who really should have won."

"Dylan Federov," Bogey murmured.

"Wow," Lil and I said together.

Bogey gave the Princess a "paws up." "That's just crazy enough to work."

"But how do we convince Gracie to have this party?" I asked.

Now the Princess stopped prancing. "Well, I haven't exactly figured out that part."

Bogey shook his head. "There's the rub."

I nodded. "And we have to do it in a way so we're helping her to do it herself."

"So we have to make her think it was her idea," Lil added.

How in the world were we going to do that?

That was the big question.

Holy Catnip!

CHAPTER 12

Holy Mackerel!

Lil and Bogey and I really liked the Princess' idea of trying to get Gracie to throw a party. But that was the easy part. Now we just had to figure out how to pass that idea onto Gracie. Plus, we had to do it in a way so she'd think it was her idea. Then she could make up her own mind about whether or not she wanted to throw that party.

Let me tell you, that's where us cats were stumped. And I do mean stumped! I looked at the Princess, and she looked at Lil, and Lil looked at Bogey. But no matter how much we all looked at each other, or asked if anyone had any suggestions, well . . . we just couldn't come up with an answer. So we ended our meeting and decided to think about it for a while. We decided to talk again tonight, to see if anyone had come up with any new ideas by then.

Hopefully one of us would. Because we didn't exactly have a lot of time to figure this out. The Fourth of July celebration was going to be on Saturday night. And here it was, already Tuesday! That meant we had to hurry!

Bogey grabbed the bag of cat treats and stashed them under the base of the exercise wheel again.

Lil pointed to the huge wheel. "So, have you boys taken it for a spin yet?"

Bogey grinned. "Not yet. Would you like to do the honors?"

Lil smiled back. "Sure, Detective Bogart. I'd be delighted."

And with that, she stepped up into the wheel. Then she reached up and grabbed onto the carpet with her claws. This made the wheel roll forward on the stand. She did it a couple more times, until she got that wheel rolling pretty nicely. Then she just trotted along, with that wheel going around and around.

Bogey flexed a front paw and looked at his nails. "So, Lil, what's the verdict?"

"It's not bad," she answered. "But it would be better if it was actually going somewhere. Why don't you come on in and give it a try?"

Bogey grinned. "Sure, why not?"

Then he jumped into the wheel beside her. Together they ran side by side for a few minutes.

The Princess scooted closer to the wheel. "Mind if I join you two?"

"Sure, Princess," Bogey said. "There's plenty of room. Come on in."

So the Princess gracefully leapt into the wheel and ran just behind Bogey and Lil. The three of them kept on running along together. And that wheel started to pick up a little more speed. The wheels in the base even started to make kind of a *whuuurrrr* sound.

"Come on in, Buckley!" the Princess hollered to me. "Join the party. This is fun!"

"Um, okay," I told her. I scooted closer to the wheel and looked for an opening.

Finally, I jumped in on one side, right behind Bogey and next the to Princess. But when I did, I felt that wheel start to wobble. Probably because I was so much bigger and weighed so much more than everyone else.

"Uh-oh . . ." I said as I watched that wheel wobble some more.

"We're off balance," Bogey yelled.

Then for some reason, we all just started running faster and faster. To tell you the truth, I don't know why. I guess it was just a natural reaction to watching that wheel start to tilt.

Maybe everyone kind of thought we could get it back on track if we made it go faster.

Unfortunately, it didn't stop that wheel from tilting at all. Instead, it just kept on wobbling and zooming around with the speed of a racecar.

"We're going too fast," Lil shouted.

"Slow 'er down, kid," Bogey told me.

But I couldn't make it slow down. Because if I slowed down and the wheel was still going really fast, I knew I'd probably go flying off somewhere.

"I can't!" I hollered back to Bogey. "It's going too fast! And it weighs too much!"

"I'm getting tired," Lil yelled. "I can't keep up this pace much longer."

So there we were, all four of us, running and running and running. For all we were worth. And at the same time, that giant wheel was wobbling all over the place. If this was Steele Bronson's idea of exercise, well, he could keep it. Because I didn't like it one bit!

Finally, Lil yelled, "I can't take it anymore. I'm going to jump!"

"Lil, no!" I barely screamed before I saw her leap off to the side.

Well, if I had thought that exercise wheel was off balance before, it was nothing like it was now. Holy Mackerel! That thing was wobbling and spinning like a tornado! And it was completely out of control.

Seconds later, that big, heavy wheel came off its base and started rolling down the hallway and straight for the front door. The Princess flew out like she'd been bounced off a trampoline. I barely caught sight of her landing safely on a couch.

But Bogey and I were still inside and still running. And that wheel just kept on rolling and wobbling down the hallway.

"Abort!" Bogey yelled. "Abort, kid!"

With those words, he stopped running and dug in his claws. He spun around one and a half times before he let go. The momentum of that speeding, spinning wheel just flung him right on out of there. I saw him go flying way up in the air before he grabbed onto the railing of our curved staircase.

With him gone, the weight shifted again. I kept on running as the whole wheel started to shake and twist while it rolled along. I was ready to jump out myself, but I couldn't tell which side would be the safest. Especially since I was pretty sure that gigantic wheel could tip over at any second. And I didn't want to be on the bottom end of things when it went down. I was sure to get flattened if I did.

So instead of jumping, I just dug my claws deep into that carpet and held on for dear life. Around and around, and side to side, I went. I watched our hallway go by in a blur. A blur that was sometimes upside down and sometimes sideways and sometimes right side up. And since it was going side to side, I even caught a glimpse of our ceiling every once in a while.

Before long, I was pretty sure that huge, heavy wheel was going to crash into the front door. I wondered if it would stop, or if it would just go right on through that big, wooden door. Either way, I didn't exactly like the options.

Behind me, I could hear the other cats shouting. Probably giving me instructions on how to get out of there. The only problem was, I couldn't hear a word they were saying. I just kept on going around and around, and side to side.

And then I felt it. That whole wheel moved a little too far to the left, and I knew it was going down. It was only a matter of seconds.

So I did the only thing an oversized cat like me could do. I leaned over as far as I could go, to make that thing fall over once and for all. Just as I felt it start to completely fall, I pushed off with my feet as hard as I could. Then I went soaring over the edge of that big, giant wheel, only a split second before it hit the ground. It landed in a really loud *thunk-thunk-thunk*! I'm pretty sure the whole house shook and the noise echoed through every single room.

Once my feet were on the ground, I tried to walk forward. But my eyes wouldn't focus and the room kept on bouncing around before me. And if I thought I'd had trouble making my feet go where I wanted them to go before, well, it was nothing like right now. Because, for some reason, they were just going all over the place when I tried to walk. In fact, I wasn't even sure I could stand up anymore. And I started to feel really, really sleepy. A nap suddenly sounded like a pretty good idea.

The Princess was the first to reach me. "Oh Buckley! Are you all right? I was so worried!"

She reached up and gave me a kiss on the nose.

Well, it was more than I could take. I flopped down on the floor and onto my side. I let my eyes droop closed. Funny, but even though I'd quit moving, it sure felt like the room was still going around and around and around. In fact, I was pretty sure it was.

From somewhere in the distance, Bogey's voice floated down to me. "Here you go, kid. Have a couple of these. These'll get you going again."

Suddenly I smelled turkey right in front of my nose.

"Just open up, kid," Bogey said. "I'll take care of the rest."

I let my chin fall open, and the next thing I knew, someone had put a cat treat in my mouth. I munched away.

"Dames," Bogey whispered in my ear. "They'll get you every time, kid."

"Dames," I sort of mumbled under my breath.

Then I heard Lil from above me. "Excellent work, Detective Buckley. That was very brave of you. If you hadn't leaned that thing over like you did, it probably would have broken through the front door."

I heard Bogey chuckle. "Yup, kid, and you would've rolled straight into the street. And probably kept on going until you hit the downtown."

Well, I had to say, I think I liked going downtown in our Mom's car much better.

I opened my eyes and leaned up on my side. I wasn't sure I was going to be moving anytime soon. And that nap idea was sounding better and better all the time. I was just about to close my eyes when the doorbell rang.

That's when I almost jumped to the ceiling. So did Lil and the Princess. Bogey sat on his haunches, ready to spring.

Holy Catnip! I'd had more than enough surprises for one day already. My heart was still pounding really loud inside my chest when the doorbell rang again.

Let me tell you, us cats can do many things. But answering the door is not one of them. So even though the person on the other side of the door kept ringing the bell, it didn't make any difference.

At least not until I heard our Mom and Gracie come in through the garage door. Then Gracie came running through the house to the front entryway. Her footsteps thudded and echoed on the hardwood floor. She was making a beeline to the front door, probably to open it. But she stopped dead in her tracks when she saw the big wheel on the floor. Then she saw us.

Her eyes went really, really wide. "Oh my goodness! What happened here, kitties? Are you all right?"

Our Mom wasn't far behind. "Oh no," she said when she ran in and saw the whole scene. "That cat exercise wheel that Steele Bronson sent over must have come off its base. Gracie, why don't you make sure the cats are all okay? I'll get the door and let the caterers in. After that, I want you to set the table, okay?"

Gracie kneeled down to where the four of us cats were gathered. "Okay, Mom. How many places should I set?"

Our Mom glanced into the dining room. "I think eight should cover it. Since I really have no idea how many people he's planning to bring with him. But his hairdresser will probably show up. And Nadia, his assistant."

"And Frank," Gracie added. "That writer." All of a sudden she sounded so sad.

"So if you set the table for eight, we'll have an extra place in case he brings someone else," our Mom told her.

"Got it, Mom," Gracie said.

While our Mom opened up the front door, Gracie turned her attention to us. "Okay, kitties, I'm going to check you over and make sure no one is hurt. That big round thing looks pretty heavy. I sure hope it didn't land on one of you when it fell."

We all purred up to her. She petted each of us and looked into our eyes. Then she put her hands around the Princess' ribcage and lifted her into a standing position.

Gracie gently ran one hand down the Princess' back and tail, and over her hipbones. She finished by running her hand down all four of the Princess' legs.

Then Gracie gave the Princess a kiss on the head. "Well, Lexie. It looks like you're all right."

Next she moved onto Bogey and did the same thing. Then

she repeated this with Lil. Gracie wanted to be a veterinarian when she grew up. And one thing was for sure, she was going to be a really good one!

"So far so good," Gracie said softly. "Though I sure would like to know what happened here. I didn't even know Steele Bronson sent over an exercise wheel. I don't like him sending over something that could be dangerous to my cats!"

That's when I realized she'd already been in bed last night when Steele Bronson had it sent over.

She kissed Lil on the head and moved on to me. She was about to put her hands around my ribs, too. But I knew my big body wasn't hurt. Not physically anyway. And I sure didn't need to be checked out.

But I did know what I *really* needed. Especially after all the drama of that exercise wheel! I needed a nice hug.

So before she could grab me, I reached up and put my arms around her neck. Then I climbed into her arms and gave her a kiss on the nose.

She giggled and hugged me tight. "I guess you're okay, too. Huh, Buckley?"

I was now, anyway. It seemed like ever since Steele Bronson had come into our lives things had gone haywire. And now he was coming to our house for dinner, too. I sure hoped nothing else would go haywire tonight.

I turned to watch people in black pants, white shirts, and black bow ties walk in and out of our house. They were all carrying food in metal pans to our kitchen. It sure looked like they were bringing in a lot of food for only eight people.

Gracie put me down. "Okay, kitties, I've got to go to work now. I've got to help get ready for this dinner tonight. On top of that, I've still got to figure out what to do about the essay contest."

She let out a very big sigh and stood up. Funny, but yesterday she had been so excited about meeting Steele Bronson. And she had been so excited about the contest.

Now it all just seemed to make her tired. And very, very unhappy. She was dragging her feet as she left the room.

But the Princess sure didn't seem tired. Not at all. She suddenly jumped up and started to prance around. Her green eyes were almost dancing. Of course, I made sure I didn't look directly *into* those beautiful, green eyes. I'd had about enough spinning for one day.

"I think I've got it!" the Princess chirped. "I think I figured out how to help Gracie!"

My jaw practically hit the floor. "You did?"

She smiled her pretty, little smile. "I think so. But I will tell you for sure later. First I've got to check out some things."

Then she turned to Lil. "Could you please help me for a few minutes?"

Lil got to her feet. "I'd be most happy to."

Then together they ran off for the family room.

Bogey grinned and shook his head. "Dames. You just never know what they're up to."

He handed me another cat treat and took one for himself. It looked like they were from the bag he kept stashed behind the table in the entryway.

I smiled and munched on my treat. "Dames. I sure hope the Princess is right. And I hope she *did* figure something out so we could help Gracie."

That's because I hadn't been able to come up with any answers yet myself. Not that I'd even had a second to think about it.

Bogey passed us each another treat. "I hear ya, kid. But tonight we've got bigger issues. We've gotta keep a tight lid on security. We could probably use Lil in on the detail, too."

I tilted my head. "Um . . . really? But not the Princess?"

Bogey glanced around the room. "Nope, kid. We need to keep the Princess hidden. There'll be a bunch of people over tonight.   And you can bet Steele Bronson will bring in reporters. It wouldn't be safe for the Princess if her picture turned up in the paper. We don't want her old owners to catch wind of where she is."

I gulped down the rest of my treat. "Do you think they might try to find her?"

Bogey nodded. "That would be my guess, kid. Even though they're in prison, you never know about their type. They're pretty slippery. They might just fool the guards and break out."

The idea of that made me sort of scared and mad all at the same time.   I remembered how horrible the Count and

Countess Von De Meenasnitzel had been to the Princess. I sure didn't want them to get their hands on her again. Not when she was safe and happy living at our house.

Bogey passed us each another treat and stashed the bag back into its hiding place. "So we'd better make sure the Princess stays out of sight tonight, kid. She'll be fine upstairs in the sunroom with Miss Mokie."

I nodded. "That sounds like a good idea. Since our Mom and Dad always keep people downstairs when they have them over for dinner anyway."

Bogey glanced around the room. "You got it, kid. And it's a good thing, too. Because we're gonna have a lot more on our plate tonight."

I raised my brows. "Our plate? You mean we'll be eating at the table?"

Bogey shook his head. "Nope, kid. I mean, we've got big things to worry about."

I sure didn't like the sound of that. It seemed to me like we had plenty to worry about with keeping the Princess safe and hidden.

I gulped. "Like what kind of things?"

Bogey glanced into the dining room where Gracie was setting the table. "Don't know exactly yet, kid. But something still smells fishy to me. And I think this Bronson character is up to something. So we need to keep our eyes on him. And his crew. The whole time they're here."

I felt my own eyes go really, really wide. "We do?"

Bogey flexed the nails on one paw. "Yup, kid. Think about it. Are you watching all that food being hauled into our kitchen? If you ask me, Bronson's got bigger plans than just a little dinner party. And you can bet he never bothered to mention those plans to our Mom. I'm telling ya, the guy's got something up his sleeve, because none of this adds up. So we'll have to be on our best guard tonight."

I sat up straight and nodded. "You can count on me."

Bogey gave me a paw bump. "Don't I know it, kid. Don't I know it."

And that's when I suddenly realized something. This dinner party sounded like it might be fun for Steele Bronson. But it sure didn't sound like it was going to be fun for our family at all.

Plus I knew Bogey was probably right about Steele Bronson having something up his sleeve. Now I wondered what that "something" was. Somehow I wasn't exactly looking forward to finding out.

Holy Catnip!

CHAPTER 13

Holy Mackerel!

That night, everything seemed to happen at once. Our Dad walked in the door at six o'clock and went upstairs to change clothes. But not before he and a couple of the caterers put the exercise wheel back on its base.

Then while he was up getting dressed, Gracie put our best collars on us. She even put the Princess' diamond collar on her, the one she was wearing when she came to us. But Gracie didn't know that the Princess wouldn't be making an appearance tonight. Because we planned to keep her safely upstairs and out of sight during the party. We'd already popped into the family room and filled Lil and the Princess in on our security plan for the night. They were busy doing something with some magazines when we found them. Lil agreed to stand guard upstairs and the Princess promised to stay in the sunroom. But first the Princess wanted to finish what she was doing before the guests arrived.

So we took off again to check on our Mom. She was rushing around as she finished getting things set up and ready. At one point we heard her say that Steele Bronson was supposed to arrive at seven o'clock. But with the way she kept zooming around, I wasn't sure she thought everything would be ready by then.

Maybe that was why she let out kind of an "*Eeeeep!*" when the doorbell rang at ten after six.

Our Mom raced to answer it. "Oh please, don't let him be early!"

Bogey and I trotted along about ten feet behind her. After all, with our extra strict security tonight, we wanted to know exactly who came in that door. And when.

But when our Mom opened the door, thankfully it wasn't Steele Bronson standing there. Instead it was an older lady with short, curly blonde hair and little, black glasses on the end of her nose. She held a whole bunch of papers in one hand and a briefcase in the other.

"Hello, you must be Abigail," she said with a smile.

"I am," our Mom answered. "I hate to be rude, but I'm in a bit of a hurry. What can I help you with?"

From where Bogey and I sat, we could feel the outside heat pouring into the house.

The lady smiled again. "I won't take but a minute of your time. I'm Polly Peychek. I am Bogart's agent."

Our Mom raised an eyebrow. "Bogart? As in . . . *our* Bogart? Bogey? Our cat?"

Polly just kept on smiling. "One and the same. He's listed you as having power of attorney. And I just need your signature on a few forms."

Our Dad came down the stairs and joined our Mom at the door. "What is it, Abby?"

Our Mom kind of sputtered. "It's Bogey. Apparently he has an agent."

Polly stuck out her hand and turned her smile to our Dad. "I'm Polly Peychek. I negotiated the contract for Bogart's cat food commercials. Long, long ago."

Now it was our Dad's turn to sputter. "Bogey was in cat food commercials?"

Beside me, Bogey grabbed the bag of cat treats he had stashed behind the table in the hallway. He passed one to me and took one for himself.

Right about then, Polly spotted Bogey. "Bogart! How are you? So nice to be working with you again!"

Bogey grinned back at her. Then he lifted his right front paw in a wave.

Polly gave him a little wave in return. "And my goodness! I see you've landed a movie role this time. With Steele Bronson, no less. Not that I should be surprised. You always cut a dashing figure on camera."

Our Mom and Dad just stood there looking at each other. They kept on saying, "Bogey has an agent?"

Polly put the papers in front of them. "I guess Bogey wants all his earnings to go to the Buckley and Bogey Cat Shelter at your local church."

I raised my brows and glanced at my brother. The Buckley and Bogey Cat Shelter had been named in our honor after we solved our last case. It was run by our feline friend, Luke. Of course, he had a whole staff of humans helping, too. Not that they fully understood that he was in charge. Either way, they'd taken in lots of homeless cats and found forever homes for most of them.

"That sounds like a great place to send the money," I told Bogey.

Bogey passed me another treat. "That's what I thought, kid. The money will feed lots of cats who stay at the shelter. That is, if there is any money."

I felt my eyes go wide. "Since we're not sure if Steele Bronson has any money to pay his actors?"

Bogey nodded. "Yup, kid. Plus I'm not sure this so-called movie is the real deal."

"The real deal?" I repeated.

Bogey munched on another treat. "Think about it, kid. Let's say he really is here to crack a code and find what it leads to. And he wants to do that without anyone getting suspicious. This whole movie business would be the perfect cover."

Holy Catnip! If that was true, that would mean he was lying to everyone. That would be pretty lousy, as far as I was concerned.

I turned to see Polly hand some papers to our Dad, just as another blonde lady showed up at the door. This one I recognized. She was Steele Bronson's hairdresser.

She waved at our Mom. "Hello, Abigail. I'm here to do your hair for tonight. And Gracie's hair, too. We need to have everyone looking their best for the publicity photos."

Our poor Mom just kept on sputtering. "What publicity

photos? I didn't even get your name."

"I'm Taffy," the hairdresser said. "And of course, Steele Bronson will be having publicity photos taken. You don't think he would pass up an opportunity for more publicity, do you? I'm surprised he didn't have photos taken at your store. Aside from the reporter who was there, he didn't get another picture taken. Very odd for him."

Our Mom touched the side of her head. "I don't have time to get my hair done. And it's just fine already."

Taffy clucked her tongue. "I don't think so. Not for pictures, it's not."

I had to say, I thought our Mom's hair looked beautiful. Just like our Mom looked beautiful. I didn't know what anyone would want to do to her hair.

But the next thing I knew, Taffy was leading our Mom to the kitchen. Taffy also called out for Gracie as well. In the meantime, our Dad kept on talking to Bogey's agent.

Pretty soon he just threw his hands in the air. "Okay, I still don't know how any of this is possible. But since the money all goes to the cat shelter at the church, I'll sign. Sounds fine by me. I still don't know how our cat even has an agent."

Polly kept on smiling. "I'll fight for a good pay grade for Bogart. Don't you worry."

Our Dad signed his name in a few places on the papers. "Good. Fine. Whatever."

With that, Polly blew Bogey a kiss good-bye and shook our Dad's hand. She turned to go and I could hear her high heels clicking down the wooden steps of our big front porch.

Our Dad shut the door and stared at Bogey for a few seconds. "Bogey has an agent . . . I still can't believe Bogey has an agent . . . He doesn't even have opposable thumbs. But he has an agent . . ."

Bogey just kept on grinning and purring. He meowed up to our Dad and our Dad's eyes went wide. He looked like he was trying to say something. But then he just threw his hands up in the air again and raced into the kitchen.

Now I wondered if I needed an agent, too. Just in case this movie *was* the "real deal," to put it in Bogey's words.

I turned to my brother. "Bogey, do you think . . ."

Bogey handed me another treat and practically read my

mind. "Don't sweat it, kid. If there *is* any money, it'll automatically go to our Mom and Dad. That wouldn't be a bad deal. Not after all they've been through. Compliments of this Steele Bronson character."

I tilted my head to the side. "Hmmm . . . that would be nice. If our Mom and Dad got some money from this."

And the more I thought about it, the more I liked the idea. Our Mom and Dad sure spent a lot of money on us cats. Now I would be able to give them some money back. That made me feel pretty good.

So I decided to do an extra good job of acting.

And that's when it hit me. I'd never done any acting before in my life! I wasn't even sure I knew how to act!

Holy Mackerel!

All of a sudden my heart started to pound really loud inside my chest. "Bogey . . . um . . . is it hard to act in a movie. Or a commercial?"

Bogey shook his head. "Nope, kid. All you have to do is look cute. And you're a natural at that."

"Oh . . . okay. Thanks," I told him.

Bogey stared at the front door. "But right now we've got bigger fish to fry."

That's when my jaw practically *thunked* onto the floor. "Fish? We have to fry fish now? I didn't know we had to cook dinner."

Bogey gave us each one more treat before he stashed the bag back into its hiding place. "Take it easy, kid. Just another expression. It means we've got bigger things going on. Especially since we'll be running a whole different kind of surveillance tonight. This time we'll be tailing people."

Well, at least I was pretty relieved to hear we didn't have to cook. But I was also pretty nervous about our new surveillance. I'd never tailed anyone before. I only hoped I could do a good job.

So I tried to calm down and act like Bogey did. Especially since he didn't even seem fazed one bit. His mind was on the job and he was already thinking about what we needed to do next as cat detectives. Just like I should be doing if I wanted to be as good a cat detective as Bogey was.

Bogey nodded in the direction of the family room. "Time

to check in with Lil and the Princess, kid. For a quick powwow. Then we'd better send the Princess upstairs. Because Bronson will be showing up soon."

So we turned and made a beeline for the family room. We found Lil and the Princess still going through the magazines that had been stacked on a coffee table. Now they were all over the floor. It looked like a few pages had even been pulled out and set aside.

"This is interesting," Bogey murmured. "You two have been busy."

Lil scooted yet another page over with the rest. "Princess Alexandra has a great idea here. And I think it will work."

The Princess flipped a magazine closed. "I guess I'd probably better get upstairs. I think I've found everything I need anyway."

"You have?" I asked her.

Bogey raised his brows and glanced at the top picture. "Care to fill us in?"

The Princess pushed a few of the loose pages together. "I would love to. Take a look at these pictures and tell me what they make you think of."

So Bogey and I did. There was a picture of cupcakes that were decorated with red and white stripes. They had toothpicks with little white stars poked into the top. Then there were more cupcakes with little American flags stuck into them. Plus there were pictures of party decorations for Fourth of July parties. Then we saw some pictures of different people giving something to someone else. In one picture it was a card. In another it was a present, and in the last picture it was a cupcake. Then we saw a picture of a little boy holding a trophy.

Bogey looked at me and grinned. "Care to do the honors, kid? Tell us what comes to mind."

Well, at first I wasn't sure exactly. But since I'm a cat detective, I figured I'd better come up with an answer. And quick. So I thought as hard as I could.

"They make me think of the Fourth of July," I finally blurted out. "Since everyone uses lots of red, white, and blue decorations for the Fourth of July. And they make me think of a party. With lots of pretty decorations and cupcakes. Plus, it makes me want to give someone a present or something. Maybe an award."

Bogey gave me a paw bump. "Good going, kid. I'd say you nailed it."

The Princess nodded her little head and smiled. "That's right, Buckley. I plan to put these pictures around where Gracie can see them. So maybe we can plant the idea in her mind about hosting a party. And awarding Dylan the trophy as the winner of the essay contest."

I had to say, it sounded like a good plan to me. I sure hoped it worked like it was supposed to.

The Princess glanced at Lil. "Let's hide these in the sunroom for now. After Gracie goes to sleep, I'll put them in her room. So she'll find them first thing in the morning when her mind is clear."

Then together, we all helped the Princess roll up the pictures so they'd be easy for her to carry. Seconds later, the Princess and Lil headed for the staircase while Bogey and I stayed behind. I glanced inside the kitchen and watched all the people running around to get everything ready for the dinner. I could smell salmon and chicken and roast beef. Plus I saw mashed potatoes and corn and pies and cakes. It sure looked like a lot of food to me.

Gracie was busy folding cloth napkins. Our Mom and Dad kept directing the caterers, and the caterers kept jumping around from spot to spot in the kitchen. I noticed Gracie and our Mom both had fancy new hairdos.

I saw a young woman wiping glasses with a towel. She had short, red hair and a nametag that read, "Angie."

"Are these all the glasses you have?" she asked our Mom.

Our Mom gave her a funny look. "There are twelve right there. That's more than enough for a dinner party of eight."

Angie shook her head. "Um . . . I guess we'll just have to use the plastic glasses we brought. Because we were told this was supposed to be dinner for . . ."

But before Angie could finish, the doorbell rang. And rang and rang some more. Whoever was out there sure wanted to get inside. In a hurry!

Our Mom glanced at our Dad.

He put his arm around her shoulders and kissed her. "It'll

be all right, honey. It's just a little dinner. It'll be over before we know it. It's a story we'll tell our grandkids some day."

Our Mom smiled and gave him a hug. "You're right, Mike. It'll be fine. Just a small group of people. No big deal."

Then together they walked out to the front entryway.

"I guess Steele Bronson is here," Gracie sort of murmured. "And he's early."

Funny, but I noticed she didn't go running out with our Mom and Dad. And she sure didn't seem excited.

But my brother and I went running out into the hallway. Then we made a beeline for the front door. We got there even before our Mom and Dad did. It was all part of our security detail.

"Okay," our Dad said when they got to the door. "Like they say in the movies, 'It's show time.'"

Our Mom smiled and opened the door. But the smile quickly fell from her face. Instead her eyes went wide and her jaw practically hit the floor. Then she gasped.

For there, standing outside our house, was Steele Bronson and Nadia and Frank.

And about one hundred and fifty other people.

Holy Catnip!

CHAPTER 14

Holy Mackerel!

I could hardly believe it! The crowd in front of our house was so gigantic that it filled our whole yard. Before we knew it, cameras were flashing. And the local TV news station had sent a reporter and a cameraman who were already filming everything. Our poor Mom and Dad practically got shoved out of the way as all these people nearly flooded our house. Pretty soon almost every square inch of the first floor was filled up. And let me tell you, there really wasn't enough room for all those people. So they were packed in pretty tight.

Plus it got so noisy so quickly that I just wanted to cover my ears with my paws. It seemed like everyone was talking all at the same time.

Bogey and I had no choice but to jump up on the table in the hallway. Otherwise we might have been trampled underfoot. We got up there just in time to see our Dad shake his head no to the TV reporters.

"We don't care to have our home filmed and on TV," our Dad shouted over the noise. "For security reasons."

The woman reporter with shiny, black hair put her hands on her hips. "I'm sorry, but this is the biggest thing to happen to St. Gertrude in a long time. And I'm not about to miss it! So we're going to film this whether you like it or not."

Our Dad's eyebrows shot to the top of his head. "No, you will not. This is private property and you need my permission to film inside. And if you don't leave my house immediately, I'll be happy to call the police to escort you out."

With those words, the reporter stomped her foot on the floor and squealed. Then she and the cameraman turned around and stomped down the porch. It didn't seem to bother them that they were going against the crowd who was trying to come inside.

And let me tell you, people just kept coming in and coming in. I saw Mrs. Peebles and the Mayor and some people from the businesses downtown. And I saw a whole bunch of people I'd never even seen before.

Steele Bronson stood by our Mom and put his arm around her. "Lovely house you have here, Abigail. How old is it?"

"Over a hundred years old," our Mom answered. "And speaking of being over a hundred . . . who are all these people? I thought this was going to be a small dinner party."

Steele Bronson waved his hand in front of his face. "I just invited a few more. What's a couple hundred people, anyway? I have that many people over to my house in Hollywood all the time."

Our Mom removed his arm from her shoulders. "Your house is probably a big mansion with room for that many people."

But Steele Bronson didn't even seem to hear her. "I'm starving. Is the food in the kitchen?"

And without waiting for an answer, he turned and made his way through the crowd to the kitchen. Of course, it was kind of hard for him to do just that. Because, just like always, everyone wanted to talk to him or get his autograph. Or shake his hand. And almost everyone had a camera, and they wanted their picture taken with him, too.

Funny, but he hadn't even asked where Gracie was. I thought that would've been the first thing he did when he walked in. Especially since this was supposed to be part of her prize for being the winner of the essay contest.

Shortly after that, I saw people walking around with plates of food. It looked like they'd already been to the kitchen.

Our Mom just closed her eyes and shook her head. "I can't

believe this," she said to our Dad. "Not only was it rude that he invited himself to dinner. But to invite this many people, too . . ."

Our Dad frowned. "Without even asking our permission. This is pretty obnoxious."

Our Mom looked up at our Dad. "But what can we do now? These are people we know from around town. I don't feel like we can just kick them out."

Our Dad ran his fingers through his blonde hair. "I know what you mean. Just because this Bronson guy has been so rude, doesn't mean we have to be, too."

Our Mom nodded. "I guess we'll have to make the best of it. It looks like the caterers brought over plenty of food. Let's let them eat and then we can kick everyone out early."

"Sounds like a plan," our Dad told her. "Let's call Phoebe and see if she can come over. We might need her help."

"Good idea," our Mom agreed. "Would you mind making the call? I'll head to the kitchen and try to do some kind of traffic control."

"Got it," our Dad said before he headed for a phone.

Then our Mom turned and tried to work her way through the crowd. In the direction of the kitchen.

It was right about then that we saw Frank walk in. His gaze went straight up to the second floor. Luckily, I spotted Lil who was now sitting squarely at the top of the landing. Exactly where she was supposed to be.

Nadia made her way over to Frank.

"Are you ready to start searching?" she asked him.

Frank sort of laughed. "No use wasting any time."

"I'll take the downstairs," she said. "Why don't you take the upstairs?"

Frank ran his fingers through his messy hair. "I'm on it. That key has got to be somewhere in this town. And if this lady is an expert on the history of this place, you can bet she has it already. It could be sitting right here in her house. And she probably doesn't even know what she has."

Nadia glanced around. "Well, we only have a few hours. So let's get cracking. Abigail and her husband are going to have their hands full for a few hours. So they won't see us searching."

I turned to my brother. "What does all this mean?"

Bogey raised his brows. "A twist in our new case for the BBCDA, kid."

I'm sure my eyes went wider than my food dish. "It is?"

Bogey scanned the crowd. "Yup, kid. And we'll need to make a slight change in our security plans."

I nodded. "Should we stick closer to Frank and Nadia?"

"Like white on rice, kid," Bogey meowed above the hubbub. "Looks like they plan to search our house for some kind of a key. Whatever you do, don't let them walk out of here with anything. Don't be afraid to use your claws if you need to."

"Aye, aye," I said as I tried to salute Bogey. This time my paw only missed my forehead by about an inch.

But Bogey didn't see it. That's because we were suddenly too busy watching Frank start to walk up the stairs. I could hardly believe it. None of the other people at the party went upstairs. I guess they already knew it would be rude and that they shouldn't go upstairs in someone's home without permission. But Frank didn't seem to care one bit about that.

Seconds later, we saw Nadia push open the French doors to our Mom's office and slip inside.

Bogey stood at attention. "We'd better get a move on, kid. I'll tail Nadia down here. You go upstairs and keep a close tail on Frank!"

"I'm on it," I meowed back.

Right away, the whole situation made me pretty nervous. Especially the idea that Frank and Nadia wanted a key that our Mom had. Because, if there was one thing I'd learned in my short time as a cat detective, it was that crooks often tried to steal keys. That way they could go back into a home or a building without having to break in. So if Frank was looking for a key, maybe he wanted to break into our house later. Or into our Mom's store.

I jumped down. Then I wove my way around and dodged all the feet on the floor. Just as I did, I noticed a red-haired, young man with a camera step through the front door. It was the same reporter with the *St. Gertrude Times* who had taken Gracie's picture after the essay contest. Our Dad had already kicked out the other reporters who tried to film inside our house. I wondered if he knew this guy had just walked in.

That's when I suddenly realized who wasn't here tonight. Tango and Bravo. And I really had to wonder why. Somehow I couldn't imagine Steele Bronson going anywhere without his security team!

I finally made it to the edge of the stairs when the red-haired reporter waved up to Frank.

"Where are you going?" he hollered. "I understand you're Steele Bronson's writer. I want to get your picture. And I wanted to tell you about my screenplay."

Frank motioned for the reporter to join him. "Come take my picture up here."

The next thing I knew, the reporter was also going up the stairs. Our stairs. The stairs in our home.

Right at that moment, my heart began to pound and I flexed my claws. Then I raced up those stairs at about a million miles an hour. I passed those two men climbing the stairs like they were standing still. When I got to the top, I sat just as tall as I could next to Lil. Side by side. Blocking their way. I glared at those men without blinking. Just like I'd seen Bogey do before.

"Well, isn't that cute," the newspaper reporter laughed. "I'm working on a *Cats of St. Gertrude* calendar. Wouldn't this make a great shot?"

And before I knew it, a bright light flashed in front of my eyes. Apparently the reporter had taken our picture.

The only problem was, I couldn't see a thing now. Except for the image of that bright light that kept on flashing in my eyes.

"It's called an afterimage, Detective Buckley," Lil murmured to me. "It'll go away in a minute."

Well, I sure was looking forward to that.

Only it *didn't* go away. That's because the reporter took another picture of us. And another.

Pretty soon I couldn't see a thing. Except for lots and lots of bright flashes of light.

"Move away from the light," Lil's voice floated over to me. "Run!"

And so I did. But there were so many bright images flashing in my eyes that I couldn't see where I was going. And I ran straight into the banister at the top of the stairs.

"Over here," Lil meowed. "Run toward my voice."

So I did. All the while, I could heard Frank and the reporter still talking. From the sound of their voices, I could tell they'd now made it up to the second floor.

"I'm a little busy right now," Frank said. "But you can drop your screenplay off at the library tomorrow. We're setting up to start filming on the new movie."

"That would be terrific," the reporter said. "But I'd still like to get your picture."

"Fine," Frank told him. "I've got an idea. Why don't you get a picture of me with one of these cats? For your calendar?"

By now, my eyesight was starting to come back a little. I could barely make out Lil and the hallway. We weren't far from the sunroom.

"The Princess," Lil meowed. "She's in the sunroom with Miss Mokie. We've got to warn her. So she can hide. We can't have her picture taken by a newspaper reporter!"

That's when a chill ran up and down my spine. We were supposed to protect the Princess. We were supposed to keep her safe and hidden.

But my eyes were still a little fuzzy and I could barely tell where I was going. So I did my best to head toward the sunroom. Then I started meowing her name just as loud as I could.

Lil joined me. And together we staggered toward the sunroom door.

"Hide, Princess! Hide!" I kept on meowing.

A few seconds later, I could barely make out the edges of the wood around the sunroom door. Then I felt the warmth of the sun when I stumbled into the room.

I could feel Lil next to me.

"Princess!" I kept on yelling. "Princess, run and hide!"

My eyesight finally came back to me, and right away I didn't like what I saw. For there was the Wise One sitting on her purple velvet couch. And across from her was the Princess. She was sleeping on the same flowered chair where she always sat.

Her head popped up and she blinked a few times as we came barreling in.

"Hide!" Lil and I hollered again.

She shook her head and tried to stand up. Then she jumped down just as Frank and the reporter came into the room. She blinked a few more times. And then she suddenly raced to hide behind Miss Mokie's purple velvet couch.

But it was too late. She'd already been spotted.

"There!" Frank said as he pointed to the couch. "I want my picture taken with that cat."

"What cat?" the reporter asked. "Not that old, weathered gray cat. She's not what I would call 'photo pretty.'"

And that's when Lil and I almost came unglued. Nobody talked about Miss Mokie like that.

Frank laughed. "No, not that old cat. I want my picture taken with that cat wearing the diamond collar. The one who just ran back there."

Without another word, Frank reached behind the couch and grabbed that little Princess. He pulled her out and sat down on Miss Mokie's couch. All ready for his picture. I could see the Princess was terrified and Miss Mokie was furious.

"Okay," the reporter said. "Say 'cheese.'"

Then everything happened almost at once. Frank held the Princess up and the reporter clicked his camera. The flash lit up the room just as one of Miss Mokie's big paws landed on Frank's hand. It was a direct hit. Her claws were fully extended, and let me tell you, they looked sharp!

Frank screamed and tossed the Princess off to the side. She ran behind the couch again and Frank put his hand in his mouth. Probably to stop the bleeding.

Then he turned and glared at Miss Mokie.

And she glared right back at him.

He started to lift his hand, like he was going to hit her. And she raised her paw again and extended her claws once more.

Frank kept watching her as he stood up. "Did you get the shot?"

The reporter's eyes were wide before he looked down at the camera. "This one looks fine. The diamonds really sparkle. But I don't think we'd better take another one."

"You and me both," Frank mumbled. "Let's get out of here."

The reporter walked out and Frank backed out of the room.

Miss Mokie smiled a smug smile. "No one grabs Princess Alexandra on my watch."

Let met tell you, Miss Mokie may have been so old that she was practically ancient. But that didn't seem to matter where she was concerned. Because, even at her age, that cat sure knew how to pack a wallop!

Lil glanced at me. "We'd better get going. We've still got to keep on eye on these two. I'll watch the reporter and see if I can get to his camera. You're tailing Frank, right?"

"I sure am," I told her. "Now more than ever."

Lil and I bowed before Miss Mokie and then raced from the room.

I paused for just a second to holler to the Princess. "Be sure to stay behind the couch, Princess! Until the party is over!"

"I will, Buckley," came her shaky voice.

And I knew she would. The only problem was, it might be too late. That reporter had already taken her picture. A picture that could put the Princess in danger.

Now the question was, what did he plan to do with that photo?

Holy Catnip!

CHAPTER 15

Holy Mackerel!

Lil raced after the reporter and I caught up to Frank. The two men had paused to talk for a couple of minutes on the second-story landing. Then the reporter headed straight for the staircase, with Lil right behind him.

But Frank clearly had no intention of going downstairs. Instead he went from room to room, looking in drawers and closets. Bogey would have said that Frank acted like a man on a mission. He took paintings off the walls and looked on the backs. He also put his ear to several walls and knocked on them. Then he listened carefully, like he was trying to see if it was hollow or not. I tailed him the whole time and watched his every move.

He seemed especially interested in any antique furniture he could find. He pulled out drawers from those pieces and glanced at the bottoms. Plus he checked out the backs and sides and underneath of any furniture that looked old, too.

And he did it all really, really fast!

I could hardly believe it! I guess he was looking for that "key" that he and Nadia had been talking about.

Not that it made any difference *what* he was looking for. Because he had no business searching around our house like that! And if he found some key in our home, well, he sure had no business taking it, either!

Finally, when he strolled right into our Mom and Dad's bedroom, I'd had enough. I knew what Bogey would want me to do. He'd want me to put a stop to this Frank guy. Once and for all. So, I decided to do just that.

But the funny thing was, I don't think Frank had even noticed me.   He must have been so busy trying to find whatever he was trying to find, the he didn't see me tailing him.

So I had no trouble getting into position. I moved about ten feet away from Frank and scrunched down. I wiggled my back end a couple of times and got ready to spring. I watched him pull out a couple of the top drawers of our Mom's dresser and search around. But I waited until he pulled out the bottom drawer, and that's when I made my move. I pushed off with my big, strong back legs. Full speed ahead! I shoved right into that drawer and pushed with all my strength.

And all my weight.

Sometimes it pays to be an extra big guy. Because that drawer closed with a really loud *thunk*! It smashed Frank's hand right between the dresser and the drawer. Really hard.

The same hand that Miss Mokie had dug her claws into.

Frank let out a loud "*Yeeeooow!*" Then he yanked his hand out, and bent over and grabbed it.

He was still bending over when I bounced onto our Mom and Dad's bed and sprung into the air. I landed right smack dab in the middle of Frank's back. Of course, I had each one of my claws out on each one of my paws. And let me tell you, I dug in deep! Plus, being such a big guy, I knocked him right down to the floor.

Then I jumped off and bounced back onto our Mom and Dad's bed. Ready for another attack.

Frank screamed again and rolled around on the floor.

He was still there when our Dad came rushing up and stood in the doorway. Our Dad took one look at Frank and the open drawers. Then he saw me on the bed, and I figured he must have put two and two together. At first our Dad's eyes went wide. But then he clamped his jaw together and his eyebrows came down low on his forehead.

Let me tell you, our Dad didn't get mad very often. And it

sure took a lot to make him mad. But I could tell he was mad right now. Really mad!

"Excuse me, but what are you doing in our bedroom?" our Dad yelled.

He grabbed Frank by the shirt collar and picked him up.

"Take it easy," Frank sputtered. "Your cats attacked me. I was only protecting myself."

"Yeah, right," our Dad said. "Listen buddy, our bedroom is off limits. You'll have to go downstairs with everyone else."

Frank held onto his injured hand. "Okay, okay. Just let me go."

Our Dad patted down Frank's pockets. "Right after I make sure you didn't steal anything."

Frank cringed. "Hey, you don't have any right to do that."

Our Dad stared straight into Frank's eyes. "Would you rather I let the police do it instead? By the way, who are you?"

"I'm Frank," he said. "I work for Steele. I'm his writer."

"Doesn't that just figure," our Dad murmured.

Then without another word, our Dad pretty much escorted Frank from the room. He sort of walked him down the hall and to the staircase. I followed them both.

"Don't come back up here," our Dad told him. "If I catch you going through our rooms again, I'll have you arrested. Do you understand?"

"Got it," Frank snickered.

He was still holding his hand as he staggered down the stairs. I could see little rips on the back of his shirt where I'd landed on him.

Our Dad stood at the top of the stairs with his arms folded. I rubbed up against his legs and sat beside him.

He reached down and petted me on the head. "Buckley, I don't know what happened up here. But if you or the other cats did scratch him . . . well, he probably had it coming. I think you were probably just protecting your family."

Boy, he could say that again!

I stood on my back legs and stretched up my Dad's side. So he would pick me up.

And he did just that. "You're a good guy, Buckley."

Well, he would know. Because our Dad was a good guy, too.

"I think we could use you downstairs," he told me. "We've sure had our hands full down there, taking care of this pack of people."

Probably just like us cats had our paws full, watching Steele Bronson and his bunch. Our Dad leaned me over his shoulder and carried me down the stairs.

And let me tell you, it was the perfect position for surveillance. Because I could see the whole downstairs as I rode along on my Dad's shoulder. I noticed Lil had stuck to the reporter and was probably waiting for him to set his camera down. I figured she'd probably try to sneak the camera away so we could get rid of the picture of the Princess. But it didn't look like she was having any luck.

Then I spotted Frank who had found his way to Nadia. Together they seemed to be whispering about something. Bogey was sitting on a table right next to Nadia. So I knew he was listening in on every word they said.

Steele Bronson was in the middle of the living room holding a big plate of food. He was surrounded by lots of women who were holding plates of food, too. He was talking and smiling, and all the women were sort of giggling.

Our Dad carried me on into the kitchen, and that's when I saw our Mom. She was busy picking up paper plates and throwing things into the trash. Gracie was right beside her and helping the whole time. I had to say, it was really hot inside our kitchen, probably because there were so many people in our house. Gracie and our Mom both had red, sweaty faces. It looked like their new hairdos had started to droop.

I didn't see any of the caterers anywhere. As near as I could tell, they must have already left.

Gracie paused and wiped the sweat from her brow. "Mom, we've been so busy that we haven't had a chance to eat. And I'm really getting hungry. Do you think it would be okay if I ate something? Now that all the guests have gotten their food?"

Funny, but when Steele Bronson announced he'd be coming to our house for dinner, I never dreamed that meant our family wouldn't get to eat. I thought they'd all be eating together.

Our Mom stopped working and gave Gracie a hug.

"Absolutely, honey. I sure appreciate all your help tonight. Have I told you today, how happy I am that you're my daughter?"

Gracie smiled and hugged her back. "No, not today. But I think you said it a few days ago. And I'm happy that you're my Mom."

That kind of made me smile, too. Because I was happy that our Mom was my Mom, too. And I was happy that Gracie was my human sister. And just to let our Dad know how I felt about him, I leaned over and gave him a kiss on the nose.

He laughed. "Okay, Buckley. I get the picture. I love you, too."

With that, he put me onto the kitchen floor. He tossed me a little piece of chicken. Then he helped Gracie scrape together some dinner from what was left of the food.

Our Dad put his hand on our Mom's shoulder. "Why don't we have a bite, too, Abby? We'll finish cleaning this up later."

Our Mom put her arm to her forehead. "Sounds good. I'm hot and starving."

Together they pulled some leftovers from the pans and took their plates to the dining room. Gracie led the way.

Just as Bogey came running up to me. Lil was right behind him.

He had a huge frown on his face. "I'll explain later, kid. But right now we've got to get these people out of here."

I gulped. "Um . . . okay. But how are we going to do that?"

Bogey grinned. "Easy, kid. Just follow my lead."

And so I did. When Bogey jumped onto the counter, I jumped up right behind him. And Lil jumped up with us. There wasn't a lot of room up there, so Bogey shoved one of the empty food pans right onto the floor. It landed with a loud *clang*!

That got everyone's attention.

Or, at least, it got the attention of the people near us in the kitchen.

Bogey nodded to Lil and me. "Okay, on the count of three, start to scratch."

I raised my brows. "Scratch? What do you mean?"

Bogey grinned again. "Scratch away, kid. Use your back feet up near your ears. Or use your front claws on your legs.

But whatever you do, put some heart into it."

Lil laughed. "All right, Bogey. Whatever you say."

Then he counted to three and we all started to scratch. I put my back foot up to my neck and gave it a good scratching. Lil used her front paw to get her back hips. And Bogey switched from scratching his ears to his neck to his stomach. But together we sat there and scratched and scratched and scratched for all we were worth.

It wasn't long before a lady I'd never seen before turned our way. She let out a little "*eeek!*" and leaned into her husband. She whispered something in his ear, and they practically ran out of the kitchen. In the direction of the front door. Seconds later, a man saw us and turned to whisper to his wife. The next thing we knew, they were on their way out, too. And they whispered to a few other people along the way. Those people also headed out in a hurry.

And so it went. The more we scratched, the more people got out of there. Pretty soon we had that whole kitchen cleared out.

Then the strangest thing happened. Once a few people had started to leave, well, other people just followed them. Then more people followed those people. And pretty soon, almost the whole crowd suddenly decided to leave. Then Lil jumped down from the counter to go tail the reporter again. Bogey and I jumped down, too, and zoomed into the hallway. We wove our way around people's legs like we were running a maze. Once we were near the front of the house, we jumped back up onto the hall table again.

That's when our Mom and Dad sort of positioned themselves at the front door. So they could say good-bye to people as they were leaving.

Some of the people were pretty nice and thanked our Mom and Dad. But others just walked out. Finally, the only people left were Steele Bronson and Frank and Nadia. And Steele Bronson's hairdresser, Taffy.

And the reporter who had taken the Princess' picture. Lil fell into place behind him and kept on tailing him.

Taffy reached up and tried to put our Mom's hair back into place. She pulled out a few pins and put them back in. But our Mom's hair just drooped all over again. Finally, Taffy gave up.

"I'll be over tomorrow," she said.

Our Mom's eyebrows went up. "Tomorrow? But Gracie and I don't need to have our hair done again."

Taffy shook her head. "Oh no. It's not for you. I have to give your two black cats a bath. And get their fur ready for being on camera."

"Wait a minute . . ." our Mom started to say.

And let me tell you, I sure wanted to hear *the rest* of what our Mom was going to say. Because I sure was hoping our Mom was going to tell Taffy that she would not be allowed to come over and give us a bath. As far as I was concerned, Bogey and I didn't need a bath! Ever. And we definitely didn't need to have our hair done.

But our Mom didn't even get a chance to finish saying what she was going to say.

That's because Steele Bronson suddenly moved in next to our Mom and Dad.

"Don't worry," Steele Bronson said. "Taffy's handled animals before. It's standard procedure for all animals on film to be bathed first. Your cats won't even know the difference."

Right about then, I'm guessing my eyes went wider than they'd ever gone before. Because he sure had that wrong. Us cats definitely knew the difference between having a bath and not having a bath! And we hated baths! That's because we hated being in the water.

Now Steele Bronson took our Mom's hand. "You'll be there, won't you, Abigail? When we film Buckley and Bogey's part?"

Our Dad looked right at Steele Bronson. "One of us will be there."

Our Mom pulled her hand away and leaned into our Dad. Just as Gracie joined us all.

Steele Bronson turned on his brightest smile. "You look worn out, little girl. And your hair is a disaster. I guess you must have had a lot of fun tonight."

Gracie just sort of nodded.

Nadia smiled. "You're a very lucky girl to have dinner with Steele Bronson. Most of his fans would give anything to have dinner with him."

Gracie looked like she was trying to force a smile on her

face. "Um . . . yeah. Very lucky."

Then Steele turned to Taffy. "You'll need to redo her hair for her part in the movie."

Gracie's mouth fell open. "My part?"

Our Mom's eyebrows came down. "What part?"

Steele Bronson stared at his fingernails. "Oh, did I forget to mention it? I'll need Gracie to read her essay again. And I'll need you in the audience, Abigail. I want to recreate the essay contest. For my movie."

For a second or two, I thought Gracie was going to start crying. It was bad enough that she'd had that awful experience at the essay contest once. But now she had to relive it?

Before anyone could say another word, the reporter jumped in. "Let me get another picture of the winner with Steele Bronson."

"Get my good side," Steele Bronson commanded as he moved over to Gracie's left.

He stood right next to her while the reporter snapped their picture. I wasn't sure, but I thought I saw a tear roll down her face.

Then the reporter turned to Frank. "Don't worry. I'll be sure your picture makes the front page tomorrow. Just imagine the headline: 'The Man Behind Steele Bronson's New Movie Being Filmed in St. Gertrude.' It'll be a human interest story."

Frank grinned. "Great. Don't forget to mention my book. It's about some research I did on my ancestors. Benjamin Franklin and Thomas Jefferson. They were both signers of the Declaration of Independence, you know."

"Sounds interesting," the reporter said. "I'll be sure to mention it in my article. Just as long as you'll take a look at my screenplay."

Then without answering, Frank turned to our Mom. "I understand you're writing a book, too, Abby."

If I thought our Mom looked surprised before, well, it was nothing compared to now.

She raised one eyebrow. "Yes, I am . . . But how did you know that?"

Frank looked out the open front door. "My publisher knows your publisher."

And without saying another word, Frank and the reporter walked out.

Steele Bronson and Nadia left, too. Without so much as saying thank you.

Taffy at least said, "Thank you for a lovely evening." Then she followed the rest outside.

I turned to my brother. "What's this business about us having to get a bath?"

Bogey shook his head. "First I heard about it, kid. But I'll be sure to send an email to my agent. Let her complain for me."

"Sure wish I had an agent," I muttered.

"I wouldn't sweat it," Bogey told me. "Because right now we've got bigger problems. Meet me in the office after our Mom and Dad go to bed."

Bigger problems? Wasn't getting a bath a big enough problem?

Holy Catnip!

CHAPTER 16

Holy Mackerel!

It took our Mom and Dad and Gracie quite a while to get the house back in shape after the party. The kitchen was a huge mess, and so was the rest of the downstairs. While our Mom tackled the kitchen, our Dad ran the vacuum cleaner. And Gracie picked up trash and straightened things up in the other rooms. I could tell they were all really hot and tired. Very tired. It was almost midnight by the time they were finished.

Gracie was half-asleep when she said goodnight. She barely had her eyes open when she thudded upstairs to bed. Lil trotted along beside her, to make sure she made it okay. I knew Lil would be spending the rest of the night in Gracie's room, keeping guard over her. Just like she always did.

In the meantime, Bogey and I sat at the bottom of the stairs and watched them go up. Lil paused for a second, looked back at us, and saluted. Bogey nodded and I saluted back. Well, I saluted pretty well, anyway. More and more my huge paws were starting to go where I wanted them to go.

Could the other cats be right? Was I going to grow into my ever-growing paws someday? Just like they did?

Our Mom and Dad locked up the house and turned out the lights. Then together they headed toward the stairs, too.

Along the way, our Mom leaned down and kissed us both on the top of our heads. And our Dad petted us.

"I still can't believe it," our Dad said as they stepped onto the staircase. "I can't believe the nerve of that guy. Inviting all those people to our house. Without our permission."

Our Mom sighed. "And without even telling us. Plus, I got the impression this dinner was supposed to be some kind of a prize for Gracie. But it certainly wasn't any great treat for her. She did nothing but help out in the kitchen all night long. Especially after those caterers took off and left us holding the bag. I don't think Steele Bronson even said hello to her until the end of the night."

Our Dad shook his head. "Well, he sure didn't eat dinner with her. I don't get it. Why was the guy even here?"

Our Mom moved up to the top step. "I have no idea. None of it makes any sense to me. But I have to say, this big, famous movie star sure is disrupting our lives."

"He doesn't have a lot of respect for us," our Dad told her. "Did I tell you I caught some guy who works for him going through our dresser drawers? Some guy named Frank?"

Our Mom stopped and her eyes went wide. "Frank? That's Steele Bronson's writer. What was he looking for? Was he stealing from us?"

Our Dad shook his head. "Well, if he was, he didn't get anything. I checked. But maybe that was what he was planning to do."

Our Mom slipped her arm around our Dad's waist. "This has been such a weird couple of days. I will be so glad when all this is over."

He put his arm around her shoulders. "You and me both."

Then they turned the corner and headed for their room.

That's when Bogey turned to me. "Lil told me what happened upstairs, kid. It's a lousy deal, them getting a shot of the Princess like that. But it sounds like you and Lil fought a good fight. And Miss Mokie, too. I have to say, that old gal's still got it."

I sighed. "We would have done a better job, but we were blinded by all those camera flashes. We couldn't see a thing. And the Princess had fallen asleep, so she didn't hear us yelling to her in time."

Bogey put his paw on my shoulder. "There's the rub, kid. The Princess should have been safe up there. Because those two jokers weren't even supposed to go upstairs. They crossed a whole lotta lines."

I nodded. "That's for sure. Especially when the Princess tried to get away and dove behind Miss Mokie's couch. And Frank went after her."

Bogey squinted his eyes and looked at the front door. "The guy's nothing but trouble, kid. It's the second time he's ruffled our feathers. First he rewrote Gracie's essay. And now this. Like our Dad said, the guy's got a lotta nerve."

I bit my lip. "You can say that again. I only hope the Princess' picture doesn't end up in the paper."

Bogey frowned. "Me, too, kid. Me, too. It could put her in some serious danger. So we'll need to tighten our security around here. Probably run more surveillance rounds and keep the Princess close. Just so she's protected."

I sat up at attention. "That sounds like a good plan to me. I sure wouldn't want anything to happen to the Princess."

I shuddered. Just the thought of her old owners finding her made my skin crawl. After all, I'd seen them in action before. I knew how badly they'd treated her.

Bogey got to his feet. "You and me both, kid. By the way, thanks for helping me get this crowd out the door tonight. That old 'scratching trick' gets 'em every time."

I smiled. "It sure did. But what was going on that you wanted to get everyone out of here so fast?"

Bogey shook his head. "I got an earful when I tailed Nadia, kid. There's more to this business than meets the eye."

I nodded my head. "That's what I thought, too. After I tailed Frank."

Bogey flexed his left front paw. "Let's talk about it in a bit. First I need to do some research. In the meantime, maybe you could check on the Princess. Make sure she's okay after that guy grabbed her."

I glanced up the stairs. "Got it. I'll go see her."

Bogey nodded at the French doors to our Mom's office. "How about meeting me in the office when you're done. We've got lots to go over on this case."

"Sounds like a plan," I told him right before I trotted

upstairs.

To tell you the truth, I was kind of glad to be checking on the Princess. After all, I'd been a little worried about her myself. I hadn't seen her since she'd run to hide behind Miss Mokie's couch. And I wanted to make sure she was all right. So I ran straight for the sunroom, where I knew I'd find her.

Along the way, I thought of all the stuff that had happened since Steele Bronson and his crew came to town. And one thing was for sure — a lot of the things he did made my family really unhappy. Gracie was miserable, the Princess might be in danger, and our Mom and Dad were really tired. And pretty mad. Plus Bogey and I had to add to our security, and worst of all, we might even have a bath in our near future! That was just for starters. Because as near as we could tell, he was searching for some secret treasure in town. Something that he might steal right out from under the noses of the citizens of St. Gertrude!

Yet so many people in town acted so giddy and excited around him. It just didn't add up. Why did my family and I feel one way around him, when everyone else in town felt another way?

Before long, it seemed like all the thoughts in my head were whirling around like a big, giant tornado. There had been so much going on that I just didn't understand. I could hardly make heads nor tails of it all.

But I knew someone who could.

The Wise One.

And since I had just about reached the sunroom, well, I figured it might not hurt if I asked her a question or two. While I was there.

Suddenly, my heart started to pound and my paws started to shake. And that was when I was just *thinking* about talking to Miss Mokie! Like I said before, maybe I got nervous because it seemed like she could read my mind. Not to mention, I'd just seen her in action when it came to protecting the Princess. And let me tell you, Miss Mokie was *not* a cat to be messed with!

Holy Mackerel!

But Miss Mokie had helped me before, and I knew she could help me again. So I took a deep breath and gathered up all my courage. I slowly stepped into the room and peeked around. Much to my surprise, the Princess wasn't even there. But Miss Mokie was sitting upright on her purple velvet couch. She was cleaning and sharpening her claws.

She stopped when she saw me enter.

I bowed to her like Bogey had taught me to do.

She waved her paw, motioning for me to get up. "Ah, yes, young Detective. So delightful to see you again. No need to stand on ceremony tonight. Not after this evening's events. I suspect you're here to see that Princess Alexandra has survived her ordeal. She's been under my personal care, of course. And I assure you, she is much stronger than you might realize."

Well, that made me feel better. "Um . . . that's good, Miss Mokie."

She gave me one of her rare smiles. "I trust you put a halt to that villain who so brazenly invaded the sanctity of our home."

I looked up at her and nodded. "Uh-huh . . . yes, I did. I went on the attack. I made him yell loud enough to get our Dad's attention. Then our Dad showed up and took the man downstairs."

Miss Mokie raised her paw and brought it down in a swoop, like a queen knighting a subject. "Splendid, young Detective. Simply splendid. Though I do regret that troublemaker managed to take a photograph of the Princess. We must all be on our guard from now on. To make sure she is protected."

I shifted my weight a little. "Boy, that's for sure. Bogey and I are already planning extra security measures."

Miss Mokie tilted her head. "Excellent. But I see that you are here for other reasons. Something else has you rather distressed."

Her words made me jump. How in the world did she know that?

Like I said before, it was almost like she could read my mind.

"Um . . . I . . . well . . ." I sort of sputtered.

But then I figured, since she could practically read my mind anyway, I might as well just spill it. Like Bogey would say.

So I did. And once I started, it felt like I had turned on the tap to our bathtub. Because the words kept falling from my mouth so fast I could barely keep up with them all.

I sat up straight. "It all started when that movie star, Steele Bronson, came to town, and everyone went crazy over him. Ladies were screaming and crying and fainting. Everyone wanted his picture and his autograph and all kinds of things. Plus it seemed like whatever he did, people thought it was wonderful. And they all went along with him, no matter what he said. Or what he did. I've never seen people in St. Gertrude act like this before."

Miss Mokie put her paw to her chin. "It's tragic, indeed, young Detective. I'm afraid I have personally witnessed such folly myself in my life."

Now I started to pace across the floor. "When Steele Bronson walked right into Gracie's essay contest, he just interrupted everything. And I do mean everything! But if anyone else had done that, they would have gotten in trouble. Big trouble. But he just stood up and announced that Gracie was the winner, and he hadn't even heard all the essays. And he especially hadn't heard *her* essay. Yet the strange thing was, when he called her the winner, everyone went along with it. Nobody said a thing. They just cheered for him and congratulated Gracie."

The Wise One shook her head. "Most unfortunate."

I kept on pacing, moving faster and faster. "Then when he said he was coming to our house for dinner, nobody even asked whether he should get permission from our Mom and Dad first. I just don't understand it . . . Whatever he says he wants, people sort of bend over backwards to make sure he gets. He's behaving very badly and yet most of the people are going around all goo-goo eyed over him."

The Wise One nodded. "Yes, it truly is a most complicated situation."

Now I sat down and started waving my paws for emphasis. "I don't understand why they're all acting this way. These aren't people who would normally just go along with things. Especially if they thought something was wrong. But when they're around Steele Bronson, they're different. It's all very strange. And it sure doesn't make any sense to me."

The Wise One sat back on her haunches and sighed. "I fear you have encountered a weakness that many humans have. A weakness that, thankfully, cats do not possess. So it makes it rather difficult for a cat to understand why humans would act this way. Humans, of course, are generally a much more flawed species. But we love them anyway, despite this weakness so many of them suffer from."

I'm sure my eyes went pretty wide right about then. "They have a weakness? Sort of like a sickness?"

Miss Mokie nodded. "I fear it's true. It *is* much like a sickness. For humans simply do not understand what makes someone valuable. Of course, us cats know quite well that it is age and wisdom that makes one important. But humans have a rather odd notion that *fame* makes a person more important."

I tilted my head to the side. "Fame?"

Miss Mokie closed her eyes for a moment. "Yes, sadly, it is so. There are those who desire fame, and there are those who worship it."

"Wow . . ." I breathed.

Miss Mokie sighed. "Unfortunately, those who worship fame treat the famous people as though they're superior to all. They may believe the famous person has greater knowledge and abilities, simply because they are famous. And they tend to let the famous one get away with all kinds of bad behaviors. In a sense, they sort of spoil the famous ones."

I could hardly believe my ears. "That's exactly how people have been acting around Steele Bronson!"

The Wise One flexed her newly sharpened claws and held them up for closer inspection. "Yet Steele Bronson would be one of those humans who desires fame. He looks for attention from others. He wants to be adored and worshipped. I would suspect that no one warned him to beware of fame."

I gulped. "You mean, we're supposed to beware of fame?"

Holy Mackerel! There were already so many things I had to watch out for as a cat detective. And now I had to add fame to my list?

"Yes, young one. You must beware of fame," Miss Mokie said. "And you must not be blinded by those who have achieved fame. Remember, just because one achieves fame, doesn't mean they deserve respect."

I put my paw to my chin. "Oh, like Steele Bronson. He hasn't earned the respect of me or Bogey. Or the rest of our family."

The Wise One nodded. "That is excellent, young Detective. For your eyes have been opened. But you must also be careful not to seek fame, just for the sake of being famous. Fame may call your name and promise many, many wonderful things. Yet being famous is rarely wonderful. Fame usually brings nothing but a false happiness. And fame can be fleeting. One might be famous one day, and not the next. Often, when fame starts to go, humans will do more and more peculiar things to hang onto it. Just to get the attention they've come to crave."

I gulped again. "So how do I stay away from this fame?"

Miss Mokie raised her brows. "Ah, therein lies the difficulty. You must stay focused on your work and do your job well. But do it for the sake of doing a good job and serving others. Rather than doing something merely so you'll become famous. On the other hand, if you become famous as a result of doing a good job, that is fine. But if you want to be famous just to be famous, then I fear you will end up terribly unhappy in the end. Fame, for the sake of fame, should never be your goal."

"Um . . . okay," I murmured. "So I just need to be the best cat detective I can be. If I become famous because I'm a good cat detective, that's fine. But I shouldn't try to be a good cat detective just so I might be famous someday."

Now the Wise One smiled. "Ah, yes. You have learned well, Grasshopper."

"Um . . . thank you," I murmured, even though I still didn't understand why she called me that.

"But now you must leave me," Miss Mokie said. "It's time for me to rest."

I bowed to her. "Thank you, Miss Mokie. Before I go, do you know where the Princess is? I want to make sure she's okay."

Miss Mokie nodded. "Of course. Very noble of you, young Detective. I believe you'll find the Princess Alexandra in young Gracie's room. Apparently she is setting up some sort of surprise."

I smiled. "Thank you, Miss Mokie. I sure learned a lot today. I hope you have a nice nap."

Her eyes were already closed when I backed out of the room. I ran into the hallway, and then I just sat still for a moment or two. I had so much to think about. And I finally understood why everyone was acting so weird around Steele Bronson.

It was all because of fame.

The bad part was, he was getting away with acting very badly around my family. And I, for one, didn't like it. More than anything, I wanted to put a stop to it. Before he hurt them even more.

That's when I realized something. If we solved our case, it might send Steele Bronson packing. Because then he might not be interested in St. Gertrude anymore. And maybe he'd go home, which meant he couldn't hurt our family anymore either. Unless he really was filming a movie.

All of a sudden, I was more determined than ever to crack that code and solve our case.

But how?

Holy Catnip!

CHAPTER 17

Holy Mackerel!

I sure had a lot to think about. And it seemed like that was *all* I was doing as I trotted over to Gracie's room. The whole house was dark, but since us cats can basically see in the dark, that wasn't a problem. Besides, the moon and the stars were shining in brightly through the upper transom windows. The temperature may have been hot this time of year, but the sky sure was pretty at night.

I paused when I reached the doorway of Gracie's room. I wanted to be extra quiet when I went inside, so I wouldn't wake her up. Especially since she had worked so hard tonight. And a growing girl like her needed her sleep.

I peeked inside the room. That's when I spotted a white paw waving at me. It was Lil. She was lying on the end of Gracie's bed while Gracie snored softly. The Princess was tiptoeing around on the floor. She had her stack of pictures that she'd taken from the magazines downstairs.

Or, at least, she had what was *left* of that stack. As near as I could tell, she'd already placed most of those pictures around the room. A picture of red, white, and blue cupcakes was on Gracie's night table. And a picture with Fourth of July party decorations was on Gracie's desk. Another picture was right next to her pink slippers. Yet another one was sitting on the end of her teal-colored bed comforter.

I watched as the Princess put the last few pictures around the room. She had a huge smile on her face. And she was so focused on her work that she didn't even see me.

Right about then, I was so proud of her and so absolutely amazed. Here she was, in hiding from her former owners. The very people who had abused her. And the people who might even find her again if her picture ended up in the paper.

Yet instead of worrying about herself, she was more concerned about Gracie. Maybe that was one of the things I liked the best about the Princess. She had once been famous in the cat show world. She could have ended up like Steele Bronson and been very rotten and mean. Not to mention, completely selfish.

But she didn't turn out like that.

Instead, she happily left fame behind for a better life. To top it off, she wasn't even the least little bit selfish. Instead, I think she was just grateful to live in a happy home where everyone loved her.

She finally spotted me and I waved to her. She waved right back. Then she looked at me with her big, green eyes and well . . . you know the rest. The room started to spin and I sort of flopped over.

Seconds later, she was by my side. She nudged me with her paw.

"Buckley, Buckley," she meowed softly. "Are you okay?"

I lifted my head just as soon as the dizziness stopped. "Funny, but that's what I came to ask you."

I pulled myself up, and together we walked down the hall. So we could talk without waking up Gracie.

She nodded her little head. "I'm okay. Except I'm a little bit scared."

To tell you the truth, I was, too. But I wanted to do everything I could to make the Princess feel safer.

I leaned closer to her. "Bogey and I will be adding some extra security measures. And well, don't forget that the Count and Countess are still in jail."

She sighed. "Thanks, Buckley. But I wouldn't be surprised if they broke out just to come after me. Because I'm sure they were pretty furious when I escaped and they went to jail. They were so mean and they thought they owned me. In their minds, they probably want to make me pay."

I stood up just as tall and straight as I could. "Bogey and Lil and I won't let them hurt you. We're here to protect you."

She smiled and looked at me again with her big, green eyes. "You're my hero, Buckley."

Then she reached up and gave me a kiss on the nose.

That was about all I remembered until my head cleared again. I found myself flopped over on the floor, and by then, she was gone. And I knew it was time for me to meet Bogey in the office.

I got up on wobbly legs and stumbled down the stairs. Then I sort of tripped into our Mom's office. Bogey was sitting on the desk and working on the computer. He had an open bag of cat treats next to him.

He took one look at me. "Dames, kid. They'll get you every time."

"Dames," I mumbled back and jumped onto our Mom's desk.

Bogey passed me a few treats. "Here you go, kid. You look like you could use a couple of these."

I took the treats and munched away. Pretty soon I started to feel a little better.

Bogey nodded at the computer screen. "Glad you made it, kid. Because we've got lots to talk about."

I blinked my eyes a couple of times and tried to focus. All of a sudden, I realized I was running short on sleep and long on being really, really tired. But if I wanted to be a great cat detective like Bogey, well, I had to look alive. As he would say.

"Okay, I'm ready," I told him and sat up straight.

Bogey got right down to business. "First, here's our new case as I see it. It's pretty clear that Steele Bronson and his gang are in town to search for something. Something that must be pretty valuable. And I'll bet it's something that should belong to the residents of St. Gertrude. Cats included."

I nodded. "Uh-huh. And for some reason, they seem to think it might be in our house."

Bogey put his paw into the treat bag and pulled out a few treats. "Maybe, kid. Maybe. His buddies were doing a bang-up job of searching for something here. But I'm not sure they believed the real item they were after was in our house."

I tilted my head. "Huh? Then why were they searching so hard?"

He passed us each a treat. "Because of something I overheard tonight, kid. When I was tailing Nadia. Right after Frank came downstairs, he and Nadia said something about an 'old broad.' They mentioned it a couple of times. And how that 'old broad' had to be here in town."

I crinkled my brows. "That isn't a very nice way to talk about a lady. And they sure better not be talking about our Mom like that. Or Miss Mokie."

Bogey waved his paw in front of his face. "You've got that right, kid. But I don't think they were. Seems to me the 'old broad' was something else. But I'm not sure what. I'm guessing it may be a very, very old painting of a woman. Or maybe a sculpture of a woman or something."

I put my paw to my chin, and for once, it went right where I wanted it to go. "Hmmm . . . So it could be something like a valuable painting. Or some kind of art."

Bogey nodded. "That's my guess, kid. Something really expensive. Something like they put in famous art museums."

I shook my head. "But our Mom doesn't have any valuable art stuff. Sure, she has some old paintings on the wall. And she has a few little sculpture things around. But I don't think they're worth a lot of money."

Bogey passed us each another round of treats. "Me either, kid. At least not the kind of money that Steele and his gang are talking about."

I took the treat in my paw. "And I've never heard of anybody in St. Gertrude having any really famous paintings or anything."

Bogey bit into his own treat. "Ditto on that, kid."

Then it hit me. "Could it be an old book? Our Mom says some old books are worth a fortune. And that could be why Steele Bronson wants to film his movie at our library."

Bogey grinned at me. "I'm all ears, kid. I like your train of thought."

Funny, but all of a sudden, I didn't feel so tired anymore. "But I still don't understand. Why did we also hear them talk about searching our house for a key? It kind of seems like they're looking for two different things."

Bogey grinned. "Exactly, kid. That brings me to the second thing I want to talk about. When they said they were looking for a key, I don't think they were looking for a house key. Or a car key."

I crinkled my brows. "I wonder what kind of key they were looking for?"

He nodded. "Remember me telling you about codes, kid? That there are two parts? There's the code and then there's the . . ."

I jumped to my feet. "The key! You said the second part was a key."

Bogey gave me a paw bump. "Bingo, kid. The thing that decodes the code is called the key."

All of a sudden, my heart started to pound really hard. "So you think they were searching our house for the key to decode the code. And the decoded message will lead to the 'old broad.' Which could be a book or a painting or who knows what?"

Bogey passed us each another treat. "Keep it up, kid. You're on a roll."

Now I gulped. "So we're in kind of a race. We've got to find this key before they do."

Bogey nodded. "You got it, kid."

Holy Mackerel! When I said this was our toughest case ever, I wasn't kidding. It was turning into a real doozie. And I was having a hard time keeping track of everything.

I scooted closer to the computer. "Okay, so what would this key look like?"

Bogey raised his brows. "That's what we've got to figure out. It could be a paper. Or a document. Or something from a book. Even a poem. But one thing I do know, is that Bronson and his bunch haven't found it yet."

I tilted my head and looked at him cross-eyed. "They haven't? How do you know that?"

Bogey glanced around the room. "Think about it, kid. Remember all that furniture and stuff Bronson bought at our Mom's store?"

I sort of gasped. "He only bought stuff from the early families of St. Gertrude. Maybe he thought this key was hidden in one of those things."

Bogey grinned. "Exactly, kid. But he didn't want anyone to know he was looking for that key."

I nodded my head really fast. "So he just pretended he was going to use that furniture for his movie set."

Bogey passed me another treat. "So if he'd found that key in all that stuff, he would have called off the dogs. Meaning, his little friends Frank and Nadia wouldn't have been here hunting through our house tonight."

"That's right," I sort of murmured. "Because otherwise they wouldn't be looking for it anymore."

Bogey stared at the French doors. "You got it, kid. But I think I found a clue that might lead us to the key."

All of a sudden, it seemed like I could hardly breathe. "Wow . . . you did? What is it?"

He pointed to the picture of the stone on the computer screen. "Take a look, kid. Tell me what you see. Right up there in the left hand corner. I enhanced the photo and made it sharper."

I scooted closer to the computer. "I'm not sure, but I think I see three lines, followed by two small 'X's.' And then I see a line and a little 'V.' What are those?"

Bogey grinned. "Roman numerals, kid. The first three lines stand for the number three. And the next symbols come out to be the number twenty-four."

I turned and looked at my brother. "Number three and then number twenty-four? What does it mean?"

Bogey passed me a treat and took one for himself. "Don't know yet, kid. But I do know we'd better figure it out before Steele Bronson and his crew do. Otherwise, we'll have some valuable treasure missing from St. Gertrude. And we'll never even know what it was."

You may have heard the expression, "Curiosity killed the cat." Well, right about then, I figured that expression was about to come true. Because let me tell you, I really thought I was going to die of curiosity at that moment. More than anything, I wanted to know what those numbers meant.

Bogey stashed his treat bag back into the vase where he always hid it. "Let's give it some thought, kid. But right now we'd better run our surveillance rounds. We're behind schedule."

I wanted to salute him, but for some reason, I just couldn't keep my mind off those numbers. What did they mean? And how would we ever figure out that part of the puzzle? Especially before Steele Bronson and his people did?

I was still thinking about it when we ran our first surveillance round that night. We zoomed through the downstairs together and then headed upstairs. Everything looked fine, so we took time out for a nap. Then we ran another set of rounds and grabbed another nap. We were just finishing up our third set of surveillance rounds when our Dad came down the stairs. Yawning.

And about to get ready for work.

He opened the front door and grabbed the paper from the porch. He rubbed his eyes and yawned again. Then he blinked a few times and unfolded the paper.

The *St. Gertrude Times*.

We could even see the headline from where we sat on the floor. "World Famous Movie Star Steele Bronson Visits Local Home For Dinner."

And right below that was a picture. A huge picture. A much, much larger than life picture.

That's when my jaw dropped and practically hit the hardwood floor.

"Bogey," I meowed in a whisper. "Do you see that?"

He clenched his teeth together. "Couldn't miss it if I tried, kid."

I sure wished I hadn't seen it. I even blinked my eyes a few times, just to make sure I *did* see it right. But no matter how I turned my head, or how many times I closed my eyes, that picture was still there every time I looked.

I felt my heart sink inside my chest.

For there, staring at us from the front page of the paper, was the Princess.

Holy Catnip!

CHAPTER 18

Holy Mackerel!

I could hardly believe it. There she was. The Princess. Staring back at us from the front page of the *St. Gertrude Times*. The caption below read, "Franklin Jefferson, the writer behind Steele Bronson's fantastic success, holds one of the family cats as he attends an event at the home of Mike and Abigail Abernathy."

As pictures went, it was a really good one. But let me tell you, nobody was going to be looking at Frank Jefferson. That's because he'd been holding the Princess forward, so she ended up being front and center in that photo. Even though Frank was in the background, what stood out was the Princess' beautiful white fur and her big, green eyes. And, the diamonds sparking in her collar.

The paper might as well have posted a caption that read, "Here's Princess Alexandra. Come and get her."

Our Dad petted Bogey and me on the head. "Look boys. Lexie made the front page."

Then he wandered sleepily to the kitchen.

I turned to my brother. "I don't get it. That reporter must have taken a million pictures last night. But why, oh why, did the paper have to put *that* picture on the front? They must have had tons of other pictures they could've used. Pictures of

Steele Bronson."

Bogey's mouth was set in a firm line. "Probably a backroom deal, kid. That reporter is the son of the guy who owns the St. Gertrude paper. So what that reporter wants to go on the front page probably *goes* on the front page."

I looked up at the ceiling. "But I still don't see why he put the Princess' picture there."

Bogey rubbed his head. "He's getting cozy with Frank, kid. Because the reporter has written a screenplay that he wants to go to Hollywood. He thinks Frank has the connections to help him. And that was probably the only picture he took of Frank. So he made sure it ended up on the front page of the paper. To flatter him."

I rubbed my own head. "All these people trying to get something from someone else. Yet the Princess isn't trying to get anything from anyone. And she might be the one who ends up suffering from all this."

Bogey sighed. "I hear ya, kid. This could set off a huge chain reaction. If this picture hits the wires and goes national, we could be in big trouble."

I gulped. "Do you really think her old owners could break out of jail?"

Bogey glanced at the front door. "Time will tell, kid. Time will tell."

A few minutes later, our Mom came down the stairs and headed for the kitchen. She and our Dad started cooking breakfast.

Then, much to my amazement, I heard singing. The sound came closer and closer. Pretty soon I figured out it was Gracie singing one of her favorite songs. She was still singing when she came bounding down the stairs. She picked up Bogey and gave him a kiss on the head. Then she picked me up and gave me a big hug.

I had to say, I needed a good hug right about then. So I hugged her back. And I gave her a nice kiss on the nose, too.

She giggled and put me down. "Do you boys know what a great day this is?"

Well, to tell you the truth, I had no idea. Though I was sort of surprised to hear her say so. Especially after all that she'd been through in the last couple of days.

I turned to my brother and raised my brows, silently asking him if he knew anything. But he just shrugged his shoulders.

Then Gracie went dancing into the kitchen.

We ran in after her. What in the world was going on?

She stopped right in front of our Mom and Dad. "I've made a decision. I would like to throw a party."

Our Mom looked at our Dad. And he shrugged his shoulders exactly like Bogey had. Then Bogey and I looked at each other again, and we both shrugged our shoulders.

Right about then, the Princess and Lil strolled into the kitchen. Lil came over and joined us while the Princess jumped onto a kitchen chair. She sat up nice and straight and sort of surveyed the room. She smiled and started to purr.

Our Mom poured coffee for her and our Dad. "Um, what kind of a party did you have in mind?"

Gracie smiled. "A Fourth of July party."

That's when my head spun around toward the Princess like metal being drawn to a magnet. Because I suddenly remembered the pictures she'd left around Gracie's room the night before. Now it looked like her plan was working.

Our Mom smiled back at Gracie. "Okay. But you're going to have a very full day. Are you sure you'll have time to throw a party on Saturday, too?"

Gracie danced around the room. "I'm not going to throw my party then. I'm going to throw my party tomorrow afternoon."

Our Mom choked on her coffee. "Tomorrow? That's pretty short notice."

Our Dad cracked a bunch of eggs into a bowl. "Maybe you could tell us about the rest of your party plans."

Gracie stopped dancing. "I would love, too. I want to have red, white, and blue decorations. And I'm going to bake cupcakes and decorate them red, white, and blue, too. Then I'm going to invite all the kids who were at the essay contest. And Mrs. Peebles. I'm going to tell them I've got a big surprise for them. And when the party gets going, I'm going to make a big announcement."

By now our Mom's eyes were wide. "Well, everything so far sounds good. What's the big announcement?"

"I'm going to announce that Dylan Federov should be the

real winner of the essay contest. After all, everyone knows his essay was the best. Then I'm going to award him the trophy instead of me."

Our Mom and Dad both sort of gasped.

Our Dad set down the bowl of eggs he'd been whipping. "Gracie, honey, you're going to give up your trophy? And the ride on the float and everything else?"

Gracie jutted her chin out. "Yes, Dad. It's the right thing to do. The only reason I got that trophy was because Steele Bronson walked in and said I was the winner. But I didn't really win that contest. Honestly, I did a terrible job that night. I don't deserve that trophy. And I don't want to have it if I don't deserve it."

Our Mom was smiling. "Are you sure about this?"

Gracie started to dance around again. "Mom and Dad, I've never been so sure about anything in my whole life. Ever since I got awarded that trophy, I've felt just awful. Because I didn't deserve it and someone else did. But now that I decided to have this party, I feel like a big weight has been lifted off my shoulders."

Our Dad finished stirring the eggs and poured them into a hot frying pan. "Well then, Gracie, I think it sounds like a wonderful idea. You'll turn it into a bit of a ceremony and make it official."

Our Mom walked over and wrapped Gracie in a big hug. "Gracie, that's sounds like a perfect way to handle all this. I am so proud of you."

Gracie looked up to her. "You are? Even though I won't end up with the trophy? And I did such a terrible job at the contest? I got so flustered when Steele Bronson showed up that I didn't even practice enough. And I can't believe I let that Frank rewrite my essay. I never should have let him do that."

Our Mom stroked Gracie's hair back from her face. "He *never* should have done that to your paper. But to answer your question, I am proud of you right now for doing the right thing. You may not have done your best at the contest, but I think you've learned a lot from all this."

Gracie let out a really loud sigh. "I've learned a lot of things I wish I'd never had to learn."

Our Mom hugged her again. "Well then, let's get your

party set up. I think we can stay home from the store today. I'll call Merryweather and Millicent and make sure they can handle things on their own. Then we can bake cupcakes and decorate."

Our Dad waved his spatula. "Don't forget to save some cupcakes for your dear old Dad."

Gracie laughed. "I'll set some aside for you."

Then she looked back to our Mom again. "Thank you, Mom. For giving me this idea."

Our Mom raised an eyebrow. "Me? Honey, I had nothing to do with this. You came up with this idea on your own."

Gracie grinned. "Uh-huh. Someone left a whole bunch of pictures around my room. Kind of like hints. It took me a little while, but I put two and two together."

Our Mom's mouth fell open. "Honey, I'm afraid I don't know what you're talking about."

Gracie winked at our Mom. "Right, Mom. Sure, whatever you say."

With those words, Gracie skipped off. Our Mom and Dad stood there with their mouths hanging open. In the meantime, the Princess just sat there purring as loud as she could. I'd never seen her look so proud.

And I was pretty proud of the Princess, too! I sure had to hand it to her. When she came up with a plan, she really knew how to make it work!

Holy Catnip!

It was so nice to see the Princess look so happy. And she kept on looking happy. That was, until she spotted the front page of the paper and saw her own face looking back at her. That's when she bit her lip and quit purring. I could tell she was upset, and probably scared. But she was working hard not to show it.

About that time, I could barely keep my eyes open. Bogey and I both dragged ourselves to our cat beds for a nice long nap. We woke up around lunchtime to see party decorations and balloons strung up in the living room. Plus we could smell cupcakes baking in the oven. Gracie announced to our Mom that she had sent emails to everyone and that all had promised to be there.

Gracie spent the rest of the day practically walking on air.

Later in the afternoon, she sat down at the computer at our Mom's desk. She had the copy of her essay with her, the one that Frank had marked up with red ink.

Bogey and I decided to join her. She giggled when he sat on one side of the computer and I sat on the other.

She petted us both on our heads. "Hello, boys. I'm typing my essay into the computer again. And I'm deciding if I want to use any of the suggestions that Frank made. I may use some, and I may ignore others. Then I'm going to read it aloud in front of my mirror. This may sound kind of funny, but I just want to prove to myself that I can read it out loud without any problems."

I had to say, that sure sounded like a good idea to me! I gave her a kiss on the nose while Bogey watched every word she typed.

She had barely finished when the doorbell rang. She saved her work and raced off to the front door. Our Mom was just coming up behind her as Gracie swung the door open wide.

There on the front porch was Taffy, Steele Bronson's hairdresser. She had her arms full of towels and she was pulling a small suitcase.

"Hello, Abby. Hello, Gracie," she said. "It looks like you both fixed your own hair today."

Our Mom smiled. "I'm afraid our hairdos weren't in great shape after last night. And Gracie and I both decided to wear our hair like we normally do."

Taffy frowned. "Oh . . . all right. But I think Steele liked your hair better the way I fixed it."

Gracie put a big smile on her face. "Well, I don't remember asking his opinion on how I should wear my hair."

Now Taffy raised an eyebrow and glared at Gracie. "I'll just have to fix your hair again before you read your essay. For the movie."

But Gracie's smile didn't dip. "We'll see."

Our Mom put her hand on Gracie's head and looked at Taffy. "What can we do for you today?"

Taffy stepped into our house. "I'm here to give Buckley and Bogey their baths. Ready for *their* part in the movie."

Our Mom shook her head. "It's all right. I can bath the boys later. You don't need to worry about it."

Taffy took another step forward, and sort of forced our Mom to move aside. "Look lady, if I don't do people's hair, then I don't get paid. And if Steele Bronson says he wants me to bath those two cats, then that's what I have to do. Otherwise I'll be out of a job."

Our Mom sort of laughed and shook her head. "All right, fine. You can give the boys a bath."

"I'll need your kitchen sink," Taffy said.

Gracie let out a little shriek. "No, you can't use the kitchen sink. Because I'm baking cupcakes and I need to use the whole kitchen."

Taffy rolled her eyes. "Whatever. Just show me to a bathroom. I'll use the tub."

"Fine," our Mom said again. "I'll take you to an upstairs bathroom."

And the next thing I knew, Taffy carried Bogey and her suitcase up the stairs. Our Mom walked in front of her, and carried me and the towels.

I wriggled around to look our Mom right straight in the eyes. I couldn't believe she was going along with this lousy plan! Didn't she know that Bogey and I were being carried to our doom?

Let me tell you, I've had a bath or two before. And it was not pretty. That's because us cats hate being in the water. So I sure wanted to avoid getting a bath today. Or any other day, for that matter. Especially from this Taffy person whom I barely even knew.

"Don't worry, Buckley," our Mom murmured to me. "You'll be fine."

I figured our Mom must suddenly be in some kind of a trance or something. Or maybe she was just really tired or stressed out and not thinking straight. Because I sure couldn't understand why she hadn't put a stop to this terrible trauma that was about to take place!

So I started to squirm in my Mom's arms and tried to get away. Then I saw Bogey waving to me. From the look on his face, I could tell he had something important to tell me. But to be honest, I didn't really care at that moment. All I really cared about was escaping. And staying away from any bath water.

"We've got to keep Taffy busy, kid," Bogey meowed over to me. "So she can't go off and search our house. For the key. Or the 'old broad.'"

"But Bogey," I meowed back. "We're talking about a bath here!"

Bogey shook his head. "Don't I know it, kid. Don't I know it. But sometimes you've got to take one for the team."

I squirmed some more. "Take one for the team?"

"Yup, kid," Bogey meowed. "It means doing something you don't want to do, for the sake of your team. That's us. We're the team and we've got to solve this case. So the best thing we can do is put up a big fuss while she's giving us a bath. It's what a good cat detective would do."

I cringed and closed my eyes. Sure, I wanted to be a good cat detective and do my part to solve a case. And I wanted to be part of our team. I was happy to run surveillance, and hunt for clues and all kinds of things.

But taking a bath was another thing altogether.

I glanced at my brother and took a deep breath.

He gave me a "paws up." "You can do this, kid. I know you can."

I moaned and cuddled into my Mom. Of all the things I've had to do as a cat detective, this had to be the worst.

Why, oh why, did it have to be a bath?

Holy Catnip!

CHAPTER 19

Holy Mackerel!

The next thing I knew, Bogey and I were in our huge, guest bathroom with the old, claw-foot tub. The floor tiles were in the shape of little, black-and-white octagons. The black tiles made an outline around everything, and the white tiles were in the middle. Funny, but I'd been in this bathroom a million times before. We usually did a quick run through this room when we did our surveillance rounds. I always thought it was kind of a nice bathroom. But all of a sudden it sort of seemed like a bad place to be.

Our Mom kissed us both good-bye before she shut the door and went downstairs to help Gracie make icing for the cupcakes.

Then Taffy didn't waste any time. She unpacked her suitcase and turned on the taps to pour water into the tub. I backed into a corner and got as far away from that tub as I could possibly go.

Suddenly I wasn't so sure I wanted to take one for the team anymore.

Bogey jumped into the suitcase and started to investigate.

But he didn't last long. Because she only needed a few inches of water in that tub to bath us. And it filled up pretty fast.

"What are you doing in there?" she hollered to Bogey.

Of course, she didn't exactly wait for him to respond. Instead she grabbed him and put him smack dab in the middle of the tub. Right into the water. I heard him land with a giant *splash!*

Just the thought of it made me howl! And I kept on howling and ran for the door. Then I reached up to the doorknob. I tried my very best to turn it, but it was too slippery.

I could hear the Princess on the other side of the door. "Buckley, Buckley, are you okay? What's the matter?"

"Help! Help!" I yelled. "This lady is giving Bogey a bath. And I'm next."

The Princess stuck her little paw under the door. "Just relax, Buckley. It'll be okay. I had to get lots of baths when I was a show cat. They're not fun, but it'll be over quick."

Well, the Princess sure was right about the "not fun" part! I wasn't so sure about the "quick" part.

By now I could smell the shampoo that Taffy was using on Bogey. And judging by the way she was working her arms back and forth, I could tell she was lathering him up good.

That's when my heart started to pound really hard and I searched frantically for some place to hide. The suitcase looked like the only place to go. So I dove straight in. It was nice and dark and safe inside there.

Then I wondered what the Princess would think of me if she could see me. Here I was supposed to be a big, tough cat detective. But I sure wasn't acting like one.

So I took some deep breaths and tried to calm down. Then I glanced around the suitcase. I noticed a piece of paper tucked into a clear plastic pocket on the side. The paper was sort of torn and not in good shape. I couldn't read it very well, but it looked like an article. Maybe something someone had printed off the Internet. I could make out a little bit of the title and the words, ". . . Missing Copies of the Declaration of Independence . . ."

Well, that didn't exactly make any sense to me. Especially since Gracie had already told me that the Declaration of Independence was in Washington, D.C. She even wanted to go see it someday.

So how could there be any missing copies?

I scooted over and took a closer look at that paper. That's when I saw someone's handwriting scrawled across the top. The words that were written there said, "Be sure to read this article, so you'll understand." It ended with the words, "Top Secret. Tell no one."

But nobody had signed their name to that note.

Funny, but I was pretty sure I'd seen that handwriting before. I just couldn't remember where.

And then it hit me. It was the same handwriting I'd seen on Gracie's essay. Right after Frank had written all over it.

So it must have been Frank who wrote those words on this paper, too.

Had I just found a clue?

My heart started to pound all over again. Somehow I knew I needed to keep this paper. So Bogey and I could look at it later.

I peeked out from the suitcase to make sure Taffy wasn't watching me. Then I reached into the pocket and carefully grabbed that paper with my claws. I pulled it out a little way, until I could grab the edge with my teeth. Then I worked at getting it the rest of the way out. It was stuck just a little bit, so I had to tug for a few seconds. But I finally had that paper free from the pocket.

And not a moment too soon.

I jumped out of the suitcase with that paper in my teeth just as Taffy reached down for a towel. I quickly tiptoed to the door while she picked Bogey up out of the tub. Then I put the paper on the floor and pushed it underneath the door. All the way out to the other side.

"Princess! Princess!" I meowed softly. "Are you still there?"

"I'm here, Buckley," came her sweet voice.

I leaned up against the door. "Could you please take this paper? And hide it in the sunroom?"

"I've got it, Buckley!" she said. "I'll hide it for you."

"Thanks," I managed to get out just as Taffy grabbed me around the ribcage.

The next thing I knew, I was practically flying through the air with her hanging onto nothing but my ribcage. She was carrying me directly into that tub, whether I liked it or not. I saw the water coming closer and closer. So I stretched out my arms and legs and all my claws. Then I searched frantically for something to grab onto. But in a split second I realized there was nothing there but open water and a big bathtub. Not a single thing I could latch onto and save myself. So now I put my arms and legs down, ready for landing.

Taffy put me into that water a whole lot faster than I wanted to go. I landed with a big *sploosh!* Water and suds went flying, and I let out the biggest yowl of my life. Then I started to scramble around in the bath water. The leftover shampoo from Bogey's bath quickly bubbled up into a huge froth. Almost as tall as I was!

But Taffy didn't seem to care. Instead she started scooping water onto me to get my fur wet. She did it so fast that I barely even noticed when she poured shampoo onto my back. She lathered me up just before I managed to make a run for it!

And I ran for all I was worth. I headed straight for the angled back of that tub. The only problem was, I was so wet and slippery that I couldn't climb up the porcelain.

Taffy grabbed me again and tugged me back into the middle of the tub. And I immediately wiggled my way out of her grasp and took off again. This time I tried to jump up the side of the tub. But it was too tall and wet and slippery.

She tugged me back and started to rinse me off.

"Hold still, will you?" she commanded me.

Well, I wasn't exactly crazy about the way she was talking to me. But I finally figured I might as well just get it over with. After all, she was almost done. So I let her finish rinsing me off. Then she wrapped a towel around me and yanked me out of the tub.

She put me right beside Bogey on the floor.

"Not exactly gentle, is she, kid?" he murmured.

I shook my whole body and water went flying everywhere. "You can say that again!" I meowed.

Now he grinned. "I thought I'd return the favor, kid. So I left a nice imprint of my claws in her left arm."

I kind of laughed. And I wanted to tell Bogey about my clue right then, but I didn't get a chance. Because Taffy pulled some tubes from her suitcase and started squeezing some gunk out. She put something flowery-smelling all over me and something else all over Bogey.

She studied us for a moment. "The secret to a good 'on camera' look is to exaggerate what you already look like. It'll be you, only amped up."

Well, I had no idea what she meant by that. But out came combs and brushes and blow dryers. Soon my fur was getting blown all over the place and I couldn't see a thing. I could only feel her doing all kinds of combing and brushing. She combed sections of my hair up and down, until I could feel big tangles in my fur. Funny, but our Mom always combed the tangles out of my fur. Not purposely put them in.

Next I tried to watch while she did something else to Bogey. But I couldn't tell what it was for sure. That's because my fur was completely poofed out in front of my face. And all I could see was a big bunch of black fuzz.

Finally, she yelled, "I'm done. Got that job over with. Hope I don't have to bath another cat for a long time."

Boy, that went for both of us. I sure hoped she didn't ever bath another cat! For the cat's sake!

I pushed some fur from my eyes. Now at least I had a little tunnel to look out of. I could barely see Taffy packing up her stuff.

She glanced at her watch. "I'm late! I've got to get back to the library. Don't forget, filming starts tomorrow!"

With that, she grabbed her suitcase and headed out of the room. She made a beeline for the stairs and Bogey and I followed her. I still couldn't see much except for things that were right in front of me.

But I did see our Mom and Gracie at the top of the stairs. They took one look at us and they both squealed and then gasped at the same time.

"What on earth . . .?" our Mom started to say.

Gracie's eyes went as wide as dinner plates. "Oh Buckley and Bogey . . . what did she do to you?"

Taffy sort of sneered and walked down the stairs.

Our Mom turned and followed her down. "I don't understand . . . I thought you were just going to give them a bath. I don't even recognize them."

Now Taffy sounded nasty. "That's because you're not in

the movie industry. Films are art, and artistic expression comes in many forms. We wanted to make the smaller cat smaller, and the larger cat larger. It's an exaggeration of their normal selves. It's an illusion."

Our Mom let out a laugh. "You can say that again."

Then she let Taffy out the door and shut it behind her.

Gracie kept on moving toward us. "Oh my goodness, boys. Have you seen what you look like?"

Well, to tell you the truth, I hadn't. That's because I could barely see anything. But I could hear Bogey sneezing, and I'm pretty sure he was blinking his eyes a bunch. I guess all those hair products were giving him allergies.

Just then I heard, rather than saw, our Dad come into the hallway. He must have come home from work already.

He and our Mom walked up the stairs to join us.

Our Mom just kept shaking her head. One minute she would kind of laugh, and the next minute she would sigh.

"What the . . ." I heard our Dad start to say when he saw us. "What happened to Buckley? Did he stick his paw in a light socket or something? And what about Bogey? Why is he so slicked down like that? He looks like he's got varnish on him."

"Steele Bronson's hairdresser styled them," Gracie said with a tone in her voice that I didn't hear very often.

I think it was anger.

She leaned down toward us and spoke very softly. "Let me show you boys what you look like. Come with me."

And so we did. She led us to the full-length mirror in her room, and we both stood right smack dab in front of it. At first, I wasn't even sure who the two creatures looking back at us were. For that matter, I wasn't even sure they were cats.

I could sort of make out Bogey's form. But he was so sleeked back with some shiny, greasy stuff that he reminded me of a ferret. Or maybe a weasel. With his fur completely slicked down like that, he looked very, very thin. I could make out every bone in his body.

As for me, well, I was the exact opposite. I was huge and round and fluffy. Every piece of fur on my body stuck out. I looked about four times my normal size! I kind of looked like a big, fuzzy, black tumbleweed! Or maybe a creature from outer space. I was so round that I almost wondered if I could roll away. And I could barely see my eyes, which were practically hidden in all that fur.

Our Mom joined us. "I can't believe this . . ."

Gracie shook her head. "Me, either. But one thing's for sure — I'm not having our cats going around looking this ridiculous."

"You're right," our Mom said. "This is ridiculous."

Gracie stood up straight and tall. "I'm going to wash all this gunk out of their fur. These boys are handsome enough without any special effects. They can look like themselves in the movie. And that will be just fine."

Our Mom smiled. "I couldn't agree more."

Me, either, I thought.

I glanced at my brother who didn't even look like my brother.

"They've got my vote, kid," he meowed. "It would be pretty tough to run surveillance in this get up."

Somewhere from under all that fur, I nodded. "They've got my vote, too. I feel like a walking fluffball."

I wanted to give Bogey a paw bump, but I couldn't see well enough to even try. Who knew what I'd bump into if I stuck my paw out now?

"Okay, boys," Gracie said. "Let's get you in the bath and get this stuff washed out of you."

I turned my head up and tried to look at Gracie.

Wait a minute. Did she just say we were going to get another bath?

Two baths in one day? How much could two cats take?

Holy Catnip!

CHAPTER 20

Holy Mackerel!

I had to say, by the time Gracie was done with us, Bogey and I both looked pretty sharp. The bath Gracie gave us wasn't even half as bad as our first bath. That's because Gracie put a big pan full of water into the empty bathtub and then stood us in that pan. So we were really only standing in a little bit of water. Then she used pitchers full of water to rinse us. She told us she'd been reading up on how to bath a cat on the Internet. And let me tell you, it wasn't so bad. I knew she wanted to be a veterinarian when she grew up. She sure was going to be a good one.

Still, she had to shampoo and rinse us several times to get all that gunk out of our fur. When she finished bathing us, she wrapped us up in warm, fluffy towels. Straight from the dryer.

To tell you the truth, my towel felt pretty nice and comfy.

I gave Gracie a big kiss on the nose to thank her. I sure was glad I didn't have to go around looking like a gigantic fuzzball anymore. It would have been pretty embarrassing if anyone other than my family had seen me like that. Especially Hector, the Siamese who lives down the street. Hector is known for being a big blabbermouth. And if he would've seen me all poofed out, well, he would have blabbed it to everyone!

Right after we were dried and combed from our second

bath, I took a long, long nap. I woke up just in time for a little late night supper. And in time to see our Mom and Dad and Gracie head for bed. Then I met Bogey in the office, all ready to run surveillance.

But along the way, I noticed the Fourth of July decorations that Gracie had hung up for her party. I saw flags and streamers and balloons in red, white, and blue. It all looked so pretty. I really hoped her party went well, because I knew she'd worked so hard to set it up. And she was pretty excited about it.

It also made me happy to see the Princess' plan fall into place. She'd come up with such a great idea, and she'd gone to a lot of work, too. Because it took a lot of time to pick out those magazine pages and set them out in Gracie's room. She'd found just the right pages to give Gracie the exact hints she needed . . .

And that's when it hit me. I stopped dead in my tracks and did some serious thinking for a moment. The Princess had pulled pages from a magazine. Could it be . . .?

All of a sudden, I had something I'd been hoping I'd have for a long, long time. Something all the great cat detectives have sometimes.

I had a hunch. A real hunch.

Just like Bogey.

I didn't even wait to finish thinking about it. Instead I ran for all I was worth to our Mom's office. Bogey was busy on the computer, and I jumped right up to join him.

I was breathing so hard I could barely get the words out. "Bogey, Bogey! You'll never believe it!"

Bogey shook his head. "I wouldn't be so sure, kid. But me first. I've just been looking at the news and it isn't pretty. There's been a jailbreak. The Count and Countess Von De Meenasnitzel have escaped."

I gulped. "They have?"

Bogey's mouth was set in a firm line. "I'm afraid so, kid."

Suddenly I started to shake in my paws. "Do you think they'll come here?"

Bogey reached his lean arm into the vase on our Mom's desk and pulled out the bag of cat treats he had stashed there. "That would be my guess, kid. They'll probably try to snatch the Princess and get out of town in a hurry."

Bogey handed me a cat treat and took one for himself.

I could barely eat my treat. "So I guess that means we'd better run extra surveillance rounds."

Bogey ate his treat in two bites. "Looks like it, kid. And it might be a good idea if we took the Princess with us tomorrow."

I raised my brows. "Took her with us? To the library?"

Bogey nodded and handed us each another treat. "Yup, kid. To the library. So we can keep her close to us. Plus if the Count and Countess come looking for her, they'll never think to look there."

I finished my second treat. "Um . . . okay. Sounds good. But how will we get her there?"

Bogey grinned and passed out another round of treats. "Easy, kid. We'll jump in our pet carriers before our Mom is ready to go. But we'll sneak the Princess into your carrier first, and hide her under the blanket. Once we get to the library, we can let her run with us. Because our Mom won't have time to take her back home."

I nodded. "I like it. That way we won't worry about her while we're gone."

Bogey grinned. "Exactly, kid. So tell me, what had you so fired up when you came flying in here?"

Now the same excitement that I'd felt earlier came rushing back into me. And I could barely hold still. I started to pace from side to side, and swished my huge tail back and forth. I finally understood why Gracie danced around when she got excited.

I smiled bigger than I think I've ever smiled. "I have a hunch."

Bogey's eyes went wide and a huge grin crossed his face. "Good job, kid! I knew you had it in you! Like I keep saying, you're going to be a great cat detective one day."

He did? That made me stop pacing for a moment. I wasn't sure if I was going to be a great cat detective or not. But it sure made me feel good to hear Bogey say that.

Bogey kept on grinning. "Okay, kid, spill it. What is your hunch?"

I grinned back at my brother. "I think I know where the

key to crack the code might be."

Bogey gave me a paw bump. "Pretty good first hunch, kid! Care to fill me in on the details?"

Now I started to pace again. "Well . . . it's like this. The Princess took pages out of a magazine to drop hints to Gracie. And that got me thinking about things like dropping hints. And that made me think about Mr. Fartheringston and how he might have dropped some hints about how to crack his secret code. And then I thought, hey, what if he used a page from a magazine, too . . ."

I paused and looked at my brother.

His eyes were huge. "That's brilliant, kid! But instead of using a page from a magazine . . ."

I nodded my head really, really fast. "He probably used a page from those books in the library. The ones he wrote."

By now Bogey was up and patting me on the back. "It was a set! The Complete Works and Diaries of Arthur J. Fartheringston!"

Bogey was still grinning when he headed back to the computer. "I think you've cracked this case wide open, kid! Now, let's take a gander at that stone again. I seem to remember some numbers up in the corner."

So did I.

Bogey didn't waste any time finding his enhanced picture of that stone. Then he zoomed in on the upper left hand corner. And there they were, those same symbols that we had seen before. Roman numerals for the number three, and then the number twenty-four."

He pointed to the picture. "I'll bet the number three is for the third book in his group."

I scooted closer to the computer screen. "And maybe the number twenty-four is for page twenty-four in that book."

Bogey grabbed a couple more cats treats from the bag. "I think you've nailed it, kid. And I'll bet your hunch is right. Let's sneak off when we're at the library tomorrow. And find this book. We'd better tear out that page, so Bronson an his bunch can't get their filthy paws on it."

Suddenly my heart started to pound inside my chest. I could hardly believe it! Here I was, still practically a rookie. And my hunch might turn out to make a huge difference in solving this case! Provided that page turned out to be the key we were looking for. Still, I was so excited I almost forgot about the paper I'd found in Taffy's suitcase.

Bogey held up a cat treat. "A toast, kid. To you! For figuring out such an important clue."

I held up a treat, too, and we clinked our treats together. Sort of like people sometimes clink their glasses together.

I munched on my treat. "Um . . . Bogey . . . there might be more. I think I found another clue while Taffy was giving you a bath."

Bogey choked on his treat. "Way to go, kid! You'll be ready to take the lead in some of our cases pretty soon."

Well, I didn't know about that. But I did tell Bogey all about the other clue. Seconds later, we were headed to the sunroom to find the Princess. We found her sitting with Miss Mokie and Lil on the purple velvet couch. Together they were looking at a crumpled, partly torn piece of paper.

It was the paper that I'd found in the pocket of Taffy's suitcase!

Miss Mokie waved us on in and told us there was no need to bow. Then she got right down to business.

"The Princess Alexandra has informed me of recent events around here. And apparently this paper might serve as a clue in your case, Detectives. Well, I am more than happy to share my wisdom and give you a summary of this paper. It is apparently an article about an 'Old Broad.'"

Right about then, I think my jaw practically hit the floor. So did Bogey's. For a moment I thought Miss Mokie was using mean words that might describe herself. But nobody spoke badly of Miss Mokie. Especially not Miss Mokie!

She blinked her eyes and shook her head. "Fear not, young ones. I would never use such a horrible phrase to describe an older female. Of any species. It's only humans who don't respect females as they gain in age. And naturally, in wisdom, too. But of course, us cats know better."

Bogey and I both let out a huge sigh of relief.

The Wise One held her paw above the paper. "No, in this case, the term 'Old Broad' is used to describe a Dunlap Broadside."

"A Dunlap Broadside?" Bogey and I asked at the same

time.

Miss Mokie nodded. "That is correct, Detectives. The Dunlap Broadsides were the first printed copies of the Declaration of Independence. But the copy that was written by hand, the one that was later signed by the fifty-six delegates of the Continental Congress, is in Washington, D.C."

"Wow," I sort of breathed. "That means a Dunlap Broadside would be really old. Almost two hundred and fifty years old."

Miss Mokie smiled down at me. "Correct again, young Detective. To uncover a Dunlap Broadside is the find of the century. It is believed there were about two hundred copies printed on that night in 1776. But only twenty-five are known to have survived until today."

"*Ooooh . . .*" the rest of us kind of murmured.

Now Miss Mokie spoke in a low, quiet voice. "Picture it, young ones. It was July 4th, 1776. A group of delegates from all thirteen colonies had just adopted the wording on the Declaration of Independence. There was excitement and tension in the air. Since they had just declared that they were going to be a free nation. And they were going to separate from England and King George. Naturally, they knew England would not release its control without a fight. In fact, by declaring their freedom, these delegates had just committed high treason in the eyes of the King. So they chose freedom at great peril. Their very lives and all their possessions were at risk."

"*Ooooh . . .*" we all said again.

The Wise One held her paw above us. "Then five men, along with John Dunlap, raced to his print shop in Philadelphia. There, he and the others set the type for the first copies of the Declaration to be printed off. As I said before, they printed off 200 copies of these broadsides. 'Broadside' was the word they used back then for a large sheet of paper that was printed only on one side. Then these broadsides were sent throughout the colonies, declaring freedom for this young nation. Freedom from a king who oppressed them. And freedom for the people to make their own choices. Yes, it was quite an event when those first copies of the Declaration went out. It would have been such great danger for those people riding on horseback across the land."

"Wow . . ." the rest of us whispered.

Miss Mokie sat back and blinked her eyes a few times. "The few broadsides that exist today are mostly owned by libraries and museums and such."

Bogey crinkled his brows. "Very old and very rare. That sounds like an expensive combination to me. I wonder what kind of dough one of those old broadsides would bring today."

Miss Mokie sat up as straight as she could. "There was one that sold at an auction not long ago. It sold for over eight million dollars."

We all gasped.

"Did you say 'million?'" I sort of sputtered.

Miss Mokie nodded her head. "That is correct, young Detective."

Bogey grinned and glanced at me. "Well, that adds up then, doesn't it, kid?"

It did? For a moment, I didn't want to answer, since I wasn't exactly sure how things added up. And I sure didn't want to look bad in front of all the other cats. A good cat detective would have figured things out, just like Bogey had.

But instead of giving up and being so sure I couldn't figure it out, I decided to try working through the situation. One step at a time.

"Well . . ." I started slowly. "If I found that paper in Taffy's bag . . . and it had Frank Jefferson's handwriting on it . . . that means he probably gave that paper to Taffy . . . and Frank told us that he was related to both Ben Franklin and Thomas Jefferson . . ."

Lil smiled and turned my way. "And Ben Franklin and Thomas Jefferson were both signers of the Declaration of Independence."

I smiled back at her. "Uh-huh. Plus, we also heard that Frank was writing a book about his ancestors."

Lil kept on going. "So he probably did a lot of research on them."

Now the Princess jumped in. "Which means he maybe learned a lot more from his research than he thought he would. Maybe he accidentally discovered the location of another Dunlap Broadside."

I turned to her and nodded. "Or maybe he found clues that could lead him to one that is hidden. Maybe he figured out some things, like the name of a town. Or a person who had it last."

Bogey tilted his head to one side. "And that led him straight to good, old St. Gertrude. A town with a big stone with a bunch of letters carved into it. Letters that we're pretty sure are a secret code. Sitting right there in our library."

I felt my heart start to pound. "And that would be the *real* reason why Steele Bronson is here, though he claims he's here to film a movie. Especially since we know he needs money. Maybe Frank let Steele Bronson and the whole bunch in on his secret. So they could help him. And they all came together in search of a hidden copy of the Declaration of Independence."

Lil let out a slow whistle. "A cool eight million plus would be a nice chunk of change. Even when it was split four ways."

I raised my brows. "I think we have a good idea what the code on the Fartheringston stone leads to. Maybe Arthur had one of the Dunlap Broadsides. Maybe it got passed down in his family. And maybe he hid it since he knew it was so important. Then he set up the code on the stone so someone would find it if he passed away. Maybe he thought his wife, Emily, would figure it out."

The Princess sighed. "But the sad thing is, she didn't. Nobody did."

Lil nodded. "Not until now. Or, at least it looks like they must be pretty close."

Finally, the Princess' big, green eyes went really, really wide. "So if Steele Bronson and his bunch find the Dunlap Broadside, what will happen to it?"

The Wise One raised her paw above us. "I fear we might never know. Bronson and his gang would likely sneak it out of town and sell it on the black market. Alas, no one in St. Gertrude would be the wiser. Though in reality, it should stay in our library. Since Mr. Fartheringston left everything he owned to his beloved wife. And since she later left everything to the library, a Dunlap Broadside would belong there."

Bogey grinned and glanced around the room. "That's why we've got to get to it first. And thanks to Buckley's hunch, we've got a great lead on finding it."

Now the Princess danced around. "So it can be framed and hung in the St. Gertrude Library instead. For everyone to see. And maybe we can all go see it, too."

Suddenly all eyes were on me. Funny, but instead of feeling proud that I'd had my hunch, I now felt like squirming.

What if my hunch was wrong, and it didn't lead us to find the key to crack the code? Then again, what if it was right but it came too late? What if we didn't find it before Steele Bronson and his bunch did?

Secret codes and hidden documents. And hunches. They were almost too much for a guy like me!

Holy Catnip!

CHAPTER 21

Holy Catnip!

That night, I hardly got any sleep at all. For starters, we added our extra surveillance rounds to keep the Princess safe. Lil even lent a paw and helped us out. She traded off with Bogey and me, so we could take turns getting naps. But when it was my turn to sleep, I just kept wondering what we would find at the library the next day. Would we find the key to our secret code? Was my hunch right? Did I figure out what book had the right paper?

Just thinking about everything was pretty much driving me up a wall. Especially after we told the Princess and the others that her former owners had escaped. Sure, the Princess didn't make a big fuss about it. And she even said she was looking forward to going to the library the next day. But I knew deep down that she was scared. And it upset me to know that she was so afraid.

I had to say, I was looking forward to the day when the Count and Countess were captured again. Until then, we would need to be on our toes. And being on my toes meant I was on edge.

Maybe that was why I jumped a mile when the phone rang the next morning. It was Bravo calling, saying he'd be picking us up to take us to the library. To start filming the movie.

If there really was a movie, that was.

Bogey glanced my way. "Look alive, kid. Be ready to zoom to our pet carriers. I'll signal the Princess."

"Got it," I meowed back. I crouched down, all set to spring into action.

Our Mom told Bravo that we'd be ready to go soon. She sighed after she hung up the phone.

"Here I am, taking another day away from my business," she told our Dad.

He grabbed his backpack, ready to leave for work. "Would you like me to take a day off and go with you? After all, I told Bronson I would be coming, too."

She kissed him good-bye. "No, but thanks anyway. There's no use having both of us miss work. Not for something like this."

Our Dad left, and our Mom called Millicent and Merryweather. While she gave them instructions for the day, Bogey and the Princess and I made a beeline for our pet carriers. I let the Princess go into mine first. Then Bogey and I carefully arranged the blanket over her. Of course, we left her face partly uncovered so she had room to breathe. Then I scooted in on the front half of the soft-sided carrier.

Bogey jumped into his, just as our Mom and Gracie walked up.

Our Mom laughed. "Well, at least somebody is looking forward to this."

Gracie shook her head. "I think they're they only ones."

Our Mom turned to Gracie. "It would be okay if we decide not to be part of this movie."

Gracie smiled. "I know. But we've already agreed to go along with this. Sort of."

Our Mom laughed. "Funny, but I don't remember that we actually agreed to go along with any of it."

Gracie put her finger to her chin. "You know, Mom, you're right. We didn't agree to any of it. We just didn't bother to disagree."

Our Mom grabbed her purse and keys. "That's about right. We haven't put our foot down at all, have we?"

Gracie shook her head. "If someone had told me a month ago that I was going to be in a Steele Bronson movie, I would have fallen over. I would have been so excited. Now here I am, about to *be* in a Steele Bronson movie. And instead of being excited, I'm dreading it."

Our Mom put her arm around Gracie's shoulders. "That's the way it goes, honey. When fantasy and reality collide."

Gracie raised an eyebrow. "Huh?"

Our Mom smiled. "When you see Steele Bronson in a movie, it all looks real, doesn't it?"

Gracie nodded. "Uh-huh."

"But it's not," our Mom told her. "It's nothing but a fantasy. The makeup, the lighting, the words that he says. It's all a very carefully crafted fantasy. And the truth is, the character he plays in a movie may be very different from what he's like in real life."

Gracie stared ahead, though her eyes didn't really seem to be focusing. "You know, that's true, Mom. Steele Bronson isn't anything like I thought he would be."

Our Mom zipped up our pet carriers. "I know, honey. As you get older, you'll learn to question things. Like they say, you can't believe everything you hear."

Gracie picked up Bogey's carrier. "Or see in a movie."

"Wise words from our Mom, kid," Bogey meowed to me.

Boy, he could say that again.

Gracie took a deep breath. "Well, we'd better get going. They're counting on us being there, and since we didn't tell them otherwise, I suppose we'd better show up. But I want to leave around lunchtime. To finish getting ready for my party."

"Sounds good," our Mom said with a smile.

Then she picked up my pet carrier and let out a loud grunt. "My goodness, Buckley, have you grown again? I don't remember you weighing this much before."

Minutes later, we were all riding in the back of that big black limo. The same one we had seen the day Steele Bronson had rolled into town.

Bravo drove us to the library, and shortly after that, we were being carried inside. The library sure looked a lot different today. There were big, black cameras and big lights and all kinds of equipment all over. Plus I saw a few local people who seemed to be helping out.

Steele Bronson was sitting in a red, director's chair with his name on the back. And Frank was sitting next to him in the same kind of chair with his name on the back, too.

Nadia spotted us the minute we came in. "Oh excellent, Abigail. And little girl . . . Gracie! So nice to see you! We're almost ready for your cats' first scene. So, if you'll take a seat with Steele and Frank, we'll get started shortly."

She pointed to a couple of library chairs right next to Frank. But our Mom and Gracie didn't go sit there. Instead, they stayed with us.

Now Taffy came over and unzipped our pet carriers. "Hold on a minute . . . This isn't right! These aren't the hairdos I gave these cats! What happened to the hairstyles I gave them yesterday? I spent hours working on them!"

She put her hands on her hips and glared at our Mom.

Gracie stood up nice and tall and looked right into Taffy's eyes. "The boys' fur is just perfect like it is. They don't need a new hairstyle."

Taffy raised her hands up. "Now I'll have to fix them all over again! It'll take me hours. We'll be behind schedule."

Gracie crossed her arms. "Oh no you don't! You will not be ruining their coats like you did yesterday. Buckley and Bogey stay like they are, or they won't be in your movie. In fact, we'll all just go on home."

Taffy put her hands to her cheeks. "I can't work with this! I will not put up with this kind of treatment!"

Gracie smiled. "And neither will we, thank you."

With that, Taffy stomped off.

I had to say, I was pretty proud of Gracie. She had stood up for us and said no. And she even did it nicely. Right about then, I sure wished I could give her a kiss on the nose.

Steele Bronson turned our way and squinted his eyes. Then he leaned over to Frank, and the two men started whispering.

Gracie reached down and took Bogey and me out of our pet carriers. She had just pulled me out when the Princess popped her head out. Gracie gasped. Then she giggled.

Our Mom smiled. "I guess that explains the extra weight. It looks like Buckley brought a friend. I wonder if Lexie wants to be in the movie."

Gracie kneeled down to pet us all. "Okay, kitties, they're

going to be filming you this morning. Then we've got to leave because I'm going to be having a party. And you're all invited."

Now I reached up and gave Gracie a kiss on the nose. Of course we knew about the party. In fact, it had been the Princess' idea. I glanced over at the Princess, who sat purring with a smile on her face.

Then the next thing I knew, Steele Bronson stood up and clapped his hands. "All right, are we ready for the first scene? I need Buckley and Bogey at the bottom of the staircase. We're going to film them running up the stairs."

Okay, to be honest, that part sounded pretty fun to me.

Our Mom and Gracie carried us to the bottom of the stairs. And the Princess slipped back into my pet carrier. Out of sight.

Once we were in position, Steele Bronson strolled over to us. "Listen boys, here's what I want you to do. I want you to ascend those stairs . . . the stairs of time . . . the stairs that have been tread on by a million footsteps. The stairs that have seen seasons come and go, and lives start and end . . ."

I glanced at my brother. "Do you understand what he's talking about?"

Bogey grinned. "He wants us to run up the stairs, kid."

"Oh . . . okay," I meowed back.

Funny, but it seemed like he could have just said that.

But apparently Steele Bronson wasn't finished talking yet. "As you're going, I want you to think of all the people who have trod those stairs. Then show me the emotion that you're feeling when you think about all that. Give me lots and lots of emotion. I want to see it written all over your faces. Make me feel what you're feeling."

I turned to my brother. "Emotion? We're supposed to show emotion? How are we supposed to do that?"

Bogey kept on grinning. "Don't sweat it, kid. Just run the stairs."

Then Steele Bronson clapped his hands and yelled, "Buckley and Bogey Stairs Scene! Take one! Ready!"

Bogey and I crouched down, ready to go racing up that big, round staircase."

Finally somebody yelled, "Action!" Just as they did, I heard a loud *thwack!* Out of the corner of my eye, I saw someone holding a small blackboard that had an even smaller strip of wood on the top. They hit the top of the board with the wood and that's what made the noise. It was so loud that I jumped straight into the air while Bogey went racing up the stairs!

Holy Mackerel! Nobody told me there were going to be scary noises like that!

"No, no, no!" Steele Bronson yelled. "That's just the clapperboard! You can't jump whenever someone claps the clapperboard!"

Bogey came running back down to me.

"Clapperboard?" I asked him.

Bogey shook his head. "Just something they use when they make movies. Don't worry, kid, it won't hurt you. Just ignore it."

Let me tell you, that clapperboard was going to be tough to ignore.

"All right," Steele Bronson yelled. "Buckley and Bogey Stairs Scene! Take Two! Ready!"

This time I knew just what to do when someone yelled "Action!" I took off running up those stairs, right behind my brother.

"No, no, no!" Steele Bronson hollered again. "You're not doing it right!"

Bogey and I came running back down the stairs. To tell you the truth, it looked to me like we were running up those stairs just fine. I glanced over to see our Mom and Gracie sitting next to Frank. While Frank talked to our Mom, Gracie watched us. And she did not look happy.

Steele Bronson waved his hands in the air. "This is not right, boys. You're not giving me raw emotion. I want awe and wonderment. Amazement, even. But you're giving me a Saturday stroll in the garden."

Before I knew it, we had "Take Three," and "Take Four," and then "Take Five." None of them was right according to Steele Bronson.

"What are we doing wrong?" I meowed to my brother.

Bogey glanced to where our Mom was sitting. "Not a thing, kid. Except for feeding into Steele Bronson's plan."

I crinkled my brows. "We are?"

Bogey nodded. "Yup, kid. Take a look. Nobody's even working the cameras. Steele Bronson is just using this so Frank can pump our Mom for info."

Well, up until that moment, I hadn't picked up on that. But I sure did now. And I put two and two together really fast.

I squinted my eyes and stared at Frank. "Let me guess. He thinks our Mom might know something that could help him find the key."

Bogey nodded. "You got it, kid. Because our Mom is writing a book on St. Gertrude history. And if anyone had any clues that could help him, it would be her."

I suddenly opened my eyes wide and glanced at our Mom. "But she would never go along with helping them find something that belongs to St. Gertrude."

Bogey shook his head. "Nope, kid. But now we know why they wanted *us* to be in this so-called movie. Because our Mom would have to come with us. Then they could quiz her up and down about St. Gertrude. And she would never even suspect a thing."

"Very sneaky," I breathed. "They're trying to fool our Mom into giving them information."

Bogey flexed his claws. "You got it, kid. She could lead them straight to the key. And not even know it."

That's when I felt something bubbling up inside of me, something I don't feel very often. If Steele Bronson wanted raw emotion, well, he was about to get it. Because I was feeling really, really mad. I'd had enough of Steele Bronson and his bunch hurting my family. And now here he was, trying to take advantage of our Mom like this. As Bogey would say, he had crossed a whole lotta lines.

Now Steele Bronson clapped his hands again. "Let's take a break, people! We'll let Buckley and Bogey practice. And Frank and I will go with Abigail to scout out locations in the library."

Bogey nodded. "Okay, kid. We've gotta zoom. Time for us to *really* go to work. Let's go follow your hunch."

I glanced up that staircase. "We'd better get that page from that book before Frank figures it out. And goes looking for it, too."

Bogey nodded. "You got it, kid. And before Bronson

decides to shoot more of his phony scenes."

We were just about to go racing up those stairs when I spotted a white streak. It was moving low and close to the baseboards.

It was the Princess!

She was breathing hard when she joined us. "Hi, guys. I'm so glad I caught you! I wanted to help you boys."

Bogey nodded to her. "Good call, Princess. We could use your smaller claws on this job. Thanks for pitching in."

And with that, we practically flew up those stairs. All the way to the fourth floor. We found those tall books right away. It sure helped that Bogey had left the initials BBCDA in the dust. In the exact spot where we needed to go.

Bogey glanced around. "Okay, kid, we think it's page twenty-four in the third book. So let's grab that sheet and get out of here."

So we did. We pulled the third book in the series out of the shelves and onto the ground. Then I used my big paws to pull the front cover open. After that, I hooked a few claws into a few pages and kept on turning them. Until I got to page twenty-four.

I had to say, I was pretty happy with the way my paws were acting. They were going right where I wanted them to go. Now I only hoped my hunch was right.

That's when I realized it was a big responsibility to have a hunch. And let me tell you, it sure took a lot of courage to follow it. Because a hunch was kind of a gut feeling about something. But a guy didn't really know if he was right until he found out for sure. I'd heard people call it a leap of faith.

Leap was right. Because when you leaped, you also took the chance of falling to the ground. Suddenly I had even more respect for Bogey than ever before. His hunches were almost always right and he wasn't afraid to take a chance. He really was one of the greatest cat detectives ever. And I was pretty lucky that he had taken me under his paw.

Bogey nodded to the Princess. "Would you care to do the honors, Princess?"

She smiled and extended one of her very tiny, but very sharp claws on her right front paw. Then she stood on the book and placed her claw about a third of the way down the page. Right next to the spine. She put a little pressure into it, and little by little, she started cutting that page out of the book.

And that's when we heard the voices.

Voices that sent chills running up and down my spine. Frank and Steele Bronson talking to our Mom. And our Mom saying, "Well, yes, Arthur Fartheringston did write some diaries and other books. I believe you'll find them up here on the fourth floor."

That meant they were headed our way! And if they got the page in our book before we had a chance to get it out, then we were sunk! We'd never find that copy of the Declaration of Independence before they did!

Holy Catnip!

CHAPTER 22

Holy Mackerel!

I could hear Frank, Steele Bronson, and our Mom moving closer and closer. I wanted to tell the Princess to hurry up, but I knew that would only make her nervous. Instead, I flexed one of my big claws and started cutting from the bottom of the page. But my claws did more tearing than fine cutting.

That's when Bogey jumped in. "Here, kid. Let me have a go at it."

Then he used his thin and very pointy claw on the bottom where I'd been working. And the Princess used her thin claw at the top. Together, they were slowly cutting that page out of the book.

Finally, after what felt like hours, they were getting close to having it cut from top to bottom. That's when I put my big paw right smack dab in the middle of the page.

"I think I can rip this out now," I told them.

I put just enough pressure on the page and pulled very gently, so that the page began to tear away from the book. All in nice straight line that matched up to where Bogey and the Princess had been cutting. I could hardly believe it! My paws had never gone exactly where I'd wanted them to go like that before. Not like they did right at this moment!

By now we could hear that our Mom and the men had

made it up to the fourth floor.

Our Mom's voice came through loud and clear. "I think you should be able to find what you're looking for from here. I'm going to head back downstairs and check on Gracie."

"But we might need more information from you," Frank told her.

"You do realize the library has a full computer system to help you look for books," our Mom answered.

"True," Frank said. "But we can always learn more from someone who knows the history of this place."

"I'm sure you'll be fine," our Mom said, right before we heard her footsteps on the stairs.

But we could still hear Steele Bronson and Frank as they walked through the aisles on our floor. They were laughing and making snide remarks. I knew it would only be a matter of seconds before they got to where we were. So I gave that old paper one more firm tug and it was out of there.

"Way to go, kid!" Bogey whispered. "Now let's get this thing folded!"

So we did. And very, very quickly. Together we managed to fold it once and then fold it again. Then we gave it to the Princess. She took the edges in her mouth.

"Now run, Princess! Run!" Bogey and I both whispered.

Bogey pointed to the back of the shelves. "Go to the end. And then make your way out of here. Take this paper back to our pet carriers and hide it really, really well."

The Princess nodded.

Bogey glanced toward the front of the aisle. "Buckley and I will get that book back in the shelf. So Frank and Bronson won't know we had it open."

The Princess gave us one more little nod and didn't wait for any more instructions. Instead, she just tore out of there as fast as she could go with that paper in her mouth. She ran to the end of the aisle while I slapped that book shut. Then Bogey and I tugged at it until it was upright again. Together we managed to push it back up onto the shelf. Right in line with the others in the group.

Only seconds before Frank and Steele Bronson came strolling down the aisle.

"Oh look," Steele Bronson smirked. "It's those two cats. I

wonder what they're doing up here?"

"Probably smelled a mouse," Frank laughed.

Then he looked down at the bottom of the shelf. "Wait a minute . . . Look how the dust has been disturbed here. Somebody else has been looking at these books."

He squinted and stared at us for a moment. "And those cats are right in front of the very books we came up here to find. I think I smell a rat."

"I thought you said those cats smelled a mouse," Steele Bronson said.

Frank put his leg and his foot right in front of me. "As long as that's the only thing they're after. As long as they haven't found the key that we're looking for."

He pointed to the letters BBCDA that Bogey had left in the dust. "What does that mean? Who left that there? Did these cats have anything to do with this?"

Steele Bronson laughed. "Seriously? They're just a couple of dumb cats. What do they know?"

Suddenly the hair on my back stood straight up. Us cats knew a whole lot more than Steele Bronson would ever know, that was for sure! Not only that, but we even knew the location of the key to solve the code. Or, at least, I *hoped* we knew the location of that key. I hoped it was being carried down the stairs and to our pet carriers right at that moment. Without any problems. Unfortunately, we wouldn't know for sure until Bogey and I got back downstairs to check.

Now Frank started to move his foot like he was going to kick me out of the way. But luckily, I jumped before he could touch me.

He stared down at me. "I think this is one of the cats who attacked me the other night. Seems maybe I owe him one."

"C'mon, kid," Bogey said to me. "Let's go to the front of the aisle and keep an eye on these two jokers."

Which is exactly what we did. And let me tell you, we got an eyeful, all right. The movie star and his writer were practically giddy when they found the books written by Mr. Fartheringston. They picked up all seven of them. But instead of taking them downstairs to check them out, they stuffed them into a black duffel bag.

"They're stealing those books!" I meowed to my brother.

"They're breaking the law!"

Bogey shook his head. "Don't I know it, kid. But they won't find what they're looking for."

A few minutes later, a very happy Steele Bronson and Frank walked right on down that aisle and headed for the stairs. Bogey and I scooted out of the way. Then we followed the men down to the first floor. We watched them laugh and joke the whole way.

Once we got back to the first floor, Steele Bronson clapped his hands. "We won't be doing any more filming today. We're going to take a break for . . . for a . . ."

"Script change," Frank finished for him.

"Yes, that's right," Steele Bronson said with a smile. "For a script change. We'll contact everyone when we're ready to film again."

Taffy stared at Frank with stars in her eyes, and Nadia put on a big smile, too.

Bogey nodded to me. "C'mon, kid. Let's head to our pet carriers. And make sure the Princess made it back from behind enemy lines."

I sucked in my breath. "Enemy lines?"

Bogey shook his head. "Just an expression, kid. Let's go make sure she's safe and sound in your pet carrier."

Well, he sure didn't have to tell me twice! Because I'd been dying to know if the Princess made it back okay. I sure hoped she wasn't stuck on the second floor or something. And I sure hoped we didn't have to go searching for her. Because this was a really big building. She could be anywhere.

So we ran all out and made a beeline to our pet carriers. But as we got closer, there was no Princess in sight. Suddenly my heart started to pound. Where in the world was she?

Bogey glanced my way. "Don't sweat it, kid. She's probably just hiding."

Now I started to run so fast that I even passed Bogey. I put on the brakes when I got right next to my pet carrier.

"Princess! Princess, are you in there!" Even I could hear the shakiness in my voice.

But there was no answer.

That's when it dawned on me that it was probably a bad idea to let the Princess run downstairs alone. Especially with the Count and Countess out there, probably looking for her.

I was just about to dive into my pet carrier and search for her when I heard a little yawn.

It was the Princess!

She popped her head up from under the blanket and smiled at me. "Sorry, Buckley. I was so tired from running and being up so late last night . . . I must have dozed off the minute I got here."

Now Bogey came running up to join us. "Have any problem hiding that paper, Princess?"

"No problem," she said with a smile. "I've got it right here beside me. It's not going anywhere."

And then she looked at me with her big, green eyes.

It was just more than I could take. The room started to spin and my heart started to pound. I just flopped on over.

The next thing I knew, Bogey was standing over me with a cat treat. "Here you go, kid. This'll get you going."

"What happened . . .?" I sort of murmured.

"Dames, kid," Bogey whispered in my ear. "They'll get you every time."

"Dames," I mumbled.

As I munched away, I wondered where Bogey had found the bag of cat treats he was now passing around. I figured he must have had them hidden in his pet carrier.

A few seconds later, I crawled into my own pet carrier with the Princess. I was barely aware of our Mom and Gracie joining us. They counted to make sure all of us cats were there before they zipped up our carriers. I rested my eyes while Bravo drove us home. I couldn't tell for sure, but it sounded to me like Gracie and our Mom were pretty happy the filming was over for today.

What there was of the filming, anyway.

I meowed over to my brother when we got close to our house. "What do you think this means? If Steele Bronson's bunch think they found the key, will they be finished pretending to shoot this movie?"

"Probably not, kid," Bogey meowed back. "Not when they open up those books they stole. And when they find the page they're really looking for is missing. That means they won't be cracking any code any time soon."

I felt my eyes go wide. "Do you think they'll suspect we have it?"

Bogey sat up tall. "Could be, kid. Or they might think our Mom has it. Or she knows where it is. Either way, I don't think we've seen the last of this bunch yet."

Bravo dropped us off at home, and our Mom and Gracie let us out of our pet carriers.

As soon as they did, Bogey murmured to the Princess. "Mind taking that paper up to the sunroom? And hiding it for us?"

The Princess smiled. "I would be happy to."

Then she went scampering off as we went to the living room to watch Gracie set up for her party. She set out the cupcakes, made the punch, and put out plates and napkins. Gracie had become such a great hostess. We were really proud of her.

A few minutes later, Lil joined us. Then the Princess came running in, too.

Our Mom smiled when she saw what a great job Gracie had done. "Do you need my help? Or would you like to handle this on your own?"

Gracie finished arranging some flowers in a vase. "Thanks, Mom. But I think I'm old enough to host this one on my own."

Our Mom kept on smiling. "Sounds good. I'll check on you in a bit, in case you need any help later."

"Thanks," Gracie said and gave her a hug.

Then she ran up to her room and changed into a nice sundress. She had barely come back downstairs when the doorbell rang. Her first guest had arrived. Pretty soon all the kids who had been contestants in the essay contest were there, including Dylan Federov. Mrs. Peebles was the last to arrive.

Gracie made sure everyone got cupcakes and punch, and right away the party started out to be pretty fun. The kids were laughing and talking. And everyone told Gracie what a nice job she did with the cupcakes and the decorations.

The only one who wasn't joining in on things was Dylan. But I figured he was going to be a whole lot happier once he found out what Gracie had in store for him.

Bogey pulled out the bag of cat treats he had stashed in the base of the exercise wheel. He passed some treats to each of us, and it turned into a real party for us, too.

After a while, Gracie held up her punch glass and tapped on the side with a spoon. It made a *ding, ding, ding* that got everyone's attention.

Then Gracie stood up nice and tall. And for the first time in days, she was smiling. Really smiling.

She looked at all the faces around the room. "If I could have your attention, please. You're probably all wondering why I called you here today. Well, I decided to host this party because I have been feeling very bad. You all saw what happened at the essay contest. And, well, I didn't do a very good job reading my essay at all. In fact, I didn't even get a chance to finish reading my essay before Steele Bronson jumped in. He declared me the winner, and . . . for some reason, all the judges and everybody went along with it."

Murmurs arose from the kids.

Gracie took a deep breath. "Well, I never felt right about being declared the winner. Because I didn't really win that contest. But we all know who should have been the winner."

Now Gracie pulled her trophy from the piano bench. "So today, I want to set things right. I want to give this trophy to the real winner of the essay contest. This person will ride on the float and read their essay on Saturday night after the picnic."

I watched as all the kids stood there, with their mouths hanging open and their eyes wide.

But Gracie just kept on smiling. "I want to award this trophy to Dylan Federov. He is the real winner of the essay contest!"

Now all eyes turned to Dylan. And let me tell you, it was not a pretty sight. Dylan slammed his plate and cup right on top of the piano. He put them down so hard I was surprised he didn't break them. His eyes were blazing and his mouth was sort of trembling.

Then he pointed at Gracie. "You have no business doing this! What do you take me for? A poor, pathetic loser? Did you think I was falling apart and my life was ruined because I didn't win that contest? So you have to take pity on me?"

Gracie gasped. "But-but-but . . . I was only trying to help! I just wanted to make things right . . ."

Dylan stomped into the hallway. "Who asked for your help? I don't need your pity! I'm not a big baby, you know!"

Well, if he wasn't a big baby, he *sure* was acting like one now. Especially since Gracie was only trying to do something nice.

Gracie stood there biting her lip. A couple of tears rolled down her cheeks.

The Princess leaned into me and meowed in my ear. "Oh no! I never dreamed my plan would backfire. Poor Gracie!"

Now Dylan went storming down the hallway. He flung the front door wide open.

Us cats all sat there in shock. The other kids stood there without moving. I figured they must be in shock, too.

Dylan flung his arms open wide. "When I need your help, Gracie, I'll ask for it!"

Then he flew out onto the front porch.

Just as two people came running inside. A man and a woman. They were both wearing hats and coats, and I couldn't see their faces. They pointed to all of us in the living room and came rushing inside.

Now what was going to happen?

Unfortunately, I didn't figure out the answer to that question until it was too late. Because, from that moment on, everything happened so fast. And at the same time, it kind of felt like it was going in slow motion.

"There she is! Get her!" the woman yelled with a strange accent.

I recognized that accent, but I wasn't sure where I knew it from. The woman flew into the living room and that's when I saw her cold, cold, ice blue eyes. She reached down, snatched the Princess in a tight grip and then went racing for the front door. The Princess yowled louder than I've ever heard her yowl before.

In a split second, the man and the woman and the Princess had all vanished. Straight out the open door.

But I did catch a glimpse of the woman's long, platinum blonde hair that fell from her hat as she left.

It was the Count and Countess Von De Meenasnitzel.

And they had just catnapped the Princess!

Holy Catnip!

CHAPTER 23

Holy Mackerel!

Gracie screamed and the other kids around us started to scream, too. Mrs. Peebles shouted for our Mom.

Ice cold fear drenched my entire body. I felt like somebody had just thrown me into a bath. And not a nice warm bath like Gracie had given us. But instead a bath filled with ice cubes.

Then all at once, I felt a whole different feeling. Something else took over inside of me. I remembered how badly the Count and Countess had treated the Princess. And I sure wasn't going to let them treat her like that again. And I definitely wasn't going to let them take her away from us.

I loved the Princess. She was part of our family.

Now my heart started to pound and anger bubbled up inside of me. Then for some strange reason, I suddenly knew exactly what to do. I turned to Bogey and he was already nodding. He knew that I knew. And we were obviously thinking the very same thing.

He sprang to his feet. "Ready, kid?"

I jumped up, too. "Ready!"

Lil must have been on the same wavelength as we were. "I'll hold the door open and get eyes on that car!" she shouted.

So while she scampered to the front door, Bogey and I jumped into our exercise wheel. We reached up, latched our claws into the carpet, and pulled that wheel down to get it started. Then we ran for all we were worth. The wheel started to spin faster and faster.

"Okay, kid," Bogey hollered. "Now lean to the side and let's tilt this thing."

And I did just that. In a matter of seconds, we had that wheel wobbling. A few seconds later, it popped off its stand and landed on the floor with a loud *ka-whump*! Then we went barreling down the hallway. Kids were jumping out of the way as the wheel steamrolled past them.

"Lean over, kid," Bogey told me. "We've got to straighten it out again."

I moved slightly to the center and we kept on running and running and running. The wheel straightened out just fine.

Our Mom was coming down the stairs when she spotted us. She jumped back in the nick of time as we rolled on by. We saw Lil right where she said she would be — holding the door wide open.

"They went left at the corner," she shouted as we bounced through the opening. "Big, silver car!"

Then that heavy, giant-sized wheel hit the front porch with a gigantic *thud!* And it went *whump, whump, whump* as it rolled right on down those steps. It was a pretty bumpy ride and a little scary, too. Especially if I thought about the way I'd crashed it last time. But I knew I couldn't think about that now. Instead, I just kept my mind on my legs, and we kept on running and running and running. I suddenly had more energy than I ever dreamed I could have.

It's funny what a guy can do when he finds out his Princess has just been catnapped.

We rolled on down the sidewalk and then hit the street at an angle. It was pretty rough going, but we managed to keep that wheel upright. Thankfully there weren't any cars coming right at that moment.

"Okay, kid," Bogey yelled. "Lean it left. We've gotta turn it so it goes down the street. Think of what we've seen people do on bikes."

"Got it!" I hollered back.

And so we did. We put our weight to one side and leaned hard. We made a pretty shaky turn, but we quickly got it

leveled out and headed straight down our street.   Our
neighbor, Mrs. Nelson, was driving home and about to turn
into her driveway. But she hit the brakes and stared at us with
wide eyes. We barely missed the side of her car as we barreled
on by.

"Okay, kid," Bogey yelled. "Step on it. We've gotta catch
up with the Count and Countess."

So we did. We ran faster and faster and rolled that huge
wheel on down our street. And we picked up some good speed,
too. Another car headed toward us and quickly pulled over to
let us go by. I caught a glimpse of the faces inside that car as
we zoomed past. All the people had wide eyes and open
mouths.

I guess they weren't used to seeing cats go by in a gigantic
wheel.

Before long, we were coming to the end of our block.

"Time to take another left, kid," Bogey hollered. "This
one's going to be a little tighter. But we can do it. Let's hope
there aren't any cars in the intersection."

I gulped. I hadn't even thought of that before. But I
figured now was probably not the time to start thinking about
it. Especially if it only scared me. This just wasn't the time to
get scared. So I just kept on moving and so did the wheel.

I saw the intersection in the very same second that I saw a
big, red pickup truck and a mailman's truck. The truck was
turning right and the mailman looked like he was going to go
straight.

"This is going to be tight," Bogey hollered.

Holy Mackerel! He had that right! We had to work our
way around the pickup before the mailman had a chance to go
through the intersection. And that big truck didn't exactly
leave us a lot of room to turn.

"Okay, kid," Bogey hollered. "We've gotta be precise.
When I say lean, I want you to lean."

"Got it!" I said as I kept on running.

The pickup truck made his turn, and we barely missed
sideswiping him by a few inches.

"Now, kid! Now!" Bogey yelled. "Lean!"

So I leaned for all I was worth. And that wheel made a
really tight turn. For a second there, I think we even went up

on one rim.

"Down, kid. Lean back," Bogey yelled frantically.

I scooted over, and we missed the mail truck by inches. I could even hear the mailman gasp right before he drove up on someone's lawn.

Finally, I could see a big, silver car about a quarter of a mile ahead of us. "It's them!" I yelled to my brother. "I see them! We're gaining on them!"

And that's when I accidentally leaned too far in the wrong direction. Because all of a sudden, we zigzagged across to the wrong side of the street.

Right in front of a police car!

It was Officer Phoebe.

She hit the brakes and stared at us with her mouth open.

"Turn back, kid!" Bogey practically screamed. "Get us back on our side of the street!"

I quickly leaned the other way and we zagged back to the other side. But I overdid it on my leaning, and we zigzagged a few more times.

Finally, I got us straightened out.

"Put the coals to it, kid. We can catch them!" Bogey yelled.

Now we heard people calling to us from the sidewalk. We saw kids and grownups and even some grandparents. Some were cheering and some were laughing. A few people were even clapping for us.

In the meantime, Officer Phoebe had turned around and was now following us. She had her lights flashing and her siren screaming.

Suddenly I wished our wheel had come with a rearview mirror.

"Bogey, I think she wants us to pull over," I hollered to my brother.

"No can do, kid. We've got to catch the Count and Countess! Go faster!" Bogey insisted.

"Won't we get arrested?" I asked.

Bogey picked up speed. "Nope, kid. We're going to lead Officer Phoebe straight to the crooks. Not only did they kidnap the Princess, but they broke out of jail, too. There's probably a reward out for them."

"Okay, whatever you say!" I told him as I picked up speed

alongside him.

By now we were getting closer and closer to that silver car. I could see the Princess in the back window. Her big, green eyes went wide when she saw us. I could see her mouth moving and I knew that she had started to meow. I was pretty sure she was probably calling for us.

It made me even more determined to get to her!

But the Count was driving, and I saw him glance into his rearview mirror. That's when he stepped on the gas. Because suddenly the car started to pull away from us.

"Faster! Faster!" I yelled to my brother. "We can't lose them!"

"I'm on it, kid," he hollered back.

A few seconds later, we heard more sirens. Then we saw a huge fire truck speeding toward us from the opposite direction. It must have been enough to scare the Count. He swerved a couple of times, just as the cars in front of him came to a stop for the fire truck.

He laid on the horn, but it was no use. Finally, he must have figured the siren and the flashing police lights might be for the Countess and him. He slowed the car down and pulled over.

But Bogey and I kept on rolling forward with the power of a freight train.

The front doors of the car flew open wide. The Count jumped out and took off running. And so did the Countess.

"Okay, kid," Bogey hollered. "On the count of three, we abort. Just like I did at our house. You take the Countess and I'll take the Count. Got it?"

And I new exactly what he was talking about. Because this was the tricky part. Running in the big, giant wheel was easy. But stopping it or having a smooth landing if we got thrown out was the hard part. Because let me tell you, our wheel did not have brakes. And we had built up a whole bunch of speed and forward motion. Plus, we still hadn't actually rescued the Princess yet. Until she was home safe with us again, we couldn't exactly relax.

So that meant we had to be perfect in our next step. Or one of us might get hurt.

Really hurt.

Not to mention, we didn't want the Count and Countess to get away!

"Okay, Bogey," I hollered. "I'm ready."

"One, two, three!" he yelled.

Then we both dug our claws in and quit running. The wheel spun around one and a half times. And we went around with it. Then we both kicked out. One on either side. I did a couple of somersaults in the air until I straightened out. I went flying, flying, flying with my claws out on all four paws. I landed right smack dab onto the back of the Countess. I bashed into her with so much force that I knocked her straight to the ground. She made a loud *smack* sound as she hit the pavement. It knocked her out cold, and made a nice soft landing for me.

In the meantime, that big, heavy wheel had rolled right up and over the Count's car. It dented the trunk and the roof and the hood with a loud *thunk, thunk, thunk!* Then it sort of bounced onto the pavement and right into the middle of the street. I could still see it rolling on and on. I wondered when it might ever stop.

If it ever stopped.

But right at the moment, I was more worried about Bogey and the Princess. So I jumped off the Countess' back and ran around the car. There I found Bogey standing on the Count's back. Thankfully Bogey had hit his mark and landed safely too. The Count was lying on the ground and he was sort of moaning.

"Way to go, kid!" Bogey said with a grin. "Wow, that was a wild ride, wasn't it?"

Boy, he could say that again.

He shook himself all over. "Remind me to send Steele Bronson a thank-you note, kid. For the wheel. Who knew it would come in handy like that?"

Well, I *sure* never knew we'd end up using it like we did. But right at that moment, I needed to know that the Princess was okay. So I jumped into the front seat of the car and called her name. She poked her little head out and smiled a very shaky smile. She was pretty scared, but other than that, she was fine.

"Oh Buckley," she said with tears in her eyes. "I knew

you'd come for me. I just knew it."

I was pretty careful not to look into her big, green eyes. Especially since we hadn't finished with our job yet. I knew I couldn't be getting all dizzy and flopping over in the middle of a rescue.

"Let's get you home, Princess," I told her.

Then I helped her jump from the car.

Just as Officer Phoebe came running up. "Buckley and Bogey! And little Lexie! What in the world are you cats doing?"

But then she spotted the Count as he was starting to get up. "Wait a minute . . . isn't that the Count Von De Meenasnitzel? He's a wanted fugitive! He and his wife escaped from prison."

She glanced quickly at us. "You cats were chasing them down? How did you know . . .?"

Before she could say another word, two firemen showed up.

"Did you see that thing?" one fireman asked. "What in Heaven's name was that big wheel that went by? I've never seen anything like it . . ."

Then they tended to the Count and Countess, just as Officer Phoebe put them under arrest.

That's when Bogey nodded at the road. "Time to head home. We've got a long walk."

And while a big crowd gathered on the sidewalk to see what had happened, us cats quietly sneaked out of there. This time we trotted home a little more slowly. Bogey and I stayed on either side of the Princess. I could tell she was still pretty scared that she'd been taken.

About a half an hour later, we got to our house. Gracie and our Mom had been standing in the front yard. Gracie's cheeks were stained with tears.

That was, until she spotted us coming up the sidewalk. Then she threw her arms into the air and screamed. She came running straight for us. Our Mom followed. Our Mom picked up Bogey and the Princess, and Gracie got me.

She hugged me tight the whole way home. "I thought I lost you," she sobbed into my fur. "I thought I lost all three of you. I didn't even care if my party turned out to be a big mess. I only cared about losing you cats. You're part of my family."

I wrapped my arms around her neck and buried my head into her long, dark hair.

They took us into our house and shut the door behind us. I couldn't remember ever being so glad to be home.

Holy Catnip.

CHAPTER 24

Holy Mackerel!

That night Gracie did not let us out of her sight. And let me tell you, us cats didn't mind one bit. I was so happy to have the Princess back safe and sound. I didn't even want to think about how close we'd come to losing her forever.

I think Gracie felt the same way. Not only was she upset about her party, but she was even more upset that the Princess had been stolen. *And*, that Bogey and I had rolled out of the house on our wheel and disappeared for a while. So when Gracie went to bed that night, she brought all of us into her room with her. While Lil stayed at the end of the bed, Gracie kept an arm over me and the Princess on one side. She kept another arm over Bogey on her other side. Then she did her very best to stay awake and keep an eye on us. The only one missing was the Wise One. But Gracie probably didn't want to take Miss Mokie out of her sunroom.

I was already pretty tired by the time Gracie had brought us to her room. And I had to say, there was nothing I liked better than to be snuggled when I was tired. So it wasn't long before I dozed off for a while.

After all, it had been a really long night. Officer Phoebe had shown up at our house shortly after she'd caught the Count and Countess. She came in to talk to our Mom and Dad, but she seemed to have trouble finding the words. Bogey and I sat nearby and watched the whole thing.

"Um . . ." Officer Phoebe started. "I'm not sure why, but I found three of your cats at the scene. And right before that, I saw Buckley and Bogey rolling in a giant wheel along the street . . . They appeared to be chasing a silver car."

Then Phoebe closed her eyes and rubbed her forehead. "If I didn't know better, I'd say they were trying to catch the Count and Countess. Since, well . . . truth be told, they actually *did* catch them."

Our Mom smiled and shook her head. "I know what you mean, Phoebe. The Count and Countess had just run in and kidnapped little Lexie. And the next thing I knew, the boys were running after her in that big exercise wheel."

Officer Phoebe peeked out with one eye. "How on earth do I explain this in my report?"

Bogey leaned my way. "Writing up that report doesn't sound too tough to me. She saw the BBCDA in action, kid. That about sums it up."

I turned and meowed to Bogey. "But she left out a lot of the good stuff. Like how we turned the corner in that wheel. And how we timed it perfectly to land on the Count and Countess."

Bogey shook his head. "I hear ya, kid. I hear ya."

Funny, but the humans never did give us credit for solving so many cases. They just didn't understand the great crime solving skills that cat detectives have.

I glanced up to see our Mom and Dad and Officer Phoebe all staring at us.

"They're meowing to us," Officer Phoebe murmured. "It's like they understand what we're saying . . ."

Our Dad laughed. "Welcome to our world, Phoebe."

Then he walked over and gave both of us pets on the head. "I'd like to think my guys were out there rescuing a damsel in distress. And if any cats could do it, it would be these two."

"What ever happened to the wheel?" our Mom wanted to know.

Officer Phoebe shook her head. "Nobody knows for sure. But we've been getting lots of reports about it. Someone said they saw it on the highway, and someone else said it was down on Main Street. And somebody else thought they spotted it rolling down the runway at the airport."

Now our Mom laughed. "So we may never know."

Our Dad rubbed his head. "I don't think we'll be too upset if that wheel is gone for good."

Boy, he could say that again. Though to tell you the truth, Bogey and I did have *some* fun with it. Once we got the hang of it out there on the street, that was.

After Officer Phoebe had left, Nadia showed up on the doorstep. I had to say, Nadia did not seem happy. In fact, she acted kind of mad.

By that time, our family was too tired to let her in.

Nadia glared at our Mom. "It looks like we'll be filming again tomorrow. We'll need Gracie, and we'd like both you and your husband to be there. Plus your two black cats. We're going to film Gracie's essay."

But Gracie shook her head. "No, thanks. I think I've had about enough of all that."

That's when Nadia's eyes went really wide and sweat beaded up on her forehead. "No! You can't quit now. You have to be there. Steele will be so upset and disappointed. You don't want to disappoint him, do you?"

"Well . . ." Gracie started to say.

Nadia *thunked* a hand to her chest. "Please, I'm begging you. Steele will be heartbroken. He's had such a rough week. Something like this will put him over the edge."

Gracie moaned. "Fine. I'll be there."

"And the rest of you?" Nadia sort of whimpered. "You'll be there, too?"

"Fine," our Dad said. "We'll all be there. But not for the whole day. It's our holiday weekend, and we plan to have some fun."

"Good," Nadia said, and suddenly she smiled a very smug smile.

She leaned into our house, and her eyes darted right and then left, before she glanced up the stairs. Then she craned her neck around to look into our Mom's office.

Our Dad took a step forward, sort of making her scoot back out onto the porch. He started to close the door.

"We'll be expecting you at nine," she said quickly.

"Fine," our Dad said right before he shut the door behind her.

I turned to my brother and raised my brows. "What was that all about?"

Bogey grinned and gave me a paw bump. "It means they didn't find the key, kid. To crack the code. And they want us out of here so they can break in and search for it."

I gulped. "They do?"

Bogey nodded. "Yup, kid. Which makes the odds even better that you did find the real key. I have a hunch that your hunch was right. But we'll find out tonight when we plug it in."

I suddenly started to shake a little. "But what will we do if they come to our house and break in? Especially if we have to go the library tomorrow?"

Bogey put his paw on my shoulder. "Don't sweat it, kid. I've got a plan."

He did? Holy Catnip!

And that was the last we got to talk about it. Because right after that, Gracie and our Mom and Dad took us cats up to Gracie's room. So she could keep an eye on us. And that's when I felt so nice being snuggled, that I must have dozed right off.

It was hours later when I woke up. Lil and the Princess were still there. But Bogey was long gone. And Gracie was snoring softly.

I wiggled out from under Gracie's arm. The Princess was sound asleep, and I was careful not to wake her. After all, she'd had a terrifying day. It was probably bad enough just to see her old abusive owners. Let alone get kidnapped by them.

So I left her all snuggled up still with a peaceful look on her face.

Then I tiptoed off the bed and carefully dropped down to the floor. Lil nodded and saluted me as I was leaving. I saluted her back. Perfectly.

I could hardly believe it! Lil smiled as I walked quietly to the hallway. Then I made a beeline for the office. I was dying to know if the page we'd found at the library was the real key or not. And I was dying to see if Bogey had already started in trying to crack the code.

I ran full speed ahead into our Mom's office. I spotted

Bogey working on the computer right away.

He waved me in and handed me a couple of cat treats from an open bag. "I'll be right with you, kid. I'm almost finished writing this."

I munched on a treat and tried to be patient. "What are you working on?"

He grabbed another treat for himself and grinned. "Let's just say I'm writing a script for this movie tomorrow."

My eyes went wide. "A script? You are?"

His grin got even wider. "Yup, kid. I wasn't too happy with the ending on the old one. So I thought I'd write a better ending."

I shook my head. "But we know it's not even a real movie. It's all just a cover so Steele Bronson and his bunch can look for the Dunlap Broadside. Plus, I'm not even sure there ever was a script. So how could there be an ending?"

But Bogey just grinned again and passed me another cat treat. "Let's just say there's an ending now, kid. A good one, too. But I'll fill you in on the details later. First we've got some other business to handle."

I crinkled my brows. "Um . . . We do?"

Bogey took a treat for himself. "Yup, kid. Starting with the email we got from Luke tonight."

I grabbed a couple of treats from the bag and handed one to Bogey. "So how is our friend, Luke?"

Bogey took the treat. "He's got a little problem, kid. Three cats were brought in to the Buckley and Bogey Cat Shelter today. They've been part of a family for a long time. So they don't want to be split up. They want to be adopted into a new home together."

Well, I had to say, I sure wouldn't want to be separated from my family!

"What happened to their home?" I asked.

Bogey shook his head. "It's a sad case, kid. They only had a human Mom, and she was very, very old. She just passed away."

I gasped. "And there was nobody left to take care of her cats?"

Bogey rubbed his forehead with his paw. "'Fraid not, kid. Luke asked us to be on the lookout for a family who could take all three."

I handed him another treat and took one for myself. "We'll keep our eyes open, that's for sure."

Now Bogey grabbed a folded piece of paper from a drawer of our Mom's desk. A folded piece of paper that I recognized. It was the page that we'd pulled from Mr. Fartheringston's book.

Suddenly my heart started to pound and my paws started to shake. At long last, we were going to find out if my hunch had been right. And if this paper really was the key that would decode the secret code.

Bogey unfolded the paper on top of the desk. Then he called up the picture of the Fartheringston Stone on the computer.

"So, kid," he said with a grin. "Here's our next order of business. Are you ready to solve this thing?"

I gulped. "Um . . . I'm ready."

Bogey passed us each another round of cat treats. "Okay, kid. I've already got us started. I've already numbered all the letters in the alphabet."

I looked at him sideways. "Huh?"

Bogey pointed to a list he'd made on the computer screen. "'A' is number one. 'B' is number two . . ."

I nodded. " . . . and 'C' is number three."

Bogey sat up straight. "That's it, kid. All the way down to the letter 'Z.'"

I tilted my head sideways. "Oh . . . okay. But why did you do that?"

Bogey nodded at the screen. "Take a closer look at the stone, kid. If you look at it right, you'll see all the letters are grouped into pairs."

I scooted toward the screen. And sure enough, for the first time, I saw what Bogey was talking about. The letters *were* all sort of together in pairs.

Bogey put his paw to the screen. "I figure the first letter in each pair is for the paragraph on the page. The second letter is for the word in that paragraph. And just like most codes, we'll take the first letter of each word. Got it, kid?"

Well, to tell you the truth, I wasn't completely sure what he meant just yet. But I figured I'd go along with a few to see what he was talking about.

Bogey pointed to the first pair. "We have a 'J' and a 'B' here. So, the letter 'J' is the tenth letter in the alphabet. That means we go to the tenth paragraph on our key."

Now Bogey moved his paw over to the paper and counted until he'd found the tenth paragraph.

I was finally starting to catch on. "And since 'B' is the second letter of the alphabet, we go to the second word in the paragraph."

Bogey nodded. "You got it, kid. And that word starts with the letter 'I.' So 'I' is the first letter in our code. Let's go on to the next pair."

Suddenly I felt chills running up and down my spine. "Got it. We have the letter 'F' and the letter 'N'. Since 'F' is the sixth letter in the alphabet, we go to the sixth paragraph."

Bogey put his paw on the paper again. "And since the letter 'N' is the fourteenth letter, we go to the fourteen word in the paragraph. That word starts with the letter 'H.'"

And on we went. One letter at a time. Back and forth. From the picture on the computer to the key on the old sheet of paper. Then together, Bogey and I cracked the code. By the time we set off to run our first surveillance round of the night, we knew exactly where that Dunlap Broadside was hidden. Right there in the library.

But we still had to get to that famous document before Steele Bronson did.

We quickly finished running surveillance on the first floor and raced up the stairs to check out the second floor. That's when Bogey told me all about his plan to save that copy of the Declaration for St. Gertrude. I gulped when I heard it. Because it sure depended on a lot of people acting just like we thought they would. And who would ever guess that his plan also depended on letting someone break into our house?

The thought of it made me shiver. But one thing was for sure, tomorrow was going to be a doozie of a day.

Now there was nothing left to do but wait until morning when we could put that very plan into place.

Holy Catnip!

CHAPTER 25

Holy Catnip!

That night, I hardly slept a wink. And I was still pretty bleary-eyed the next morning when Bravo arrived to pick us up. This time Nadia came with him. She held the front door for us while our Mom and Dad carried Bogey and me out to the limo. Gracie walked quietly behind us. The sun was bright in the sky and the outside air was already heating up. It was going to be another hot day. Though I had a feeling the temperature wasn't the only thing that was going to be hot today. Oh no. I figured things would be heating up at the library very, very soon . . .

Bogey meowed over to me from his pet carrier. "Check it out, kid. Nadia just slipped a piece of tape over the door latch."

I turned to see her following us to the limo. "Why did she do that?"

"So the door won't lock, kid. It'll shut just like normal. And our Mom and Dad probably think the door locked automatically. Like it always does. But with that tape over it, the latch won't slide closed."

I felt the fur on my back stand on end. "So all they have to do is push the door and it'll open right up?"

"You got it, kid," Bogey meowed.

I shook my head. "That's very sneaky. So it'll be easier for her to break into our house and search for the key. When she and the others come back."

"Bingo, kid," Bogey meowed. "I'm sure they plan to pull the tape off when they're done. And shut the door behind them. So it would lock just fine."

I kept on staring at our house. "And nobody would even know they'd been there."

"But not this time, kid," Bogey told me. "Lil plans to tail them and Miss Mokie will nail anyone who tries to mess with her. And the Princess will stay hidden. But it will be a very short visit. Just long enough to get caught red-handed."

I could hear the grin in his voice, and I knew exactly what he was talking about. Of course, everything depended on how things went with Bogey's plan. I was glad we'd put the real key in my pet carrier last night after we'd finished with it. I could feel that paper under my blanket, along with a printout of what we'd found when we cracked the code. Just the idea of it made me smile. Nadia and Steele Bronson's bunch could search our house all they wanted. But they would never find what they were looking for.

Our whole family was pretty quiet as Bravo drove the limo to the library. Along the way, I could see people putting out flags and other decorations for the Fourth of July celebration tomorrow.

"Do you have your essay?" our Dad asked Gracie.

"Uh-huh," she answered him. "I found a nice, new copy printed off for me this morning. Right on my desk. Thanks for putting it there."

Our Dad's brows went up. "I'm not the one who put it there. It must have been your Mom."

Our Mom smiled at Gracie. "It wasn't me. Maybe you put it there after you rewrote it on the computer. Remember, you were working on it the day before your party. Maybe you just forgot, with all the things that have been going on."

"Hmmm . . ." Gracie murmured. "I'm pretty sure this is a new copy. It wasn't folded like my other copy was."

I could tell Bogey had another big grin on his face right about now. Because we knew who'd put that new copy on her desk.

"Did you practice reading it any more?" our Mom asked softly. "I know life has been so crazy lately that you probably didn't get much time to practice."

Gracie sighed. "I read it aloud once after I fixed it and printed out my copy. I took out most of the things that Frank guy wrote on it."

Our Dad put his hand on her shoulder. "I think that was a smart move."

Gracie turned to stare out the window. "I'm not looking forward to seeing the other kids. Especially Dylan. I don't know why he got so upset at my party. I guess he didn't like it when I tried to make him the winner."

Our Dad leaned over to Gracie. "Maybe Dylan thought you felt sorry for him. Some people don't like having people take pity on them. It hurts their pride and makes them feel small. Even so, it sounds like Dylan really went overboard."

Boy, our Dad sure had that right!

A few minutes later, we arrived at the library. Our Mom carried Bogey in his carrier and our Dad took me in mine. Gracie followed along with her head down as we all went into the building.

Once we were inside, Nadia pointed to a corner. "Just leave your cats over there for now. We won't need them for a while, so they can stay put."

Our Mom and Dad set us down with our pet carriers side by side. Then they turned and headed for the auditorium.

But Gracie came back and unzipped our carriers. "I really need you two boys to be there for me today. Just like last time. Except it's going to take a lot more courage for me to get on that stage today. Especially with Dylan being so mad at me. And I'm not sure, but I think the other kids might be mad, too."

I poked my head out and gave Gracie a big kiss on the nose. Just to let her know we'd be there for her. She gave us both a nice hug, right before Taffy came over.

Taffy scowled at Gracie. "I've got to fix that hair of yours before you go on camera."

"My Mom already fixed my hair this morning," Gracie said firmly.

Taffy let out a loud *huff* and put her hands on her hips.

Gracie ignored her and ran off to join our Mom and Dad. They were standing close to the auditorium entrance and talking to Officer Phoebe.

Officer Phoebe raised an eyebrow. "I got the strangest email last night. It said I should be here today. But there was no name on the email. Only the initials BBCDA. Seems I've seen those initials somewhere before . . ."

Before she could say another word, Nadia directed everyone to go into the auditorium. Bogey and I watched all the people wander inside, until there was no one left in the main room of the library. A few seconds later, we saw Nadia run out and make a beeline for the front door.

Bogey glanced at me and grinned. We knew exactly where she was headed — to our house.

And that's when Bogey and I raced for the auditorium. Because let me tell you, now more than ever, we wanted to make sure our plan fell into place.

Once we got into that huge room, we could hardly believe it. Everything looked almost exactly like it had for the original contest. The judges were there. And the kids in the contest were all sitting up front. I saw lots of the same people sitting in the audience, too. Bogey and I even slinked through the room exactly as we had on that first night. And we moved into the exact same spot where we hid for the original contest. Right under the chairs in the front row.

Gracie was already on the stage and standing in front of the microphone. She had her head down and she was holding her essay in front of her. She looked very, very sad.

I sure wished I could run up and give her a nice hug. But I knew I couldn't just yet. Still, it didn't stop me from waving at her. To let her know that Bogey and I were there for her.

Steele Bronson paced around just below the stage. He had bags under his eyes, and for once, his hair wasn't perfectly in place. In fact, it was really kind of a mess. I got the feeling he hadn't gotten much sleep.

I whispered to Bogey. "Do you think Steele Bronson was up all night, trying to crack the code?"

Bogey grinned. "Looks like it, kid. I'm guessing it didn't go too well. Probably because he had the wrong key."

That's when I smiled. "He had the wrong key *because* we

had the right key."

Bogey gave me a paw bump. "Thanks to you, kid. And your hunch. I'm proud of you. You're on your way to becoming a topnotch cat detective."

Suddenly I felt kind of warm inside. I knew I wasn't as good a cat detective as Bogey was, but I *was* getting better. I'd already had my first hunch. And thankfully, it had been right. Now I could hardly wait to have more hunches. Just like Bogey did.

I nearly jumped when Steele Bronson clapped his hands. "Quiet on the set. Little Girl Reads Essay Scene! Take one! Ready!"

Seconds later, he yelled "Action!" and somebody clapped the clapboard again.

Gracie looked up and held her essay papers in front of her. Then she read it right into the microphone. This time she read it perfectly.

"My name is Gracie Abernathy and I am proud to be an American," she said with perfect inflection. "It makes me smile every time I see the red, white, and blue — the flag that is the symbol of our great country. When I see our flag, I am so happy that our forefathers and mothers started this great country, a place where people would have freedom. Of course, they risked everything they had — their homes, their belongings and even their own lives — to create this great nation of ours."

She paused and took a breath. "Sometimes it's hard for me to imagine, but once upon a time, there was no country named America. In fact, the United States is leas than two hundred and fifty years old! And while that seems pretty old to me, believe it or not, as a country, that's actually pretty young! Then again, it took a lot of years to grow and become this nation of fifty states. Especially since we started out very small, with only thirteen colonies — Massachusetts, New Hampshire, Connecticut, Rhode Island, New York, New Jersey, Delaware, Pennsylvania, Virginia, Maryland, North Carolina, South Carolina, and Georgia."

Gracie paused for a breath. "Sometimes I try to imagine what life was like back in those original thirteen colonies. At first, the colonies were under the rule of England and King

George II. But then, when King George III became king, little by little, our history changed forever. Just like my life changed forever this last week. The week that Steele Bronson came to town."

Suddenly Gracie's eyes went wide. She hesitated for a moment, but she didn't quit reading.

Now her voice took on a whole different tone. "You see, when Steele Bronson showed up at my Mom's store on Monday, I was so excited I could hardly stand it. That's because Steele Bronson was my favorite movie star. And judging by the way everyone reacted when he got here, I think he was a lot of people's favorite star."

Murmurs rose from the crowd.

I leaned over to my brother. "So far so good. She's reading your script."

Bogey grinned. "And she's doing a bang-up job, kid."

I raised my brows. "So besides solving our case, we finally figured out how to help Gracie, too. But are we helping her to help herself?"

Bogey nodded. "Close enough, kid. It still depends on whether she keeps reading or not. Let's hope she keeps going till she gets to the good part."

Thankfully, Gracie blinked a few times and then read on. "Of course, Steele Bronson counted on everyone acting like they did around him. Because people sort of forgot themselves, since they were all so excited to see him. Especially when he claimed he had come to St. Gertrude to film a movie. The only thing is, he lied to us all. He's not really here to make a movie. In fact, if you take a look, you'll see the camera isn't even on right now."

Gracie's mouth fell open wide. She pointed to the camera halfway up the stairs to the right of the room. Gasps and murmurs rose from the audience.

Now Gracie started to read really fast, like she wanted to see what else her new essay said. "Steele Bronson is really here because he and his bunch thought they had figured out the hidden location of a very important historic document. Right here in our town."

Steele Bronson suddenly stomped down to the stage. "Cut! Cut! Cut! I don't know where you got that garbage, but that's about enough of that!"

And that's when I saw something I hadn't seen in a long, long time. I saw fire in Gracie's eyes, because she was clearly very mad. So instead of stopping like Steele Bronson had told her to do, she just kept on reading.

"You see," she practically shouted, "Steele Bronson's writer, Franklin Jefferson is related to both Thomas Jefferson and Ben Franklin. He was doing research on both of those men, since they were both signers of the Declaration of Independence. And that's when he learned that about two hundred copies of the Declaration had been printed up on the night of July 4th, 1776. Those copies were called Dunlap Broadsides. Those copies were sent out to the thirteen original colonies to announce that America had declared her independence. And today, there are only twenty-five of these copies known to exist. But people are still on the hunt to find the rest of these lost copies, since they are worth a fortune. The last one sold at an auction for over eight million dollars!"

Steele Bronson raced up onto the stage. He tried to grab Gracie's essay away from her. But she jumped to the side and held it away from him.

"Enough of this!" Steele Bronson yelled into the microphone. "Cut, cut, cut! This is not part of the script. If you people don't want to cooperate with my movie, I will have no problem replacing you." Then he tried to grab Gracie.

Before we knew it, our Dad was on his feet. He scooted down his row, then into the aisle, and headed straight for the stage.

"Listen, Bronson," he shouted. "You will not speak to my daughter like that! And you'd certainly better not touch her."

I glanced at Bogey. "Now?"

Bogey nodded. "Now, kid."

Then together we ran across the floor in front of the stage and raced right up the steps. We actually got to Gracie before our Dad did.

The people in the audience started making all kinds of noises. There was a whole lot more gasping, and a little shrieking, and lots and lots of talking.

Finally the Mayor stood up. "Back down, Mr. Bronson. Let Gracie finish reading her . . . essay . . . or whatever this is. I want to hear what she has to say."

Steele Bronson started shouting and raising his fist in the air. "This is libel! This is slander! I'll get you for this! All of you! I demand that you stop this charade!"

The Mayor smiled at Gracie. "Please, if you would, Gracie? Go on."

Bogey stood on one side of her while I stood on the other. Then we sat up nice and tall. We made it pretty clear that neither Steele Bronson nor anyone else should come near her.

Our Dad pulled Steele Bronson off to the side so Gracie could finish reading.

Gracie put her papers in front of her again and spoke directly into the microphone. "Through Frank's research, Steele Bronson and his bunch caught wind of a hidden Dunlap Broadside right here in St. Gertrude. And they wanted to come here and look for it, but without anyone suspecting what they were really up to. That's why they pretended to be filming a movie here."

Gracie glanced at the audience before she kept on reading. "Once they found it, they planned to leave town with it. Then they planned to quietly sell it and make a lot of money. Even though the copy belongs here. At our library. But that didn't matter to Steele Bronson and his group. Because they were willing to do whatever it took to find that document. Including breaking into someone's house. Now, here's the part of my story where I'd like to talk to Officer Phoebe. If you and the police would please go to my house right away, I think you'll find we suddenly have some burglars. That's because Steele Bronson's bunch have broken into our house and are searching it right now . . ."

Suddenly Gracie gasped and put her papers to her chest. "Mom and Dad, I think this is for real."

With that, Officer Phoebe jumped up and so did our Mom. She looked at our Dad and he mouthed the words, "Go with Pheobe!" Then Officer Phoebe and our Mom raced from the auditorium while Steele Bronson pulled out his cell phone. I'm pretty sure he was going to call Nadia and warn her. But our Dad grabbed his phone from him.

I glanced at my brother. "It's all going just like you planned."

Bogey's mouth was set in a firm line. "We're not out of the woods yet, kid.   Gracie's gotta finish reading the rest. Otherwise we're sunk. And she looks like she's about to fall apart."

Well, let me tell you, that was an understatement! Because Gracie had started to cry and she was hugging herself with her arms. I knew that she was about to go running off that stage any minute now.

But if she did, our whole plan would fall apart. In a very big way! That meant we had to get Gracie to pull through, no matter what!

But how?

Holy Catnip!

CHAPTER 26

Holy Mackerel!

There we were, just sitting on the stage and watching Gracie get more and more upset. Pretty soon she'd be crying so hard she wouldn't even be able to read! Then our plan would fall apart right before our very eyes. Everything depended on her reading the rest of Bogey's "script."

Somehow we had to get Gracie to go on.

Bogey nodded to me. "Okay, kid. You know what to do. You're the only one who can pull her out of this. Time to go to work."

And the funny thing was, I *really* did know what to do. I'd seen Gracie upset and scared many times before. So I knew exactly how to help her.

Gracie needed a hug. A really good hug. And if there was ever a cat who could give her a good hug, it was me.

So I ran to her and reached up her side. To get her to pick me up. And she did just that. She leaned down and let me climb up into her arms, just like she always does.

I quickly wrapped my arms around her neck. Then I purred as loud as I could. I was purring so loud I probably sounded like a lawn mower.

"Thanks, Buckley," she whispered into my fur. "I needed that. I think I'd like to go home now."

But I grabbed onto her even tighter. Then I pulled back and licked away a few of her tears. And I gave her a really big kiss on the nose.

That's when Gracie giggled. Just like she does lots of times when I give her a kiss.

Then I leaned over and grabbed her essay papers with my teeth. I pulled them up and out of her hands. I brought them up higher and sort of put them in front of her face.

She laughed and leaned back from the papers. "Buckley, what are you doing?"

But I just pushed the papers even closer to her. Then I wiggled them around before I lowered them and stared into her eyes.

Gracie gasped. "You want me to keep reading, don't you, Buckley? That's what you're trying to tell me, isn't it?"

She took the essay papers from my mouth and I gave her another kiss on the nose.

"Okay, Buckley," she said softly. "If that's what you want me to do, I'll do it."

I wrapped my arms around her and gave her another good hug. Just to let her know it would all be okay.

Gracie took a deep breath and moved back in front of the microphone. I jumped down to the stage and she wiped away her tears.

Then she started to read again in a shaky voice. "Now, you might all be wondering why Steele Bronson's bunch even wants to break into my house right now. Well, they are looking for a key. But it's not a regular key. You see, they're looking for the key that cracks a secret code . . . the code that is written on the Fartheringston Stone on the second floor of our library."

Gracie gasped again and looked at Bogey and me with wide eyes. More gasps and murmurs rose from the audience. I even heard a few people say, "So that's what's written on that stone!"

Gracie turned back to her pages and read faster now. "There are two parts to every code. The first is the code itself, and the second part is the key that is used to crack the code. The key can be almost anything. A letter, a page in a book, or another document. In this case, once the key was used to crack the code, it would lead to the location of the hidden Dunlap Broadside.   One that had been passed down in Arthur Fartheringston's family.   That's because Arthur was related to Benjamin Franklin."

I heard *oooohs* and *aaaahs* from the audience.   I sat up a little taller at Gracie's feet.

And she kept on reading, even faster than before.   "Of course, Steele Bronson and his group figured this out before they came to St. Gertrude.   The only thing they were missing was the key.   They knew it could be anything or hidden anywhere.   So as soon as they arrived in St. Gertrude, they came to my Mom's antique store.   They were especially interested in meeting my Mom since everyone knows she is sort of an expert on St. Gertrude history."

She paused and took a deep breath.   "In their quest to find the key, Steele and his bunch bought up all the old furniture from St. Gertrude settlers that was at my Mom's store.   Of course, they were hoping to find the key hidden inside somewhere.   And then when I was reading my essay the first time on this stage, Steele Bronson interrupted the whole thing. He declared me the winner, even though he hadn't heard all the essays.   And even though it wasn't his place to pick a winner.   But he did that so he could declare that part of the prize would be his coming to my house for dinner.   That was just an excuse so his people could search our house when we weren't looking.   In case my Mom had the key at our house."

Now Gracie sort of frowned.   "It was a really lousy deal, since my essay wasn't the best.   I've felt pretty bad ever since I got that trophy.   And I didn't even do anything wrong.   The grown-ups did something wrong, by going along with what Steele Bronson said.   But when I tried to set things right, it backfired."

Suddenly tears filled Gracie's eyes.   She paused for a moment to wipe them away.

The audience made different sounds now, angry sounds. And I could hear Steele Bronson practically hissing from the side of the stage.   But our Dad kept his hand on the movie star's arm.

Then Gracie finally smiled, like I hadn't seen her smile for days.   "Unfortunately for Steele Bronson and his bunch, the code he was so desperate to solve was cracked by someone else first. Compliments of the BBCDA . . ."

Gracie squinted at the page and stared at it for a moment.

Then she glanced at me and Bogey before she read on. "So now, if you would please follow my cats, Buckley and Bogey, we will lead you to the hidden copy of the Declaration of Independence. The Dunlap Broadside."

Loud murmurs and more gasps rose from the audience. Gracie giggled and smiled at Bogey and me. We nodded back to her and then took off at a nice trot. We ran down the stage steps and Gracie followed us. Along with our Dad, who still had a good grip on Steele Bronson. Then the Mayor and Mrs. Peebles followed him. And after that, everyone in the audience followed along, too.

Once Bogey and I got outside the auditorium, we ran straight across the main room. We made a beeline for the fireplace. Gracie kept up with us, and our Dad followed close behind.

We reached the fireplace and Bogey pointed to some shelves next to it. "Ready to climb, kid? I think this is a job for a big guy like you."

"Aye, aye," I said.

Then I saluted him perfectly. No problem. My big, giant-sized paw went exactly where I wanted it to go. Did that mean I was growing into my paws? For a while, anyway?

Then I scaled those bookshelves like I was climbing up our cat towers. I jumped right up onto the fireplace mantel. I tiptoed across the mantel and stopped smack dab in front of Mr. Fartheringston's painting. I could tell he was smiling at me from his painting.

And that's when I remembered the words we had uncovered last night. Right after we had used the key to decode the letters on that stone. They were the words Mr. Fartheringston had written in a secret code. We were pretty sure he must have left them for his wife. But for some reason, she must not have figured it out.

Because the code had spelled out, "I have a secret behind my smile, my dear. I will always be smiling down upon you."

Right away, Bogey and I had known he was talking about his painting that had been over the fireplace mantel. It had probably been there long before he even passed away. And inside he'd hidden a copy of the Dunlap Broadside that had been passed down in his family.

What a nice man he must have been. And what a hero he was going to be for leaving a copy of the Declaration of Independence to our library.

I reached up and pushed on the bottom of his painting with my big paw.

"What's he doing?" Mrs. Peebles demanded. "He's going to knock that painting off and ruin it."

Our Dad moved next to the fireplace. "Then maybe we could give Buckley a little help."

Our Dad reached up and grabbed onto the frame of the huge painting with his strong arms. Then he lifted the painting off the wall. He carried it over to a library table and set it down. Then he turned it over and studied the back. It was completely covered with a very old and very big piece of wood. Before I knew it, Bogey jumped up and tugged at a nail that was holding the wood in place.

"I think he wants us to take the backing off," Gracie said.

The Mayor pulled his Swiss Army knife from his pocket. And before long, he and our Dad had worked the nails from the back of the frame.

Then I leaped off the mantel and jumped up to the library table to join Bogey. Everyone gathered around to see as Mrs. Peebles carefully lifted that piece of wood off.

And there it was. Staring back at us. A very large and very old sheet of paper. One that read, "In Congress, July 4, 1776. A DECLARATION By the REPRESENTATIVES of the UNITED STATES OF AMERICA, In GENERAL CONGRESS Assembled." At the very bottom it read, "Signed by Order and in Behalf of the Congress, JOHN HANCOCK, President. Attest, CHARLES THOMSON, Secretary." And finally, it read, "Philadelphia: Printed by John Dunlap."

Oooohs and *aaaahs* rose up from the group. Everyone around us clapped and cheered. Bogey and I gave each other paw bumps, while our Dad just kept shaking his head.

"Wait till Abby sees this," he muttered over and over.

And seconds later, she did. Our Mom came running up and hugged Gracie and our Dad.

She was a little out of breath. "Phoebe caught Nadia and Frank. They'd already broken into our house. And the police caught Steele Bronson and Taffy, too. They were trying to make a getaway just as I got back here. Bravo and Tango helped the police, because it looks like they knew nothing about all this."

"Glad the crooks were caught, honey," our Dad said. "But you might want to take a look at this . . ."

Our Mom looked down at the document and suddenly her eyes went so wide I hardly even recognized her. She *thunked* her hand to her chest and seemed to have trouble breathing.

"Is that *really* what I think it is? Do you know how rare those are? And how valuable?" she sort of sputtered.

"Oh yeah. I know," our Dad said.

Our Mom choked and coughed a few times. "You mean, that's what all this nonsense was really about all week? That's why Steele Bronson was *really* here and why he put us through so much?"

Our Dad nodded. "He thought you might accidentally give him some clues to help him find it."

"So who did find it?" our Mom asked.

"Well . . ." our Dad started to say. "That part is a little fuzzy . . . Gracie announced it in an essay that she says she didn't write. And Buckley and Bogey, well . . . they sort of led us to this . . ."

For a moment our Mom just stared at our Dad. "Let me guess. Somewhere in there, the letters BBCDA came up."

Our Dad sighed. "Oh yeah."

Our Mom smiled and laughed. "Maybe it's best if we just don't think about all that right now."

"Deal," our Dad told her.

Gracie leaned down and whispered to us. "I'd really like to know who I have to thank for that . . . um . . . essay. I'm not sure who the BBCDA is, but I wonder . . . Sometimes I think you cats are a whole lot smarter than anyone knows. But I think I know."

I reached up and gave her a kiss on the nose while Bogey purred up to her.

Then she hugged us both.

Holy Catnip.

CHAPTER 27

Holy Mackerel!

The morning of the Fourth of July dawned bright and sunny. Of course, we had to get up early. That's because Gracie insisted that Bogey and I be allowed to ride on the float in the parade with her. So our Mom and Dad drove us down and made sure we were nice and secure on top of that big float.

Right after we'd uncovered the Dunlap Broadside, Dylan Federov made a beeline for Gracie and apologized. She forgave him, and Mrs. Peebles declared that both Gracie and Dylan were the winners of the essay contest. They would both be riding on the float and reading their essays after the town picnic.

Mrs. Peebles had smiled at Gracie. "Is there any way the library can thank you, Gracie?"

That's when Bogey immediately pushed the last page of Gracie's essay up to her. He turned it over and pointed to some small typing on the other side.

Gracie squinted her eyes and read it aloud. "I would like the library to adopt the three cats who were just taken to the Buckley and Bogey Cat Shelter. They were part of a family and should stay together. Then the library will have three cats again, just like when Emily Fartheringston lived here."

Mrs. Peebles' mouth had dropped open. "All right then,

young lady . . . I'll see that it's done."

And that was how the library came to be home to Agatha, Poe, and Doyle. A black cat, a white cat, and a three-legged, tiger-striped cat, all named after famous mystery authors. All three had shiny, short fur and green eyes. Luke arranged to have them brought over right away, and the cats were so happy they got to stay together as a family. Plus they were looking forward to spending time with all the people who read books at the library.

I only wished they could have joined us on the float. Because I have to say, it was a lot of fun riding on that float. The whole thing was covered with red, white, and blue streamers, and lots and lots of flags. Those flags waved in the breeze as the float moved down Main Street. The very street where we'd first seen Steele Bronson's limo creeping along. The funny thing was, everyone had practically forgotten about Steele Bronson and his group. The last we'd heard, they were still in jail.

But to tell you the truth, I really didn't think about him much today. Instead I just had fun waving to all the people, and some cats, too, on the sidewalks. It was almost as fun as running in our big, giant wheel. But a whole lot slower.

Dylan leaned over to Gracie. "I still don't understand. How did you figure all that out? And how did you get your cats to run to that painting like they did?"

But Gracie just smiled. "It's kind of a long story, Dylan. And it's complicated."

Dylan smiled back. "You know, Gracie, I'm going to nominate you for class president next year. You'd be a really good president. You're very smart and you're very kind. You always think about others instead of yourself. And you're very fair. It seems like you really want to do the right thing, even when it's hard to do. My grandfather would be proud of you."

Gracie kind of gasped. "Well thanks, Dylan."

He nodded toward us. "I think your cats might become famous after all this."

I glanced at my brother. "Do you want to be famous?"

He grinned back at me. "Not on your life, kid. How about you?"

I remembered what the Wise One had told me about fame

and I shook my head. "No, thanks. It doesn't sound all that great to me."

But I did want to be the best cat detective that I could be. Just like my brother. And I sure hoped I'd have more hunches in the future.

I crinkled my brow.   "There's one thing I don't understand," I said to Bogey.

He pulled out a bag of cat treats and passed us each a treat. "Spill it, kid. I'm all ears."

I munched on my treat. "Why did Arthur leave his wife a message in a secret code? Why didn't he just tell her about the Dunlap Broadside he had hidden?"

Bogey finished his treat and passed us another round. "Probably to keep it hush-hush, kid. So the rest of his relatives couldn't get their greedy paws on it when he passed away. If he'd put it in his will, the rest of the family would've put up a big fuss. Or someone could've broken in to steal it."

I tilted my head to the side and thought about this. "It's true. She might not have ended up with it."

Bogey nodded. "You got it, kid. So he kept it hidden and gave it to her in a secret code. So nobody would know about it. Not even Emily. Until she figured things out."

I shook my head. "Too bad she didn't crack that code."

Bogey munched on another treat. "I hear ya, kid. I hear ya."

I glanced around at all the people who lined the street to watch the parade.   "Well, if I ever want you to know something, I'll just tell you. I won't put it into a secret code."

Bogey gave me a paw bump and grinned. "I like your style, kid."

Later that day, the library held a dedication ceremony for their newly framed Dunlap Broadside. It now hung in the main room, not far from Arthur Fartheringston's painting. The funny thing was, it had been there the whole time. But nobody even knew it was there.

Our whole family was honored for uncovering it. Half the town showed up for the festivities, including the three new library cats. Everyone clapped when Mrs. Peebles announced us.

"Thanks to the Abernathys, we can enjoy our very own

copy of the Declaration of Independence. A document that
went out almost two hundred and fifty years ago, on this very
day. A document that changed our history. Can you just
imagine all those people on horseback, riding day and night to
deliver copies of this to all the colonies? Their very lives were
in danger, just by helping to declare that the United States was
an independent nation. What a brave bunch. Much like
Gracie was so brave yesterday, standing up there on stage and
reading all that to us."

Then Mrs. Peebles raised one eyebrow. "There are still a
few details that I'm a little hazy on. I'm not quite sure how
Gracie managed to get her cats to lead the way. And, I'd love
to know how Gracie decoded that stone."

Our Mom smiled. "Let's save it for another day. Our
family has had a very big week. Right now we'd just like to
enjoy the Fourth of July."

Of course, our Mom didn't know that we'd planted the page
from Mr. Fartheringston's diary in Gracie's room last night.
And we'd also printed out a copy of the decoded message and
left it next to the diary page. Just so Gracie could explain it
later if she needed to.

Then, that night, our Mom and Dad and Gracie went off to
the town picnic. Gracie was going to read her *real* essay, along
with Dylan.

And us cats had a celebration of our own. Gracie still had
her decorations up and our Mom had left us a nice, tuna
birthday cake. After all, that's what the Fourth of July really is
— a very big birthday party for our nation. We had just started
to gather in the dining room when I saw the Princess helping
the Wise One come down the stairs. So I raced up the stairs to
help. The Wise One had a hard time balancing on her tottery
legs, so I let her lean on me for extra support. Sometimes it
does pay to be an extra big guy.

Once we were all together, it turned into quite a party. The
Wise One and Lil told us lots of stories about the olden days.
Later, our Mom and Dad and Gracie came home early, to be
with us. So we wouldn't be scared when the fireworks started.

Gracie picked me up and hugged me tight. "Oh Buckley,
this turned out to be the best Fourth of July ever!"

And then she started to spin. I really hoped she might be

getting over her spinning phase, but it looked like she hadn't just yet. I hung on for dear life as we went around and around and around.

Finally, she put me down. The room kept on spinning as I tried to stand still. Just then, a pair of big, green eyes came into focus right in front of my face. And my heart started to pound really hard inside my chest.

It was the Princess.

"Buckley," she said in her sweet voice. "I never did thank you for rescuing me the other day. This is the second time you saved me from the Count and Countess. If you hadn't shown up when you did, well . . . I don't even want to think about what could've happened."

Neither did I. Not that I could do much thinking right about then anyway. Not after the Princess gave me a kiss on the nose. That's when I just couldn't take it anymore. I went down like a sack of cat food.

The next thing I knew, Bogey was standing over me. "Dames, kid. They'll get you every time."

"Dames," I sort of mumbled.

Bogey waved a cat treat over my nose. "Here you go, kid. This'll get you going again."

"Thanks," I managed to say as I munched on my treat.

Then he passed me a second treat. "Here's an extra, kid. I'm gonna need you to be alert pretty soon. There's something I want to show you on the computer. As soon as our family goes to bed."

"There is?" I sort of squeaked.

"Yup, kid. I got a strange email. It looks like we might have another case for the Buckley and Bogey Cat Detective Agency."

Another case? Already?

Holy Catnip!

About the Author

Cindy Vincent was born in Calgary, Alberta, Canada, and has lived all around the US and Canada. She is the creator of the Mysteries by Vincent murder mystery party games and the Daisy Diamond Detective Series games for girls. She is also the award-winning author of the Buckley and Bogey Cat Detective Caper books, and the Daisy Diamond Detective book series. She lives with her husband and an assortment of fantastic felines — including the *real* Buckley and Bogey, who run surveillance on her house each and every night.

CPSIA information can be obtained
at www.ICGtesting.com
Printed in the USA
FSOW01n1809060416
18860FS

9 781932 169317